I0835892

Other Works by Maggi A Petton

Historical Fiction

The Queen's Companion

Sofia's Song (sequel to *The Queen's Companion*)

Heaven's Daughter

When Rain Remembers

Poetry

Psalms of the Broken Hearted

Psalms of a Contemplative Heart

Embracing the Sacred Wound

Searching for Home

Searching for Home

A Novel of Historical Fiction

By

Maggi A.Petton

Mercury HeartLink
www.HeartLink.com

Searching for Home
A Novel of Historical Fiction

ISBN 978-1-949652-49-9
Publisher: Mercury HeartLink
Silver City, New Mexico
Printed in the United States of America

Layout and cover design by Pamela Warren Williams

Mercury HeartLink: consult@heartlink.com

For Peggy and Emma, holders of my hope . . .
and in memory of my mother, Lucille,
who was always there.

Chapter One

Olivia

"Mama!" she called out. "Mama, please." She heard the whimper in her own voice and felt powerful waves rock the ship. Sick. She was so sick. Her body was on fire with fever. "Mama," she cried. "Where are you?"

The ship rose and fell and with it so did the moans and groans of those around her. Because so many passengers had fallen ill, there was no escaping the overpowering stench of death.

"Make it stop, Papa. Make it stop just for a while so I can rest." But her parents could not stop the ship from violently tossing their daughter about any more than they could stop the pox from leaving scars on her body. In fact, Olivia Russo's parents would never again be able to answer their daughter's pleas. The ship rocked, and with it, Olivia's seven-year-old body was thrown against her mother's cold body.

Mid-May 1854

Olivia Russo jolted awake and grunted as her body rolled against the barrel filled with corn meal. She was drenched in sweat, and the bouncing movement of the wagon confused her. It took a moment for her to release the dream and the memory of her ocean voyage from Italy more than ten years ago. The heat within the covered wagon and the jostling over ruts and rocks were so similar in her sleep to the fever and roiling of the ship that, at first, she could not place her surroundings.

Sunlight streamed into the wagon through the opening at the front. A shadow moved across the sun's rays.

"Everything okay back there?" Sam hollered.

"Fine, Sam. Fine," Olivia called back. "Just a bad dream. Think I'll head out and walk again." She had walked all morning and most of the afternoon. It was unusual for her to rest in the middle of the day, but Molly had mentioned her pallor and suggested she rest. Olivia was grateful for the opportunity because she was bone tired in a way she hadn't been since the start of their journey just a little over a month ago. She had not slept well the night before.

She poked her head out from the puckering string of the wagon canvas and drew in a full breath. "Stuffy in there," she said, referring to the stifling air inside the wagon as she stepped over the seat of the wagon where she sat next to Molly. Usually, the women walked alongside the wagon, lightening the load for the oxen and talking about everything under the sun.

"None too fresh out here either," said Molly. "Looks like a storm might be headed this way, though. That should cool things down some."

Squinting, Olivia looked ahead and saw the dark clouds in the distance. It was nice to be at the head of the train. Being first opened the vast plains and prairies to an unobstructed view. More than that, the first wagon avoided the dust kicked up by all the other oxen and wagons in front of them.

"We'd best settle down for the night before that storm is on us. Hard enough on the oxen without pushing them to pull through mud," Sam said.

Sam and Molly were husband and wife. They were on their way to California to join the hunt for gold and were kind enough to allow Olivia to travel with them on her way west to marry. A wagon train of many hopeful gold seekers had left Council Bluffs, Iowa nearly a month earlier.In all, there were nine families and sixteen wagons. Traveling was slow, but Olivia preferred solid ground and the potential threat of Indians to the known dangers of a ship on the ocean.

"I need to stretch my legs," Olivia said to both Sam and Molly.

Sam nodded, reached over, and held up his hand. Olivia took it and stepped over the side of the wagon where she grabbed hold of the seat and lowered herself until she was close enough to the ground. A small jump and she was off. The wagon kept moving, and she fell in place beside it. Rufus, the Clayton's dog, ran up to her.

"Hello, Rufus," she said, bending to rub his head behind the ears. "Care to walk with me for a while?"

The dream unnerved Olivia, and she knew that walking would help her let it go. She remembered walking long hours with her mother in the hills surrounding Palermo. Those memories sustained her through the heartbreaking months following her parents' deaths on the ship that brought her gaunt, emaciated, and scarred body to the states. The smallpox outbreak on the ship had taken out more than half the passengers and a good number of the crew. Olivia's parents were buried at sea, along with so many others. She had been too sick to be present. Why she had survived when so many had died was a mystery to her.

The ship was kept in quarantine offshore for weeks once it arrived. Her aunt and uncle were waiting for her on the island where the doctors examined her and finally declared her healthy enough to enter the country.[1] She loved her aunt and uncle. They loved her, too. But they were not her parents, and at first, she was angry and bitter at finding herself in a strange, new place without them.

"Why did we have to leave Sicily?" she screamed at her aunt one day. "What is so wonderful about this place that we had to leave home?" she yelled in Italian. "I hate it here!"

Her aunt, who was her mother's sister, was patient and understanding. She let Olivia rant and rave and run crying to her room. Later she arrived and softly knocked on Olivia's door.

"I brought you some cookies, Bambina," she said as she cracked the door.

Olivia, her face red-eyed and puffy from crying, kept her face to the wall as she lay on her bed. Her aunt came to her, sat on the edge of the bed, and placed the plate with cookies and a glass of milk on the nightstand.

"When your mother was little, these cookies would always cheer her up. She would get so upset about things she felt were unfair." Aunt Maria placed her hand on Olivia's back and rubbed gently. "I remember one time, she saw a young boy from our village pick up a cat by the tail and swing the cat around and around. She tried to stop him but could not get near. Other children were standing by and laughing. They thought the whole thing was very funny."

Olivia rolled onto her back and looked at her aunt.

"She cried her eyes out for days over that cat, then she got

---

1 Willrich, Michael (2011) POX; An American History Dollar, Clyde D. (1977) The High Plains Smallpox Epidemic of 1837-38: Western Historical Quarterly Vol. 8, No. 1

(Author's note: While the facts of ship smallpox protocols are recorded, the timeline of Olivia's ship would not be accurate and falls between the aforementioned historical records. Olivia is a fictional character.)

so angry at the other children for laughing. Your mother always had a deep sense of right and wrong," Aunt Maria said.

Aunt Maria's eyes drifted to the window and beyond into memories of her own. She smiled and brought herself back. "Always such a strong sense of justice, your mama."

Her aunt looked down into Olivia's eyes. "You are so much like her, you know," she continued. "And so, dolce bambina, I thought you might be enough like her to feel better with her favorite cookies."

The anise cookies covered with vanilla frosting were Olivia's favorites.

"How did you know?" Olivia asked her aunt.

"How could I not, mi amore? You are your mother's daughter."

Olivia smiled, sat up, and reached for a cookie.

"It tastes like home," she said.

"I miss her, too," Aunt Maria said reaching for a cookie.

Rufus barked and darted off after a rabbit startling Olivia and returning her to the present. Sam was pulling the oxen to a halt. He jumped down from the wagon and walked back to the second wagon in the train.

"Bob," he called, "looks like we ought to hold up for the night soon. Storm's moving pretty quick this way. Close enough to evening that we can stop and try to get things battened down."

Bob nodded, and Sam ran back up to his wagon. "Molly, let's take it on over to that open spot up ahead. That's enough for today." Sam went up to the oxen and led them off the trail while Molly took the reins. Olivia darted up to help Sam guide the beasts.

Sam and Molly were godsent. When she knew she needed to make her way to California, she placed an ad in the Council

Bluffs paper, where she had discovered that many of the wagon trains heading west began the trek across the plains. The group of nine families had left Council Bluffs, Iowa on April 14, 1854, a day before the last recommended day for venturing across the plains and into the mountains of the west. A later departure put them at risk for heavy snow in the mountain passes that their wagons needed to cross.

When their wagons were finally in a circle, the pioneers began their routine of settling in for the night. The women got the fires and cooking started, while the men tended the oxen and horses and made whatever repairs were needed to the wagons.

Molly and Olivia worked well together. They'd found quickly how much they enjoyed each other's company and complimented each other's skills. There could not have been more different looking women, but they seemed like sisters at heart. Molly was slender and of medium height. Her hair was light, tending toward a dark blonde, although it was getting lighter as she spent more time outdoors. Even with her hat on, the ends of her hair were growing lighter and lighter. Molly's eyes were blue—the kind that changed with the sky. When there were no clouds, her eyes sparkled with the intensity of their blueness. When the sky turned gray, so did Molly's eyes. Molly's complexion was quite fair and flawless. When she worked, her cheeks turned a bright red even with mild exertion, giving her a healthy glow. Her laugh was full and free and more infectious than Olivia had ever heard.

Olivia had the thick, black hair of her ancestors. Her eyes were dark brown, and her skin held just a hint of olive tones that all but disappeared as the sun darkened the places that were not covered by clothing and a hat. Her nose was almost classically Roman, and her cheekbones were high. Olivia's mouth was blessed with strong, straight teeth, and her smile lit up all the outdoors. On occasion, Olivia was self-conscious about her smallpox scars, but she had grown accustomed to the stares and questions about them. She had scars on her face, but fewer there than others on the ship. The majority of her scars were on her arms and torso. Her Aunt Maria had long ago helped her to overcome her discomfort about both the scars and the questions.

"Mi dolce, sometimes people are uncomfortable when it comes to things they do not understand, things that frighten them," Aunt Maria had said. She reached her hand up to stroke Olivia's cheek. "There is a story of courage and survival behind each scar on your beautiful face. Don't be afraid to share it. Soon enough people will see only the light of Olivia shining out from those beautiful brown eyes."

Olivia and Molly joined the other women of the wagon train in preparing dinner. With little exception, the women of the wagon train got on quite well together. Each evening as soon as the wagons circled, all the women went straight to work to provide the evening meal as quickly and efficiently as possible. Several fires were burning, and Dutch ovens were soon hanging over those fires filled with cornbread, beans, meats, and even a pie or two if berries could be found. Olivia unhooked the butter churn from the back underside of the wagon. The swaying motion of the wagons did the work of churning the milk throughout the day, thus saving much of the churning by hand. Olivia skimmed off the cream into a bowl, poured the buttermilk into a pitcher, and proceeded to churn the cream to make the butter. In the morning, she'd milk the cow into the churn and start the process all over again.

The women chatted while working, and as soon as the men returned from tending the animals, the group filled their plates and sat around the fires to eat. When the weather was good, fiddles and harmonicas found their way to the fires after dinner.

The wagon train children loved to sing and dance. Sometimes their parents would join them. At the end of the evening, guards were posted, and everyone else turned in for the night.

Molly looked warily at the sky. "Maybe it'll be a mild one," she said as the sun was obliterated by the approaching clouds.

Olivia looked to the western sky and smiled. She paused in her churning and said, "I'd be happier with a dry one!"

Molly laughed. "You have a wonderful sense of humor, Olivia. I am so glad you are traveling with us."

"It's nice to have my humor appreciated," Olivia replied. "You have no idea how many stodgy, disagreeable folks I met on the way to Council Bluffs from New York." She shook her head with the memories. "I really had begun to despair that my entire trip across country would be plagued with grumpy men and women whose mouths looked like they had just bit into a lemon!"

Molly laughed out loud as she placed the Dutch oven with biscuits onto the fire to begin cooking. As Molly's laughter rang out into the ring of wagons and fires, Alice Whitcomb, whose fire was closest, straightened up and said, "Laughing already, you two?"

Alice and her husband, Bob, had been in the wagon directly behind them all day. Alice always looked tired but never complained. The couple traveled with their four children. The youngest, Ben, was a tow-headed two-year old, but the oldest was Sally, who at thirteen, was strong, capable, and able to help drive their second wagon. Ben was the youngest among the entire group and the darling of all.

Bob Whitcomb was one of three farmers in the group, the others being the Allens and the Grovers.

Nearby, but only because that's where her wagon was in the line, Esther Warren sniffed and said, "With that storm headed this way, I really don't see what there could possibly be to be happy about." She shook her head in disdain. "I guess the laughing will stop soon enough once that storm starts."

Molly looked at Olivia and winked.

Olivia smiled and whispered to Molly, "Guess we know who to ask if we want to make lemonade." To Esther, Olivia said, "I do feel bad for the children. They do so enjoy singing and dancing around the fires after dinner. The storm will prevent that."

Again, Esther shook her head, but this time added an eye-roll. She had made it clear early on that she did not appreciate or enjoy children of any age. As the wagons were readied in Council Bluffs, two of the children watched, wide-eyed, as Chester Warren packed Esther's harmonium in their wagon under her watchful eye. That night, in celebration of completing their first day of travel, out came a banjo and a couple of harmonicas. When the children asked Esther to bring out her harmonium, she'd responded with a huff and said, "That instrument is for praising the Lord and will never be used for such frivolity and unholy noise." She put the fear of God into all the children about staying away from their wagon. Poor Margaret Allen, who was only six years old, was so frightened by Esther's demeanor that she burst into tears and ran into her own wagon not to be seen again until the next morning. Even then, she avoided all eye contact with most of the adults until Hollis Johnson, one of the carpenters on the wagon train, squatted in front of her and held out a wooden toy he'd made for her, a ball and cup with a string attached to them. He showed her how to swing the ball up and try to catch it in the cup. She was delighted and gave Hollis a big hug.

That night Olivia brought out her father's accordion, which had been on the boat with them from Italy. It was the only large thing she'd brought with her, other than her single trunk filled with clothing and some personal items. Whenever the evening chores allowed, Olivia brought out the accordion. William Johnson and Abigail Meadows, both eight years of age, watched intently as Olivia played the reed instrument. In the first week on the trail, Olivia began to give them pointers on playing the keys and moving the bellows. Both were quick learners and, in the month of travel across the state of Nebraska, had mastered several tunes on the squeezebox.

Olivia slept on a blanket in a small section of the wagon. The heavy canvas generally protected her well from the elements, but in the worst of storms the wind lashed at the material with such force as to rip the ties from the flaps. During those storms, Olivia spent the night just holding the canvas down or a quilt at the opening to keep their provisions dry. Sam and Molly generally slept under the wagon for protection from the rain.

Now, as Olivia huddled inside the wagon during the storm, she covered her accordion to keep it dry in case the oiled canvas leaked. She set her mind on thoughts of Stewart and Sacramento. She and Stewart Anderson had begun corresponding more than a year previous. Her friend, Anna, had given her a letter from Stewart that had been written to her brother. Anna and her family knew the Andersons because Stewart's father had been the pastor of their church. Anna's brother and Stewart were close friends when they were growing up, but Stewart and his family had left New York for a church position in Sacramento, California when Stewart was twelve years old. Anna's brother and Stewart remained in touch, and when Stewart's letter arrived, he had asked Anna if she knew any young women who might be interested in corresponding with him. Anna instantly thought of Olivia.

Stewart's letter to William was tucked in Olivia's bag, but she had memorized it long ago. She closed her eyes and pictured the neat handwriting.

October 21, 1852

Dear Will,

It is with a sad heart that I write to tell you about the death of my sweet mother. She fell ill a few months after my father's passing and never recovered. She was a good mother, and I was blessed to be her son.

So, I guess I am orphaned here in California. It is not so bad. I have taken a job with a logging outfit in the Sierras. Although all the rage is about the rush for gold here, I am appalled at the greed and lack of sensibility of many of the gold seekers. John Sutter, upon whose land the discovery of gold started the rush to California, was a friend of my father's. When he came to pay his respects at my father's passing, he told me that he wished he'd never found the gold—at the very least, he wished he'd thrown the nugget back into the water and never said a word about it.

Logging is hard work and is dangerous, but I have learned much already and am stronger for the effort. There is something about the forest that draws me to her embrace. I feel at home here, especially when the work stops and quiet settles around me. It is then that I feel myself at one with nature as the birds resume their chirping and the scent of pine fills my nostrils.

I am not certain I have the temperament of a true logger, but I do find that I enjoy the work. It is exhausting and yet satisfying in a way that surprises me. I think I can be good at it.

Please congratulate your sister on her marriage. I remember Anna as a young girl, always following us around. I hope she is happy. If you feel it appropriate, you might ask her if she knows anyone who might be willing to correspond with me. My days are filled with the company of men, and since my sweet mother has gone, I do yearn for the tenderness of a woman's perspective.

Please give your family my warmest regards and do cherish your mother while you have her.

Fondly,

Stewart Anderson

Olivia's eyes still misted as she remembered Stewart's sweet letter to his friend. She instantly felt connected to this man she had never met because he spoke so tenderly about his mother. Her heart ached with the loneliness of her own long-ago loss. On the spot, she decided she would write to him.

A loud crash of thunder combined with a crack of lightning made Olivia jump. The strike was close, and she hoped everyone in the wagon train was safe. The storm was right on top of them. A gust of wind blew the blanket from the opening of the canvass, and Olivia jumped up to hold it up again. An hour or so later, as the storm began to wane and the winds died, she uncurled her stiff fingers from the material. Her hands ached from holding them so tightly. It was still raining, but the rain was falling straight down. A few spots in the canvass had begun to leak, so she placed some pots under the drips, sat down, and curled against a bean sack. She was asleep when the rain finally stopped sometime in the night.

It was still dark when Olivia heard the Colonel's horse trot into the camp. The Colonel was hired in Council Bluffs for his knowledge and experience in running wagon trains from Iowa to California over the past two years. His name was John Dawes, but everyone just referred to him as Colonel. He had been injured while fighting in the Regular Army during the Mexican-American War in 1847 and was discharged due to a severe limp caused by the injury. Not married, he was willing to lead wagon trains of less than the sixty people that most wagon masters demanded. He charged a bit more, but at twenty-five dollars per wagon, he made enough to be content and seemed to know what he was doing.

Molly and Sam already had their sleeping rolls ready to store in the wagon when Olivia emerged. She placed them inside the wagon and climbed down to greet the early day. The night guards fired their rifles at four every morning to rouse the sleepers so that they could be fed, packed, harnessed, and ready to go before the sun was up."How about some coffee, Colonel?" Sam asked.

"Don't mind if I do. Thank you kindly, Sam." The Colonel was a stocky fellow with dirty brown muttonchops. He never seemed comfortable talking with the women in the wagon train, but that seemed more out of lack of experience than fear or dislike.

"How'd you manage in that storm last night?" Sam asked.

"Oh, probably better than most of you, I'd venture," the Colonel answered with a chuckle. "Found me a nice little rocky place about a mile ahead. Managed to tent my rubber sheet across a couple o' big boulders and stayed pretty dry."

"Morning all," Olivia said as she set to help Molly with the cooking. Everything was muddy or dripping from the storm. It was difficult to get the fire started, but the air was fresh and delicious after being washed so thoroughly.

"Dig that trench a little deeper, Molly," Olivia said.

Molly nodded knowingly.

Olivia returned and sprinkled a touch of gunpowder onto the twigs that were the driest. Molly struck the flint and instantly got the powder to spark and pop. The fire grew slowly but enough so that Fred Allen, Joseph and Abigail's oldest child, was able to light a twig to start another fire.

The Colonel had nodded his greeting to Olivia and continued

talking with Sam. "If they keep moving this direction, we might run into a pretty big herd of buffalo," Colonel said as he accepted a tin of steaming cup of coffee from Sam.

"I'll be sure to let the hunters know," Sam said.

"I expect Brewster to throw a fit again," the Colonel said, shaking his head. Horace Grover and Bob Whitcomb were the only hunters in the party. But the Colonel hired a man named Jack Brewster at the urging of Chester Warren. Brewster was a professional hunter who'd often traded with Chester, who was a merchant. The Colonel was reluctant, but he made it abundantly clear to all that he would only allow the necessary killing of buffalo encountered on the prairies.

"Some breakfast for you, Colonel?" Molly asked.

The man shook his head and turned back to Sam. "I'll bring your cup back soon," he said."Why don't you take the lead, again, today. Keep an eye out for the buffalo. If you see dust on your horizon, that means there could be a stampede. That's trouble."

Sam's eyes opened wide, and his jaw dropped. "What should we do if there is a stampede?"

The Colonel shook his head. "Pray they veer away from the wagons. Outside of that, not much you can do."

Sam reached up and scratched his beard. "Damn," he said.

Sam was anxious all morning long worrying about stampeding buffalo. "Of all the things I knew we might face—wild Indians, wolves, coyotes, snakes, raging rivers, and treacherous mountains—stampeding buffalo never crossed my mind!" he confessed to Molly and Olivia.

"Don't think of them as a murderous herd, then," Olivia said, trying not to smile. "Think of them as dinner and blankets rushing to our aid."

Sam looked at her, caught the sparkle in her eye, and could not help but smile and shake his head. "Dinner and blankets," he mumbled. "Damn."

Nonetheless, as the lead wagon, Olivia, Molly, and Sam kept a watchful eye on the horizon for any sign of dust. In the early afternoon, black splotches began to dot the prairie in the distance.

"Buffalo," Sam said. "See them?"

Molly squinted and smiled. "Calm buffalo."

Olivia had been walking and pulled herself up onto the wagon to get a better look. "So many of them! There must be thousands."

As they neared the hill where it appeared most of the buffalo grazed, they tried over and over to estimate the numbers. It was too difficult. But when they reached the crest of that hill, they gave up the attempt. Spread out before them as far as they could see into the distance, the very hills were blackened—so dense with buffalo that the sheer magnitude of them was impossibly overwhelming.

Hours later, the train left behind the forest of meandering, black beasts. The buffalo had moved off the path as Sam's oxen approached. The great animals did not seem to care that a small wagon train parted them down the center.

When they finally made camp that night, Sam was visibly relieved. The three hunters and Colonel Dawes had remained behind with horses, a couple of oxen, and an empty uncovered wagon. They waited until long after the others' wagons were safely west of the herd before they started their hunt. The plan was to approach the buffalo from the west so that if they stampeded during the hunt, they would, hopefully, drive to the east.

The wagon train dogs were the first to arrive at the camp

with all the signs of a successful hunt. They dragged the entrails of the slaughtered buffalo clamped in their teeth like long red ropes. Most hunkered under wagons and growled if anyone came near. The hunters followed soon after with the slaughtered carcasses of four buffalo and hides. Voices of the Colonel and Brewster could be heard yelling in the distance. As the wagon with the bison made its way to the edge of the wagon circle, both men and women gathered around to begin the process of cutting up the meat for drying, stewing, and frying.

"Colonel told him right from the git go that he weren't goin' to tolerate no senseless slaughter," Bob Whitcomb, Alice's husband, said when Sam asked about the argument off in the distance.

"That what all the hollerin's about?" Alice asked her husband.

"Yup. Guess he figured he was hired on as a hunter, and he had the right to kill as many buffalo as he wanted. He wasn't any too happy when the Colonel aimed his rifle at him and told him any unnecessary slaughter would not be tolerated."

Sam jumped up on the wagon and helped lift a large shoulder of meat down to a large oilcloth for the women to begin cutting. "I agree with the Colonel. It seems a sin to kill an animal just for the hide and leave the rest of it. I swear the Colonel got a bit choked up when he talked about coming across whole prairies strewn with full carcasses of rotting buffalo shot just for their skins." He heaved a leg over the side of the wagon to Chester Warren, whose wife Esther looked like she'd rather be anywhere else. The first person in the group who had playfully commented on their names, Chester and Esther, was admonished with a look of disdain from Esther. No one dared mention the similarity again.

"Is it any wonder," Olivia said, "the Indians don't care to have us here if we are plundering the land and food supplies?"

Flies had begun to gather around the blood and meat, so all hands were needed to work as quickly as possible. Grunting, hacking, and lots of blood accompanied the work.

"I don't give a fig about no Injuns," said Chester. "And I think the Colonel is wrong to set such a harsh condition for a hunter."

Olivia's sense of justice rose up, but she swallowed hard remembering the fight.

"If he wanted a slaughter for hides, he should have gone off on his own, or with another train," Molly said. "He was paid to help us hunt along the way and knew the rules before we left Council Bluffs."

The Warrens both glared at Molly, then turned a condescending eye on Sam. Their look implied that he had no control over his wife.

Sam just smiled and said, "She's something, isn't she?"

Esther snorted and pursed her mouth, and Olivia looked up at Sam and said, "She sure is, Sam."

The yelling in the distance stopped, and it wasn't long before the Colonel rode up to the group, tied his horse to a nearby wagon, and started cussing at the flies. "We'll make do with the hunters in our party," he said as he pulled out his blade to assist in butchering. "Mr. Brewster has decided to part our good company."

Chapter Two

May 20, 1854
Dearest Olivia,

I write to you by candlelight from my cot in the Sierra Camp. It is sleeting madly here, and I expect we will wake up to plenty of snow. You should be well into your journey as I write, and I can't help but wonder when, or if, you will receive my letter at Fort McPherson. I trust you are traveling well and safely.

Although I was only twelve when my parents and I traversed this grand country, I remember so much from those endless days. I was not happy to be leaving my friends in New York, and I am fairly certain I was a recalcitrant young boy. My poor parents!

The things I do look back on from that trip make me wish I could be journeying with you. Sometimes, when I am working in the forest, a smell or a sound will bring back some of the sights and remembrances of that time. While I am sure I found it tedious then, I wish I could have appreciated the flow of the prairies as they rolled into an infinite sky or the sounds of the grass as the wind swept her blades to and fro. There was a place, it might have been Wyoming, where some of the grass was dried and filled with spent seed pods of some sort. I never knew what they were, but they made a most particular sound in the wind. They rather clicked, as I recall. There were acres and acres of them softly clicking and tapping in the wind. I wish now that I knew what they were!

There are wolves in the forests here. I don't remember seeing many wolves on our journey, but I do remember the coyotes. We have them here as well, and I will never forget the first time I heard a pack of them near our camp in Nebraska. All my hair stood on end as they yipped and yapped their signals to each other. Funny how life changes. Now, at night in my bunk, I hear the coyotes and feel as if all is right with the world.

Mostly, as tonight, I remember the smell following a rain. The water-washed air always invited my deepest breaths. There is something so special, so sweet about the fragrance that lingers after a rain. I hope you will remember to look forward to inhaling as deeply as possible as you endure some of the storms you will undoubtedly pass through.

My candle sputters, and the storm here seems to be drifting off to the east. Perhaps the same clouds will pass over you as you head west to me—to us.

Good night, my darling.

Stewart

May 30, 1854

My dearest Stewart,

Your letter was waiting for me at Fort McPherson. I was so happy to find it there.

I am learning so much as I journey across this land. My hope is that my lessons will help us in our life together.

Thank you for encouraging me to appreciate the land—and not just push to get across it. The words from your letter sing in me as I scan the angles of the prairies and how they cut across the sky or how the hills roll softly into one another. The whisper of grass song in the breeze is as near to a lullaby as I remember. And those clicking seed pods are from the yucca grass. I made sure to find that out for you. At night, when crickets chirp and fireflies twinkle, I feel so blessed for their music and magic. Fireflies! Such a marvelous invention!

Are there fireflies in California? Oh, I do hope so! I can imagine sitting on our porch after the sun has set and watching them flit and sparkle as we unwind from our days.

Meanwhile, the days are long and tiring on this journey, but not unpleasant. Mostly, the others are good and kind people. Everyone is generous and helpful—well, almost everyone. I do wonder what makes some people so disagreeable, or if they are just born with temperaments that do not respond to kindness. It truly is very sad. Sometimes I find myself thinking, "There, but for the grace of God, go I."

So far, we have been blessed with mostly fair weather, only occasional rainstorms and minor mishaps. There is a sense of family among us. I guess that should be expected because we see each other at our worst and our best. But, I suppose, much remains to be seen as the hardest and most dangerous part of our trail is ahead of us.

The children of the train are a blessing. I am especially fond of little Ben. Although only two, he is smart as a whip. He has the biggest blue eyes. Some evenings, when we are gathered around the fires and the instruments are brought out, Ben will shyly come over to me and climb into my lap. I love the weight and feeling of him resting against me. He is such a sweet boy. When he falls asleep, his mother, Alice, comes and lifts him from my lap to put him down for the night. I have quickly come to look forward to Ben's cuddling in the evening. Perhaps we will have a little one of our own one day.

There are nights I am so tired, but sleep will not come. The howl of coyotes, worry of Indians, sometimes the snapping of the canvas in the wind will keep me on edge. At those times, I listen for the wind to whisper your name, and it helps to calm me until, at last, I drift off.

With love,
Olivia

Olivia preferred to walk next to the wagon in the early hours of the day. Generally, the train was moving by six in the morning. Parents had learned to just let the little ones sleep until they woke. Since no one slept well, it just made life easier to allow the children to sleep when they could.

In the cooler air of the early morning, Olivia appreciated the beauty of the land. The grass, so still in the morning, looked like a blanket woven across the prairie. As the sun rose, she loved to watch the colors change in the sky, especially when there were clouds painted on the endless canvas overhead.

She imagined sunrises and sunsets with Stewart and clung to the hope that he imagined the same with her. Often, on mornings as beautiful as these, her hand automatically slipped into her pocket to the rosary beads that had once belonged to her grandmother. After her grandmother had died, Olivia's Aunt Maria had left Sicily with her husband, an American who had been studying abroad and with whom she had fallen in love. Michael Blake had stayed in Italy with Maria, knowing that she would not leave until her mother, who was ill, had passed on. Olivia still remembered watching her grandmother's fingers work the beads almost continually until her last breath. The beads were her most cherished possession.

The sounds of the animals and wagons had become rhythmical, almost musical to Olivia—the oxen snorting; their hooves padding the hard ground; pans and pots clanking in the wagons; and wheels turning, grinding, and in need of grease. Everything became a symphony heralding their arrival. She and the others were not oblivious to how noisy their band was as they made their way across the plains, and it was lost on no one that they moved slowly under the watchful eyes of Indians all along their route. Olivia was able to spot them more readily and had become less anxious and fearful that they intended anyone harm in their party.

"Ready for a little company?" Mildred Clayton asked as she and Molly caught up with Olivia.

Olivia smiled and nodded. "It really can be beautiful, can't it?"

Oh, I suppose," Mildred said and chuckled. "When it isn't so danged tedious."

In spite of her attempt at appreciation, Olivia had to agree that some days the monotony of the plains grew tiresome.

"I am looking forward to a change in scenery," Olivia said.

"As am I," Molly agreed. "I do confess to feeling wary of the mountains, though. I've heard stories about so many things." Her eyebrows creased as she appeared lost in thought.

"What kinds of things?" Mildred asked.

"Oh, the usual, I suppose," Molly said. "Cholera, snow, the fever, the bears."

After walking, each pondering all the things that might go wrong, Olivia said, "I am looking forward to seeing the Pacific."

"I hear it is quite different from the Atlantic, though I have never seen an ocean at all," Mildred said. "John and I were both born and raised in Iowa and never lived more than ten miles from where our parents lived." She paused a moment, then continued. "One day a traveler stopped to have his horse shod and told John about the gold in California. Next thing I knew, we were moving to hunt for gold and start a new life!"

"I am grateful to have your husband along," Molly said to Mildred. "We were beginning to worry that not a single blacksmith had signed on with us."

Olivia agreed. "Can't imagine anyone making this journey without one."

"I was pretty reluctant," Mildred said. "It was hard to think about leaving the place where I'd spent my whole life.

Now I am glad we came. Mark really seems to be coming into his own on this trip. A woman can't ask for more than that for her only child."

"I think he has his eye on Betsy Fowler," Olivia offered.

Mildred smiled knowingly. "You may be right, Olivia."

Again, they walked without talking for a bit, listening to the sounds of the wagons.

"Do you hear that odd clanking?" Olivia asked.

"I thought it was just the wagon wheels making a funny noise," Molly said. "But it is different. Wonder what it is?"

Mildred laughed. "Let's take a necessity break over in those bushes, and I'll show you what it is."

Molly and Olivia looked at each other and shrugged. "I'll get the blanket," Molly said as she darted over to her wagon.

The women in the group routinely went together in groups of three to attend to their personal needs. That way, two of them could hold up a blanket for privacy while the third attended to her needs. When they were safely in the bushes, Molly and Olivia held up the corners of the blanket to hide Mildred.

"Here is what's making the noise," Mildred said as she raised her apron and the gingham dress she wore over her other dresses.

"My goodness, Mildred," Molly exclaimed. "How many dresses are you wearing?"

"Oh, I think I always have on at least four plus my apron," Mildred replied. "It was the only way to be able to bring everything I needed to pack and keep the weight down on the wagon. Because we had the blacksmith wagon full of tools and supplies for repairs, our family wagon got heavy pretty quick. That," she said, "is why I had to do this."

Mildred lifted her second and third layers of dresses to reveal hidden pockets sewn into her under dressings. They were filled with silver utensils.

"Oh, Mildred!" Olivia exclaimed. "How are you carrying all that weight?"

"I just couldn't leave my mother's good silver behind," Mildred said, her eyes misting over with tears. "She was so proud of this silverware, and it is the only thing of hers that I have. I had to find a way to bring it. Please don't tell John."

"Your secret is safe with us, Mildred," Molly said.

Olivia nodded. "Be careful with such a load, Mildred. You do not want to exhaust yourself once we start our climb."

Olivia looked out over the landscape of Ash Hollow and sighed. The hills were changing and were becoming more interesting, less monotonous. A plume of dust caught her eye, and it wasn't long before the Colonel rode into view. He stopped when he reached Sam. Olivia walked over to hear what he was saying.

"Best prepare for some trouble up ahead," he said. "And your women might want to shield their eyes."

"What is it, Colonel?" Molly asked.

The Colonel directed his remarks to Sam, seemingly ignoring Molly's question. "Injuns up ahead," he said. "Most likely they will let us be. I run into 'em before. They don't take kindly to greedy white folks traveling with nothing but buffalo hides. Long as they can see our meats drying on the traveling racks and our few hides drying, we should be fine."

The Colonel had insisted that much of the buffalo be cut into thin strips and hung from poles designed to dry and display the meat in plain sight. Although he'd only been accompanying wagon trains for a couple of years, his reputation with theNatives is what made traveling with him safer than with hunters like Mr. Brewster.

"Tie up the flaps on your wagon so's the Indians can see we got nothin' to hide," the Colonel said. "And, like I said, you might want your women folk and young 'uns to cover their eyes."

Olivia could not imagine why he mentioned the women's eyes twice, but she knew that asking him again would not result in an answer. She watched the man gallop off to the wagons behind them one at a time to tell them all the same thing.

"Sam," Olivia said, "a hand up, please."Sam reached down and pulled Olivia onto the wagon bench. She and Molly tied up the canvas flaps to reveal the contents of their belongings. When they returned to the seat with Sam, Olivia looked ahead and saw many horses with riders lined up on the horizon. The Indians were Pawnee. Around twenty of them waited at the top of a rise.

"I can't imagine why he would not want us to look at the Indians," Molly said.

"Perhaps the Indians have strange customs where women are concerned," Olivia suggested.

As they neared the Indians, Olivia could not help but notice how erect they sat on their horses. Many of them had long, thick black hair adorned with feathers. Some of them had shaved heads with hair sprouting shortly from the top. Many wore beaded breastplates, but some were bare chested. All of them looked fierce, and Olivia felt a shiver of fear.

Sam was quiet as they neared the rise where the Indians waited. As they got closer, he said, "I don't think covering your eyes has anything to do with seeing the Indians."

"Isn't that Mr. Brewster's horse and mule?" Olivia asked.

Sam nodded, and the Colonel rode up to the front of the train, then slowed down and kept pace at the lead. One of the Indians nodded to him, and the Colonel nodded back but just kept moving.

Olivia looked north, past where the Indians lined the path and saw at least forty buffalo dead or dying on the prairie. When she looked back to their path, their wagon was coming to the end of the line of Indians. As they passed the last one on her right, her eyes beheld a sight that filled her with horror.

"Oh, dear God," Olivia said. Her eyes opened wide, and one hand flew to her mouth in a feeble attempt to keep her from retching.

Molly grasped Olivia's free hand and buried her face in Sam's shoulder.

There, tied to a makeshift crossbar, was Mr. Brewster. His face was all that identified him. He had been skinned alive and hung to dry in the sun.

The skins of at least twenty buffalo were piled beneath him. His own skin rested in long strips on top of them.

Olivia looked into Brewster's eyes. They were open, and he looked directly at her. He was still alive. She vomited over the side of the wagon.

Every evening after supper since the wagon train had left Council Bluffs and except for the nights there was rain, the guitars, fiddles, and mouth harps came out, but not this night. Cookware clanged as the women cleaned up the Dutch ovens, pots, pans, plates, and utensils. The oxen, horses, and mules snorted or whickered or flicked their tails at insects. That night, no one brought an instrument out; no happy conversation or song rose with the smoke of the fires.

As the campfires spit their sparks and then lowered their flames for lack of fuel, Chester said, "Guess the Injuns made off alright with Mr. Brewster's hides. They stand to make a pretty penny off his load."

A few of the others grunted, some clearly thinking the same. The Colonel said as he stood. "The Indians consider what Mr. Brewster did a desecration. To them, the buffalo is sacred. They kill only enough of them to survive, and they use every part of the buffalo they kill. Afterward, they have a ceremony to honor the buffalo. I don't know what they will do with the hides or the rotting carcasses, but I guarantee they will not sell them to anyone."[2] He turned and walked away from the group.

One by one, the remainder of the party left to turn in for the night, although very little actual sleep was found.

Her rosary beads moved in a slow procession through Olivia's fingers all night long.

---

2 The Buffalo War: Some U.S. Government officials actively sought to destroy the buffalo population to starve Native peoples. Early trains, full of "hunters" would slow to the speed of buffalo and shoot as many as they could from the train. "Buffalo" Bill Cody was hired to kill bison. He killed more than 4,000 in two years.

Chapter Three

Olivia's hand automatically reached for the touch of Stewart in her pocket right next to her beads. There was the letter she had found waiting for her when they had stopped at Platte Bridge Station. It smelled of pine and sawdust. She took it out, smelled it, and began to read as she walked. The warmth of his words washed over her as she read.

June 5, 1854

My Darling Olivia,

I pray that you are safe and well in your travels across this great land of ours. It must be so different from anything you experienced in Italy or New York.

Life here seems suspended as I await your arrival. Days that used to pass quickly now drag endlessly as I long for you to be here with me. The photo you sent of yourself so long ago is fading. My heart is anxious for the real flesh and blood of you to replace it. I imagine, with such aching, touching your sweet face with my hand, holding you in my arms, and pulling you close to me.

I am working on a project that will, I hope, make you very happy here. I cannot imagine us living in the camp and would not want to subject you to the roughness and rudeness of many of the loggers. Do not misunderstand. They are good men and hard workers, but many of them lack the common courtesies and refinements that come of being raised by a kind, loving, strong, and decent woman.

There is a women's boarding house in Sacramento. I have made arrangements with the owner to have you stay there when you arrive.

Her name is Miss Clark.[3] *Miss Clark operates the Vernon House in Sacramento on J Street. It is near the Sacramento River. When you arrive, she will send word to me in the camp. The pastor who took my father's place in our church will marry us. He is looking forward to meeting you. I have planned a honeymoon in San Francisco. It is not New York, but it may be the closest you will get out here in the wild west. Whenever you arrive, my outfit has given me leave to take as much time as I wish for our honeymoon. Of course, there is much ribbing about my getting married, but it is all in good fun.*

My candle is near sputtering, and I will fall asleep with thoughts of you. Lately, my dreams are of you, and that makes my nights sweeter than nectar.

Travel safely, my love. I wait.

Yours,

Stewart

P.S. I am sorry to report that there are no fireflies in California.

June 30, 1854

Dearest Stewart,

I was so happy to find your letter waiting for me at Platte Bridge Station[4] *when we arrived there at the end of June. We rested*

---

3 The Vernon House was first a Post Office. In 1853, it was turned into a three-story brick structure and called the Jones Hotel. From 1855-1856, Miss O.J. Clark operated a boarding house there and renamed it The Vernon House. Sold again in 1865, the original owner repurchased it and renamed it The Brannan House. Women proprietors operated boarding houses there until the early 1870s.

4 Platte Bridge Station was later renamed in honor of Lieutenant Caspar Collins after his death in the Battle of Platte Bridge in 1865.

there a few needed days. I posted a letter at Platte Bridge Station for you. *I hope you will receive it soon.*

There was a very disturbing event prior to our arrival at the Station. I did not mention it in the letter posted from there but feel I can mention it now. In Ash Hollow, we were confronted by something that has been difficult for our little band to talk about. In fact, it was so horrific that I am at a loss for words. I am fine, as is everyone in the company, and I will find a way to tell you of what we witnessed, but for now it may be better left for a time when we are no longer feeling threatened by the presence of Indians. Perhaps I will be able to speak of it once I am in the safety of your embrace. For now, I prefer not to dwell on the image.

Our goal is to reach Independence Rock by July 5th, and it looks as if we will meet that goal.The children are looking forward to climbing the rock and inscribing their names upon it. We will spend a few days there so that the cattle can graze and have access to the fresh water in the Sweetwater River. I plan to use the time there to learn to improve my skills with my rifle. I don't know if I will need that particular skill, but Sam and several others have insisted that simply carrying the Hawkin will not protect me. Perhaps I will be able to provide our group with a rabbit stew or a deer for dinner.

This journey has challenged me and is, I believe, making me a stronger, better woman. I hope you will think so, anyway, and not be put off by a rifle-wielding woman! I promise I will not attempt to learn to spit tobacco!

More when I can. Know that I think of you and pray for your safety and well-being continuously. I have read and reread your letter from Platte Bridge Station. It is already wearing thin from my unfolding and refolding of it.

Yours, Olivia

Chapter Four

The summer days were beastly hot and humid. The women were cranky while working over the fires. Men, dripping with perspiration, worried about the toll on the oxen and mules. Children whined, often crying inconsolably. One particularly bad afternoon, Bob Whitcomb walked to where the women were working to both console the children and check in on Alice, whom he'd noticed was looking very tired.

"The Colonel has allowed that we might camp here for the rest of the day," he announced.He looked around, shook his head, and smiled. "We are a bit ahead of schedule, so a rest might be the best for humans and beasts alike."

Alice looked gratefully at her husband and mouthed the words "thank you."

He saw the exhaustion in her face and nodded. "Now," he shouted, "I expect every child of mine to help set up the extra canvases and rubber tarps for shade. After dinner we will all relax and try to have as good a time as we can. Is that understood?

He looked around at his children, who had all been fussing a minute before. None of them responded.

"That means no more whining!" he said, trying to be firm.

Sally, who had tried but failed to keep the children happy answered, "Yes, Papa."

He smiled at his oldest daughter and turned back to tend to the animals.

Sally and the older children quickly pulled out all the available material to create shade between and around the wagons.

"Olivia," Alice said, "why don't you take the younger ones to explore the river? You know how they love throwing stones."

"Are you certain?" Olivia asked. "I don't want to abandon you with all the cooking."

"I can't imagine anyone eating too much in this heat," Alice said. "Besides, I would consider it a great help to know the children were in good hands."

A couple of other women nodded, so Olivia reached out to little Ben, who eagerly grabbed her hand, and she called to all the little ones near her. "Let's have a march to the river!" she hollered.

When they reached the river, they found several wonderful surprises. A curve in the river carved out a shallow, rocky place where it was safe enough for even the youngest to get into the water to cool off. Soon, the whining and crying that had seemed impossibly endless a few minutes earlier, turned into shouts of joy and play. Olivia removed both hers and Ben's shoes and waded into the water with him.

"Oh," she said with a sigh. Then without a thought about how it might look to anyone, she sat right down in the river in all of her clothes. "Aaaah."

Jeremy, Adam, and Rebecca Meadows; John Johnson; and Margaret and Henry Allen all stopped and looked at Olivia with obvious confusion. She laughed out loud. "Have you never seen an adult sit in the water?" she asked. Then, without hesitation she began to splash them.

Ben shrieked happily and began splashing as well. Soon, the whole group was drenched, cool, and happy. When the older children arrived after putting up the shade structures, Olivia was sitting on a rock in the river sopping wet. They stopped, taking in the scene with a combination of amusement and amazement.

"Well, what are you waiting for?" Olivia yelled to them. "Shoes off and get in!"

The men and animals started to arrive a short time later.

When Hollis Johnson saw where Olivia and the group of children were playing in the water, he drove the oxen and mules farther downstream to the water. When the animals were watered, the men drove them back up to the campsite. Much to the surprise of the women, the men offered to retrieve the children for dinner.

Dinner cooked and waiting, Alice grumbled about the men disappearing. "Where in the world are they?" she said out loud. "I guess I will fetch them," she announced, shaking her head in irritation.

Alice could not believe her eyes when she arrived at the river. Olivia, along with every single man and child from the wagon train, was in the river and soaking wet from head to toe. She could not help but smile at the sight of them, and the sounds of laughter filled her heart with joy.

Bob looked up and saw his wife standing on the shore. He walked out of the water dripping wet, picked up his wife, and started to carry her into the river.

"My shoes, Bob! My shoes!"

Olivia moved quickly to pull off Alice's shoes. She tossed them onto dry ground, whereupon Bob moved out into the deeper water and set his wife down bottom first. At first, she shrieked, then quickly gave into the blessed coolness of the water and submerged herself.

Except for the Warrens, the other women ran down to the river after hearing Alice scream. Eyes and mouths agape, they took in the scene. One by one, they removed their shoes and walked into the water—the meal forgotten until much later.

Later, after the meal had been eaten, Olivia was cleaning up. Her clothing was still damp, but she had no intention of changing. The wet clothes kept her cool as she washed the dishes and put things away. She had insisted that Molly and Alice head back to the river with the children and was sitting writing a letter to her aunt when little Ben toddled up to her and held out his fisted hand. Alice had come up with him from the river and was watching him.

"Hello, my little darling," Olivia said to him. "What do you have?" She held out her hand. "Do you have something to show me?"

Ben opened his fist and dropped a handful of daisy petals into Olivia's palm.

"He picked them for you," Alice said. "He insisted on giving them to you right away." Olivia looked at the crumpled petals in her hand. "They are so beautiful, Ben! You picked these for me?"

Ben's head bobbed up and down.

"I will keep them forever and ever," Olivia said. "These are the most beautiful flowers I have ever seen." She reached her free arm out and lifted him onto her lap. "I will keep them in this special box," she said as she opened the box where she kept her writing papers and pen. "Every time I open my writing box, I will think of you."

He wrapped his chubby little arms around Olivia as far as he could. She kissed the top of his head and closed the box. When she looked back down at him, he was sound asleep in her lap. Olivia smiled, looked up at Alice, and whispered, "He is fine here, Alice. Go back down to the river with the others. Ben and I both might just take a little nap."

The river gave everyone relief from the daytime flies, but there was little escape from the nighttime mosquitoes.

The blood sucking bugs were hard enough on the adults in the group, but the children were miserable. Everyone was covered in bites. The cries of mothers yelling at their children to stop scratching went unheeded because it was impossible not to rub and itch at the multitude of red bumps.

"It almost looks as bad as the pox on some of the children," Olivia said, as everyone sat around the campfires swatting and slapping at the hordes of flying insects landing everywhere.

"I hear there are cases of smallpox on some of the trains ahead of us," Bob Whitcomb said.

"Cholera, too," Alice added. "I hope we are lucky enough to avoid the illnesses. Mountain fever can be survived, but it sounds as if the smallpox is painful and tough to survive in the wilderness."

"Smallpox is dreadful," Olivia said.

"You have survived it, haven't you, Olivia?" Alice asked. "Those are pockmarks on your face?"

Olivia nodded and her eyes drifted to the fire. She was no longer afraid to remember or talk about her voyage, but she knew that the danger of pox was very real on their journey. She did not want to overly frighten anyone. She instantly regretted her comparison of mosquito bites to the deadly disease.

"It was long ago and aboard a ship from my home in Italy," she said. "Once the first case appeared, there was no escaping. We were trapped in the steerage of a ship in the middle of the Atlantic. My parents did everything they could to protect us from the contagion, but in the close quarters of third-class cabins there was no way to avoid the spread of the disease."

"You survived, though," Molly said. "And you have very few scars. So, it is possible to live."

"It is," Olivia said. "I was quite lucky. There is no explanation for why I suffered a mild case when both of my parents had extreme cases and died."

Little Ben yawned. He'd stumbled over to where Olivia sat near the fire and had been leaning against her thigh. "Up, Livia," he said and lifted his arms to be pulled into her lap.

Olivia smiled and reached for Ben, pulling him up to curl in her lap. She knew he would be asleep soon.

When Ben was comfortable, Olivia continued. "I was lucky

in more ways than so many others. I did live and was not left with the multitude of grossly disfiguring marks on my face. My torso, arms, and legs bear the majority of pockmarks."

Esther Warren was busying herself, putting away hers and Chester's items, but turned at Olivia's last remark. "Does your betrothed know about your scars?" she asked. Her voice was without compassion and, in fact, held more than a touch of accusation. Olivia felt the assault in the question. If she had not been holding Ben, she might have confronted the woman for her rudeness. Olivia felt the discomfort of others around the fire, took a deep breath, and quickly answered Esther as civilly as she could. "Of course he knows, Esther."

"That must have been so awful," Molly said. "I can't imagine being that sick on a ship and waking up to find your parents dead!"

Olivia moved quietly to let the campfire smoke drift over her and Ben, careful not to wake him. The smoke seemed to keep the mosquitoes at bay. Images of the severity of the smallpox aboard the ship made her stomach lurch. Her parents both had extreme cases. Her mother was not even recognizable her face was so red and swollen with the angry pustules. "There were so many things about that time I remember," Olivia said, shaking the memory from her mind. "It was hard to leave Italy. I was seven, and it was the only place I'd ever known. It was so beautiful there. Palermo is on an island, and everywhere there was the sea. Still, I was excited for the adventure of a voyage and life in a new country that promised so much."

The breeze shifted and instantly the insects bombarded Olivia. She waved her hands over Ben's face to keep them away. Even though she kept her body covered with long sleeves and long skirts, the bugs found their way inside her clothing.

It was odd more than anything to awaken to the cold of my mother's body, but I was too sick to really understand that she was dead until I was better. There were so many times I wished I had died, too."

"I'm glad you didn't," Molly offered as she reached over to take Olivia's hand.

"It took a long, long time," Olivia said, "but I'm glad, too." Alice came and took Ben from her. She stood up. "And now, I will be glad to try to hide under anything to get away from these blasted bugs!"

"Sleep well, Olivia," Molly and Sam said in unison.

"Sogni d'ora," Olivia said. The Italian phrase meant dreams of gold, and when she had first explained the saying to Molly, it took on a whole new meaning as they headed for the gold fields of California.

Esther's question, however, kept Olivia tossing and turning well past midnight. Each mile closer to Stewart brought her more worry that her scars would be more than he had bargained for. Perhaps, she wondered, that is why it was so easy to fall in love from three thousand miles away.

Chapter Five

"The Colonel says we'll be crossing the North Platte this morning," Sam said as he joined the women after checking on the oxen. "He says it's running pretty swift, so everyone needs to be extra cautious. All the children should be in a wagon or carried across."

Hours later, after following the North Platte out from where they had camped, they came to the recommended crossing point. Hollis and Betty Johnson were in the lead and began the descent down the riverbank with great caution. The current was fast, but they managed well into the middle of the river. There, the current nearly tipped the wagon, but the oxen found footing and managed to pull ahead before the wagon toppled.

"Joseph," Abigail Allen called from the far riverbank with all of their children who had been carried across. "How is it?"

"Not too bad," Joseph called back. "Heeyah!" He yelled at the oxen and snapped the whip. Just as the wagon was caught by the current, the oxen lurched forward and pulled the wagon onto the river bottom.

Each wagon experienced the same frightening wobble at the deepest section of the river. With only two wagons remaining, and most of the children across the river, the fearful mood began to lift. John Clayton descended the bank and was just about to reach the current when he heard a scream.

"John!"

He heard his name called, but he turned toward his wife's voice and did not see her.

"Mildred!" Olivia called, her face a mask of horror. "Mildred!"

Sam had just driven his team down the bank, and he saw Mildred lose her footing and disappear beneath the water. "Molly," he called to his wife, "take the team and hold 'em here."

Molly and Olivia grabbed the oxen yokes and tried to hold and calm the beasts as Sam jumped from the wagon and dove in the direction where Mildred disappeared beneath the water. Downriver Mildred's hand popped up from the water, but just as quickly disappeared again beneath the surface.

On the opposite side of the river, John got his team on solid ground and ran into the river screaming his wife's name. "Mildred! Mildred!"

Nearly half an hour later, Sam hauled a sobbing and drenched John out of the river almost a mile downstream. When they reached the wagon train, John was still trying to convince Sam that they had given up too soon.

"Mildred is a good swimmer," he said. "It makes no sense." His voice broke as he tried to figure out why she was unable to swim to the bank. "She is a better swimmer than me. She had to have made it out somewhere."

The wagons had all crossed and everyone else was accounted for.

Colonel Dawes sat down next to John. "We need to keep moving, John. I am sorry."

"I can't," John said. He was still weeping. "I know she made it. We need to wait—give her a chance to get to us once she gets out of the water. She swims better than anyone I know!"

Dawes looked around at the others in the group. Mildred was well liked, and all heads bobbed up and down. The Colonel looked back down at John and said, "We'll wait here until after the midday meal, then we have to keep moving."

"She'll be here," John said as he stood up and moved back down to the riverbank. "I know she will. She's a better swimmer than me."

John started walking downriver again, calling his wife's name.

Olivia and Molly shared a pained look, and Olivia nodded. "Colonel Dawes," Olivia said. When the Colonel did not respond, she said louder and more urgently, "Colonel Dawes."

The Colonel started, "Sir," he responded, then realizing his mistake turned crimson, lowered his eyes to the ground and mumbled, "Ma'am."

"There is something that you should know," she began, then turned toward the sound of Mildred's name echoing up from the banks downriver.

The Colonel waited, saying nothing.

"Mildred wore several dresses beneath her apron," Olivia said, turning back to the Colonel. "But, more than that, she had sewn numerous pockets into those dresses and filled them with her mother's silver."

"Mildred!" came the faraway and strangled sob from farther down the river.

The Colonel removed his hat, ran his fingers through his greasy hair, and shook his head. "Blasted woman," he cursed at the ground. "Got sucked right down. Never had a prayer of coming up no matter how good a swimmer she was." He put his hat back on his head and went off in search of John Clayton, still shaking his head.

July 12, 1854

Dear Stewart

So, your betrothed is now fairly adept at shooting a rifle. Sam now insists that I carry one as I walk alongside the wagons. How can it be that I actually feel braver as I walk with a weapon at my side? I have not yet been able to kill a rabbit or deer for our dinner, but I am certain my skill will permit me to if given a chance.

A godsend along our way, after a nice rest at Independence Rock was a most fascinating phenomenon. A bit more than a day out from our rest, we came across an icy spring under which was pure, solid ice! [5] *I wonder if it was here when you and your family made the crossing. The children were in heaven, using chunks of them to lick and cool themselves. Some of the adults joined the children as well. It was such a treat to have ice water to drink! I am so fascinated by finding ice in the middle of summer!*

South Pass in the Wind River Mountain Range was difficult terrain. As we neared it, it always appeared as though we would be upon it by day's end. From a distance, the upper ridges looked as if great sheets of lace had floated down to lay among the trees. The white was, of course, snow, but I could not help but imagine angels dropping down to create the lace-like weaving between the trees. It took us quite some time to get through the South Pass, but we did manage. Though I found the mountains beautiful, I shivered at night with the cold. It was hard to believe that it was summer in the gusty, cold winds we endured.

Because South Pass is the point at which the continent is divided, many of the children were excited to spit on either side of the divide. I had great fun with them. Isaac and Caroline Fowler's three girls, Betsy, Jane, and Mary could not stop giggling about the mere fact that spitting was allowed. I joined them in spitting on one side of the divide and yelling, "Give our regards to the Atlantic!" then running a short way, spitting again, and screaming, "Tell that Pacific we are on our way!"

There are apparently several cutoff trails that are being used by

5 Ice Slough was actually a small subsurface tributary that drained into the Sweetwater River. Travelers looked forward to Ice Slough on the Oregon Trail. Today there is little ice left, and the slough is only accessible via private land.

some of the wagon trains, but Colonel Dawes wishes to stick to the *one he knows best. Fort Bridger will be our next stop, and then we will veer northwest to stop at Fort Hall before we pick up the southern route of the California Trail.*

The mountains are more intimidating than I imagined, but their beauty is more magnificent with each mile.

More soon.

Your Olivia

Chapter Six

August 13, 1854

Dearest Stewart,

It has been so long since I have written to you. Please forgive the absence of a letter. I hope to post this one from Fort Hall when we arrive there. We are stopped at Clover Creek encampment at Belmont. I suppose that the town was called Clover Creek when you passed through it some years ago. There is talk that the town will soon be called Montpelier, but that is just speculation for now.

Our mountain adventure took a heavy toll on a good many in our party. Oh, Stewart, the trials some of these families have endured!

Both Isaac and Caroline Fowler succumbed to mountain fever within days of each other. We stayed camped because we were in a decent place when the illness made it impossible for them to continue. The Fowler children were so frightened after the death of their father. Their mother had symptoms of the fever before her husband died and was already too ill to continue by the time we buried poor Isaac. I suppose it might be a comfort someday for the children to know that their parents were buried side by side on the mountain. Still, it was heartbreaking to see silent tears drip down the faces of those three little girls when we pounded the makeshift cross into their mother's grave and said goodbye.

Horace and Mary Grover, whose past was littered with an unknown number of stillborn children, instantly adopted the Fowler girls. It was an act of kindness I shall not soon forget. Mary slipped up behind the girls and placed her hands on their shoulders, knelt down, and when the girls turned toward her, she pulled them into her arms and said, "You have a home with me and Horace for as long as you want. We will take care of you now."

The oldest child, Betsy, crumbled into Mary Grover's arms and wept.

Joseph Allen, one of our farmers, also died of the fever. He left his wife, Abigail, with five children. The oldest, Fred, is only nine, but has already tried to take up his father's load. The other men in the train often check in on him to make certain he is managing.

I suppose I have waited to tell you the hardest of the deaths among us. Oh, the grief of losing a child! Charles and Lillian Meadows lost three of their eight precious children. The nine-year-old twins, Caleb and Connor, became ill with the fever. One of their younger boys, Adam, who was only five, was climbing up onto the wagon to ride with his father when he slipped and fell under the wagon wheel. He was crushed by the wheel before his father could halt the oxen.Lillian is a brave, sweet, strong soul. She takes care of the things that need her attention, but part of her heart seems to have been buried with her children back up the mountain. She has given herself wholeheartedly to her remaining children, but she seems to have aged years in just a few short days.

Chester Warren was bitten by a snake. We had to amputate his leg just above the knee. Colonel Dawes tried to convince him to remove the leg earlier, but Esther was certain that her prayers would be answered by God and that the venom would miraculously leave his body. As Chester became more and more delirious, several of us women forcefully held Esther while her husband's leg was sawed off. Colonel Dawes carries many medical supplies, and Chester was fortunate that chloroform was among them. I cannot imagine the horror of having a limb sawed off without it. Many of us have taken turns changing the dressing on Chester's leg. He gets stronger every day and seems to have passed the point where there is concern that he will die.

Esther's demeanor has changed ever so slightly. She has become dependent upon others in the party for her care, so is forced to respond more politely, but it is clear that courtesy and gratitude are not her strong suit. She is unable to tend to the oxen and refuses to learn to drive her own wagon. I, because I am the only single person in the group, have volunteered to drive her team. She spends most of her time sitting silently next to me. Her lips move, and I think she is in constant prayer. I fear God will tire of her company soon, and she will begin to lecture me.

The jostling and jolting of the wagon were so terribly uncomfortable for Chester that Molly and I made a swinging bed in the back of the wagon. We tied blankets to each end of the frame and had Sam and Bob lift him into it. That seems to have made the journey more comfortable for him. He smiled at me yesterday when I was changing his dressing and thanked me for such good care. Perhaps his wife will not be far behind in a change of outlook!

More later . . .

Chapter Seven

"Good Morning, Miss Olivia," Chester Warren's weak voice greeted her.

"Good morning, Chester. I had hoped not to wake you. You seemed to be sleeping so soundly," Olivia said.

"It was a good night."

"I'm glad," Olivia said and smiled. She finished removing the bandages made from one of Esther's many dresses. It was crusted with blood.

"How bad is it?" Chester asked weakly.

Olivia poured some whiskey onto a cloth and dabbed it across the wound. Colonel Dawes had the opportunity, on one of his earlier trips west, to observe a surgeon remove the arm of a young man who'd been shot through the bone. He knew the importance of leaving enough skin to cover the stump for healing. The skin was beginning to adhere to the stump.

"Well, I will feel better when we get to Fort Hall and a doctor can look at it," Olivia said, "but to my untrained eye, I think it is looking better each day."

Chester Warren reached out and rested a gnarled hand on Olivia's arm. "You have been a godsend, Miss Olivia. I thank you for your kind and gentle care."

Olivia looked at him. His face was lined with pain. He had developed dark circles beneath his eyes and had lost quite a bit of weight. She felt the quiver of his hand upon her arm and placed her hand on top of his.

"Your strength and courage during your ordeal had been admirable," she said. "It has been my pleasure to care for you."

"I did not want to come on this trip," Chester said softly.

"Esther insisted that God wanted us to set up our store in California. I should have put my foot down when I still had it."

Chester smiled wanly at his own joke, but Olivia heard the regret in his voice, saw it in his eyes. She reached her hand up and placed it on his shoulder.

"Greed," he continued. "I gave into her will and greed, as I always have."

"We all do things we regret in hindsight, Chester," Olivia said softly. "Don't punish yourself."

"I—I," Chester started and stopped. He struggled to find words and finally said, "I apologize for my wife," he began. She—"

Olivia stopped him. "There is no need. All is well." She smiled and patted his hand, turning to complete her work and rebandage his stump with clean dressing. "All you are to think about is getting well. That is your only concern."

Molly arrived with a plate of eggs and a slice of bacon and handed them up to Olivia, who assisted Chester in eating the meager meal.

Before she left him, she asked, "How is your pain? Do you need something for it?"

Chester shook his head. "Not so bad this morning. I will try to do without, I think."

Olivia picked up the bloody rags and said, "I will check in on you a bit later. Please call up to me if you need anything. I'll be driving your team, so I will hear you," she reminded him.

"Bless you, Olivia."

Chapter Eight

A weary, bedraggled wagon train arrived at Fort Hall, Idaho, in late August. The trail from the Bear River to the Portneuf River that led them to Fort Hall was a difficult one, but the now seasoned travelers managed. Olivia drove the Warrens' wagon with the only two oxen they had left. Although the Warrens' had begun with four sturdy animals, one was set upon by wolves in the night, and the other broke its leg and was put out of its misery with a shotgun to the head. Olivia still smiled remembering the night that the group feasted on the Warrens' slaughtered ox.

"Sorry about your animal, Mrs. Warren," young William Johnson had said to Esther about the ox that broke its leg. "It's real tasty, though! Thank you."

Esther had harrumphed at William, which he took as a "You're welcome" and helped himself to another slice of fried meat.

Fort Hall was a combination of whitewashed and log structures. Their blacksmith shop was one that many wagon trains counted on for major repairs, but Olivia was often thankful that their small group traveled with John Clayton. As an experienced blacksmith hoping to set up business in California, his knowledge and skills were invaluable along the way. John and his son Mark were well cared for by the women of the group, who tended to their meals since Mildred's drowning. John quietly accepted the care from them but seemed most uncomfortable doing so. He never mentioned his wife's death, but it was obvious that he was lost without her. Mark seemed to be doing well. He and Betsy Fowler had become quite close since their parents' deaths.

Olivia halted the Warrens' wagon next to Sam and Molly's and put on the brake. Olivia waited for Molly, and the two of them disappeared into the wagon to check on Chester. Sam took care of his own oxen and was just unhitching Warren's beasts from their yokes when Colonel Dawes arrived with a litter and two soldiers. Esther Warren was with them and was issuing instructions for them to exercise caution.

Several minutes later, Olivia and Molly emerged from the wagon along with one of the soldiers.

"Be careful!" Esther demanded.

"Yes, Ma'am," the young man answered as he reached up to lift the poles of the stretcher.

Olivia watched as the two men gingerly managed to extract the litter holding Chester Warren. The soldiers carried him into Fort Hall with Esther walking alongside as Sam, Molly, and Olivia tended to the Warrens' oxen and belongings.

August 31, 1854

Oh, Stewart. I am heartbroken.

I need to write of something that has had a terrible effect on the whole of our group. We were descending the big hill just before arriving in Belmont. The hill is so treacherous that many wagons simply tumble end over end because it is so steep in its descent. The men rode the wagon brakes hard, and we moved very slowly. Even so, we had several mishaps. The Claytons' wagon lost control on the way down the hill. The brake handle snapped off in John's hand and the wagon pushed their mules, startling them into a frantic run. They bolted off the path in a panic and the wagon bounced up and rolled over onto our little Ben, whose mother had just set him on a rock *a good distance from any perceived danger. She had been gone from his side for less than a minute to run back to her daughter, Sally, who'd tripped and tumbled several feet down the steep hill and was crying. In that moment, the panicked shout from John Clayton turned everyone in his direction. We all watched in horror as little Ben was crushed and died instantly.*

Poor Alice is ghastly white and shivers constantly. She has not spoken or eaten. The company took turns in vigil with Alice over Ben's tiny body all night. We buried him near the trail and covered his grave with many rocks to prevent the animals from digging him up. John is a carpenter, and his distress over his wagon killing Ben is palpable. He stayed up all night and made a beautiful cross with Ben's name and age and the date of his death. Oh, Stewart, I am heartbroken. Even so, I cannot even begin to imagine how Alice will cope with this loss.

Some of the most treacherous of our journey lies ahead of us. I am closer to you each day, and happier for our nearness. Thoughts of you will hold me through this time.

With love,

Olivia

Chapter Nine

Olivia walked for as much of the day as Chester Warren wished to sit up front and drive his oxen for short periods of time. She had placed a sack of flour next to him to help him with balance because he was still unaccustomed to the loss of his leg. They had spent a few days at Fort Hall, and the doctor there announced that Chester was fortunate to have had some very skilled and knowledgeable lay people to tend to his amputation. He was healing well and was able to obtain a pair of crutches.

The trek since leaving Fort Hall had been filled with interesting rock formations. The next major destination was the City of Rocks as they moved southward toward the Humboldt River. Though it might be days before they reached the rocks, Olivia found herself searching for them shortly after they left Fort Hall.

Molly joined Olivia for much of the walking, hoping to lighten the load for their oxen and the wagons that were in need of more and more repairs. Some of them needed to be abandoned.

"Do you ever worry that we have come this far only to die before we reach our destination?" Molly asked Olivia as they stopped to offer a prayer at yet another roadside cross.

Olivia placed her arm around Molly's shoulder. There was nothing she could say to reassure Molly because she had wondered the same thing and did not want to give voice to her own fear that she would never make it to California. In her darkest moments, when she did think about this journey, she could not help but think of her own parents' unsuccessful voyage across the ocean. They had left Italy with such hopes. Would Alice have allowed this trip had she known that Ben would die? Would any of us? Oh, what a tremendous price to pay. Olivia shook the painful thoughts from her and looked over her shoulder at Alice Whitcomb walking beside her wagon.

"I believe we will make it," she said to Molly, "but I do worry that Alice may give up the attempt."

Molly, too, gave a furtive glance over her shoulder. "I wish there was something we could do for the Whitcombs."

Alice had refused all company and companionship since they had buried Ben. She made it clear that she did not wish to speak about what had happened and preferred to be alone. Even her children had learned to let their mother be alone with her sorrow. The evening prior, Bob had apparently made an attempt to break through his wife's anguish. It was dark, and they were outside of the perimeter of the train. Olivia and Molly were inside their own wagon, making some adjustments to the supplies. They did not hear what Bob had said, but they could clearly hear Alice's answer. It was full of her pain and her anger.

"Faith?" Alice had cried out. "You want me to have faith? Fine. I have faith. So what? What does that even mean anymore? Am I supposed to believe everything will be alright? What does that mean? What will be alright—my soul?" Her voice increased in volume as she spewed out all of the horrible thoughts and feelings that had become locked inside her. "Things here on this trail will be alright? Can anyone on this journey even believe that anymore? You want me to just trust that God is taking care of things. Does that mean I should just accept that all the children who have died on this abysmal journey are part of some greater plan? Where is my responsibility, then? Do I just sit by and watch the sickness and the dying and the horror and keep smiling? How am I supposed to take care of my children—keep them safe, feed them, clothe them,

protect them from things I cannot see? I don't see God offering to help—no matter how much or how little faith I have. You want me to have faith, Bob? Fine, I have faith. For all the good it has done on this cursed trip, I have faith. Meanwhile, this is the life I have—this harsh, painful struggle of a life is where I live—and my faith has ceased to give me comfort, or peace, or a moment's worth of rest! "You need me to have faith, so I will tell you that I do—no matter that it is a ragged, fraying thread of belief—but this life has been wearing away at that thread and soon it will snap and disappear because I am too tired, too weary, too enveloped in darkness to hold that thread together," she said, her voice starting to lose its strength and anger. "I have faith, but for how much longer I cannot say because I cannot see the point. I no longer have the eyes, or the heart, or the soul to cling to something that abandoned me when my baby was killed before my eyes."

All went silent then. Even the crickets had stopped chirping. Olivia and Molly knew that many in the wagon had probably heard Alice's rant. And many probably felt the same. They both wiped the tears from their eyes and resumed their task.

As they walked the next day, Olivia commented, "She has neither spoken nor cried. It has been a week. Perhaps it is time to do something."

Molly looked quizzically at Olivia.

"Let's just walk with her. We don't need to talk if she does not want to, but we could just be with her. She does not need to walk alone."

Together, Molly and Olivia turned and walked back to where Alice walked by herself. They fell in on either side of her and simply walked in silence.

The three women walked together all day long and all the next day. On the morning that they saw the City of Rocks in the distance, Alice had still said nothing but seemed to have accepted the companionship of Olivia and Molly walking next to her.

"It is not necessary to watch over me," she said late that morning as the two women continued to trudge beside her.

"We really just want to be with you, Alice," Olivia said, slinging her rifle over her shoulder. "Ben is missed, and we all share in his loss."

Alice still hadn't cried over Ben's death. At first, she was in too much shock, then her grief turned inward as her anger at herself became punishment for not protecting him better.

"You do know," Olivia continued, "that only a miracle could have prevented his death under those circumstances."

"I should not have left him there. I should have placed him further away or kept him with me when I ran to attend to Sally," Alice said. There was no doubt that she had been over and over the many ways she could have prevented her son's death.

"Alice," Olivia said softly. "You may live in that moment for many years. Accidents are always filled with the regrets of 'if only.' It was an accident, and that sweet child would be heartbroken to know that you blame yourself."

"I always will," Alice said so sadly that Olivia felt her heart break with the raw, honest reality of Alice's pain. "I am only putting one foot in front of the other for the sake of my other children." She sighed long and heavy.

"Una preghiera," Olivia said without thinking.

"What does that mean?" Molly asked.

"It's something my grandmother used to say," Olivia smiled. "Preghiera means prayer. My grandmother would often sigh, especially after she got sick. I asked her about it one day. She said, 'un sospiro puo essere una preghiera.'" She shifted the Hawkin so it rested on her shoulder. Her memory brought her back to her grandmother's bedside. Finally, she said, "It means that a sigh can be a prayer."

Olivia nodded. "What a beautiful thought," Molly said. "Sometimes there are just no words."

That night as the women prepared dinner, Olivia said, "Alice, I know you have been too broken to realize it, but Sally is blaming herself, too. Eventually, you will need to help each other understand that neither of you is to blame. If you can't forgive yourself for you, then perhaps you can help your daughter know that she is not to blame."

Alice looked startled by Olivia's statement about Sally, and she turned to look at her daughter. For the first time, she saw the pain in the girl's face. She stopped and looked Olivia in the eyes. "I didn't realize," she started. "I . . . I . . . thank you, Olivia."

"You would have figured it out on your own, Alice," Olivia said. "Molly and I spent some time with her at Fort Hall. She was being very protective of you, but she needs you, too."

"Thank you, both." Alice said. "I can't help but blame myself. As a mother, I needed to believe that I could protect my children by sheer will. This journey has smashed that belief in more ways than I ever could have imagined. I feel as if I may never believe in anything again."

"Then know this, my friend," Olivia continued. "I will believe for you, and I will hold the sweet memories of you and your child for you, until you can return to that sweetness on your own." She slipped her free arm through Alice's and continued without another word.

Chapter Ten

They reached the unique rock formations of the Twin Sisters late that afternoon. The City of Rocks[6] was an amazing and unique area of natural rock jutting out of the ground. Olivia, Molly, and Alice hiked into what looked to be a secluded area to relieve themselves. Olivia was taking care of herself as the other two women held the blanket. She heard a horse whicker and became alarmed. She lowered her dress and cocked her rifle, then quietly warned her friends to be quiet and motioned to them to go for help. She silently peeked around a large rock into a small area filled with bushes. There she spotted two men, two horses, and one young Indian girl.

The girl could not have been older than ten or eleven years of age. The men, large, filthy, and oblivious to Olivia, held the girl between them. One was behind the child and had his hand over the girl's mouth, although she did not look as if she had the strength to holler even if her mouth had been uncovered. The child was in rags, nearly naked, and clearly had been so physically abused that it was a wonder she was alive.

"Keep her quiet," the taller of the men said as he clambered up on a large boulder. He had clearly heard the arrival of the wagon train and was trying to get a clear picture of what they might be up against.

---

6 When the trails opened in the 1840s, City of Rocks was just north of Granite Pass. Granite Pass was in Mexico, less than a mile from Oregon Territory. After 1850, the Pass became part of Utah Territory, and in 1872 an Idaho-Utah boundary survey error placed Granite Pass in Idaho Territory. With the completion of the transcontinental railroad in 1969, the overland wagon routes began to pass into history.

Olivia was struck by the eyes of the young girl. It was as if she had disappeared, or died, only her heart continued beating and her breath remained as an afterthought. The scene so enraged Olivia that she did not think before stepping out from behind the rock and demanding that the man holding the girl release her instantly.

Both men were so startled that the tall one on the rock lost his balance and tumbled down, landing on his backside and hitting his head on the very same rock. The one holding the girl startled, throwing his hands up reflexively letting the child go. She instantly crumbled into a heap in front of him.

The man who had fallen got up and was rubbing his head. He pulled his hand away from the back of his grimy hair to find it covered with blood.

"Son of a bitch!" he said. Then he looked directly at Olivia and smiled. "Sweetheart, you know you ain't got the guts to do anything with that there shotgun." He laughed.

Olivia's eyes darted back and forth between the two of them. The tall one seemed to be in charge. His hair and skin were so dirty he looked as if he hadn't been in a bath or a river for months. She could smell them both from where she stood.

The young girl opened her eyes and saw Olivia. For a brief second, Olivia saw that the child expected Olivia to shoot her. Keeping her shotgun trained on the men, Olivia took a step toward the girl to try to let her know that she was aimed at the men. The girl made no attempt to move.

"Olivia!" Molly said from behind her. "Oh, dear God!"

"Molly," Olivia said, "help the girl over here."

"Now, what you want with a nasty Injun girl. She ain't nuthin' to nobody," the tall one said.

The man who had held the girl was short, stocky, and

just as filthy as his partner. Olivia saw his eyes dart toward his holster and pistol, which were on a blanket about two feet away from him.

"Do not assume your friend is correct," Olivia said. "I will shoot you if you make a move toward your gun."

He turned to look at his friend whose pistol was holstered on his waist. Olivia looked at him, too, and saw his hand fly down to his gun. Olivia did not stop to think but reacted and fired at him before his gun was out of his holster. She was already cocking her shotgun again when the short fellow flung himself toward the blanket for his own weapon. Another shot rang out before Olivia's firearm was ready.

A bloom of blood grew on the blanket next to the still holstered gun. Bob Whitcomb stood behind Olivia. His own rifle was still smoking. Alice was with him, and her face was a mask of fury and pain. She ran over to the young Indian girl whom Molly had covered with her body during the gunfire. Molly sat up just in time to see Sam running toward her. He fell to her side and pulled her into his arms. The Colonel arrived, and he and Bob checked to be certain that the two men were dead. One of them was still alive, but barely.

Alice Whitcomb pulled the nearly unconscious Native child into her arms and began, at last, to weep.

They camped at the City of Rocks until the taller kidnapper died. He was shot in the groin by Olivia. She had not taken the time to aim and just shot at him instinctively. His last hours were spent in agony, but not repentance. He told them only that his name was John and that he and Gabe had picked up the girl in California. He had no idea what tribe she was from, and he didn't care.

Bob Whitcomb had taken aim and shot the other man

through the heart. He was buried in the place where he died. John Clayton made two crude signs for the men's graves that let any passersby know that they had kidnapped and raped a young girl. He put the dates of death and their first names on the wood. There was no comparison between these pieces of wood marking these graves and the one he had made for Ben Whitcomb.

The kidnappers had very little by way of belongings, but Colonel Dawes took the horses and weapons. The rest of their travel gear was so filthy that no one wanted to touch it.

Alice Whitcomb and her daughter, Sally, worked together to help care for the young Indian girl. Somehow, taking care of the poor child seemed to build a healing bond between Alice and Sally. Colonel Dawes was unable to determine the child's tribe, but calculated that once they reached California, they might be able to find someone who could help. Meanwhile, the child was recovering and seemed to relax into the safety and comfort of the Whitcomb clan.

Days later, the group arrived at the Humboldt River. The cattle grazed, and the company removed what items they could for the long trek beyond the Humboldt River and into the Forty Mile Desert, which would tax their oxen and mules. There would be no water for many days until they reached Carson. There had been restrictions on the amounts and weight of items that might be brought on the journey. For the most part, these rules were followed, but back in Council Bluffs with nothing but the plains ahead of them as far as they could see, folks could just not fathom the difficulty of the trek through vast miles of emptiness. Most had never seen a mountain. The thought of leaving precious articles behind was too painful. They were full of hope and promise and dreams of gold, and their faith in God to protect them had been so pure and innocent when they embarked across the plains when the journey began.

Meanwhile, Alice and her daughter, Sally, kept a watchful eye on the young Native girl, who was beginning to physically heal of her cuts and bruises, which had resolved into a myriad of colors—from purple to yellow. It was obvious, from the day of her rescue, that she had been repeatedly raped. At first, she tried to walk with Sally, but the effort always left her exhausted and in tears. Sally rode with her in the wagon, and together the girls found ways to communicate with one another.

After having spent months under the watchful eye of so many Indian tribes, it seemed incongruous to see the child in the garb of white children. The child had the long, black, straight hair of her people. Her skin, the parts not suffering the trauma of bruising, was a deep, burnished bronze. As the swelling reduced, her eyes took on an almond shape, their deep blackness hiding her pupils. Her nose was tiny and flat, and beneath it her lips were still swollen and cracked. Behind them were slightly crooked, but very white, teeth.

"She is very sweet," Alice said to Olivia one evening after supper had been eaten and the women were cleaning up. The instruments were tuning up for an evening of music, and the child, who had kept to herself, sat near Sally away from the campfire.

"She and Sally have become inseparable," Olivia said. "It's good to see them venturing out of the wagon." As the girls searched out everything they could find to learn each other's language, Sally understood the child's name to be Little Deer.

Alice looked over to where the girls sat. Though Little Deer still made no eye contact, she seemed most at ease when she was with Sally.

"I'm not certain that everyone is comfortable with Little Deer in our midst," Alice said as she looked around. Esther

Warren kept her distance, and her disapproving glare had made it clear she was not happy to have the Native girl with the group. Alice remained sensitive to the situation, even as others in the train appeared to have gotten over their discomfort of the situation. "I know it may cause trouble to be discovered by Indians with an Indian child," she said, "but what were we supposed to do, shoot her?"

"You did the only thing any of us could have done, Alice," Olivia said. "If you hadn't taken the child in, I would have."

"I wonder how your future husband would take to you arriving with a child?" Alice asked with a smile. She reached for cups to fill with coffee for the children. As an afterthought, she said, "Hope we don't run out of beans entirely before we reach Sacramento. Don't think we could get anyone to drink the water without them."

Olivia chuckled. "I am amazed at what we have consumed on this trip, but I must say that rattlesnake surprised me the most." She was scraping out the Dutch oven to clean and asked, "Is Little Deer sleeping any better?"

"She is still unable to fall asleep at night unless Sally sings to her and holds her hand," Alice said. "But she wakes up crying less. I cannot imagine what she went through with those monsters." Alice shook her head at the memory of the City of Rocks. "Monsters," she muttered.

The day prior, Olivia had engaged in a conversation with Colonel Dawes, who had ceased ignoring her since the death of Mildred Clayton. She conveyed to him her regret that neither of the men killed at the City of Rocks were alive to be turned over to the authorities in California.

"I am afraid, Miss Olivia," Colonel Dawed replied without looking at her, "that those men got the only justice they would ever see from anyone 'ceptin' maybe the Injuns themselves."

"Why? What do you mean, Colonel? Surely, they would have had a trial where we all could have testified to what happened." Her indignation sizzled just beneath the surface of her skin.

Dawes grunted, then said, "To my knowledge, the people of California don't much care what happens to the Indians. May not be fair, or right, but not much protects the Natives from us paleface folk."[7]

Olivia could not believe her ears. "Surely you cannot be serious, Colonel!" She was incensed by the information and ready to explode. She waited for him to retract what he said.

"Wish I was, Miss Olivia," was all the Colonel said. With that, he got up and walked away from her, clearly not interested in pursuing the discussion further.

For the first time since leaving New York, Olivia felt a tremor of fear about the land she was about to call home.

---

7 It was not until 1860 that California passed an amendment to the Act for the Government and Protection of Indians (approved April 18, 1860). The amendment declared that Indians who were not already indenture/enslaved could not be kidnapped.

Chapter Eleven

For days after learning about the lack of justice for Indians, Olivia fumed. She, Molly, Sam, Bob, and Alice engaged in several conversations about the issue as they walked. Little Deer began to appear more frequently at the edge of the campfire in the evenings. Although Sally stayed with her, Little Deer still shied away from the group at large and preferred to lean against the wheels of the Whitcomb wagon.

"It's nice to see her come out of the wagon, even just for small bits of time," Molly said as she hung a pot over the fire.

"I think it is a good sign," Alice said. "Have you noticed that she and Sally are beginning to learn each other's language?"

Olivia looked over at the girls, who were sitting in the shade of the wagon.

"Hair," she heard Sally say as she reached out to touch Little Deer's hair. "Hair," she repeated.

Little Deer reached up and took a handful of her own hair, pointed to it, and repeated "hair," and then said, "*hana*."

Sally repeated the word *hana*. Little Deer nodded her approval and then repeated the word hair. Sally smiled and nodded.

Throughout the meal preparation, as they ate and even afterward, Olivia caught bits and pieces of the language lesson. Along with Sally, she'd learned the words for eye, *sutu*; nose, *huku*; and mouth, *awo*.

When dinner was done and the instruments began to arrive around the fires, Olivia pulled her accordion onto her lap and said to Alice, "I'm glad Little Deer has you and Sally to care for her. I can see her face beginning to relax a bit." It was the first time Olivia brought her instrument out since Ben died. Fingering a few chords, she looked up and saw William Johnson headed her way, looking as enthusiastic as ever. Before long, Olivia turned to find Sally and Little Deer inching closer as well. Little Deer seemed mesmerized by the instrument; her eyes were opened wide.

"Sally," Olivia said, "reach your free hand over and press one of the keys."

Sally did so as Olivia pumped the bellows. Little Deer had not let go of Sally's other hand but scooted a bit closer. When she was close enough, Sally took the girl's hand and pressed it into the keys of the accordion. Olivia squeezed the bellows gently, and Little Deer let out a tiny squeal of delight.

As Little Deer became more and more engrossed in the sounds from the accordion, she released Sally's hand without seeming to notice. She allowed Olivia to guide her fingers to different keys and even play several of them together. Little Deer and Olivia became as one, with Olivia working the bellows and Little Deer pressing the keys. Even young William seemed to realize the significance of what was happening because no one had been able to engage Little Deer over the days, except Sally. Everyone heard the child wake up screaming in the night and watched her cower and cry when any of the men happened to get too close to her.

Oliva had just helped Little Deer through a single key version of a lullaby. As the last note died out, William clapped his hands. Sally joined him and was beaming ear to ear. Little Deer looked quickly to Sally. Slowly, her mouth formed a shy smile. For a brief moment the child's eyes glistened with life and excitement, then she quickly reached for Sally's hand and scooted back away from Olivia. It was another healing episode for Little Deer and the Whitcombs.

Chapter Twelve

The Sink of the Humboldt River[8] was a day behind them, and Olivia was picking through the remains of an abandoned wagon for burnable wood. She'd fashioned a sling of sorts to carry anything she could find to burn whether it be sage, twigs, old wagon parts, or buffalo chips, when she heard the cry from Chester.

"No!"

She and Molly ran over to find that one of his oxen had collapsed and died. Molly looked up at Esther, who somehow managed to look more inconvenienced than anything.

"I'll get some help, Chester," Olivia said and went to hail the Colonel to gather some of the other men to help unhitch the dead ox. Even an emaciated ox weighed as much as a thousand pounds.

The carcass of the dead ox would lay with the bones of previous animals that died along the way. Olivia had lost count of the many piles of sun-bleached bones they had passed since entering the Sink of the Humboldt.

Now, with only one ox left to pull their wagon, the Colonel was advising Chester to leave as much as he could behind.

"This one poor ox won't make it another day pulling all you got in there," the Colonel said.

Esther glared at the Colonel. "We have removed everything we can spare, Colonel. There is nothing else we intend to leave."

"It is entirely up to you, Chester," the Colonel continued, "but I must warn you that we'll not stop again on your account.

---

8 The Humboldt Sink is actually a mostly dry lake bed where the Humboldt River ends. Reaching The Sink was considered a hopeful sign, but once there, it meant many days without any water. The Sink is eleven miles long and four miles wide.

These good folk have shown you every kindness, and I'll not impose another delay on them because of your hardships."

"Chester," Esther said, "tell the Colonel we have sacrificed enough and will not tolerate such threats!"

Chester looked at the Colonel, then at Olivia. His eyes indicated he was tired, weary, and in pain. Olivia had nursed him through the majority of his amputation and recovery. She had gained a respect for his ability to endure the pain that must have tortured him for the past month. With all the others, she wondered how he would respond to the Colonel's words.

"Colonel," Chester said, "you will please ignore my wife, tie up the canvass on my wagon, and remove anything you think we can live without."

"Chester Warren!" Esther cried out as she stood and nearly toppled off the wagon. "Don't you dare!"

"Silence, woman!" Chester shouted. "Help these good folk deliver us from our stubbornness. When we are ready to move on, you will walk with the others!"

"Colonel," Chester continued, "we are most grateful for the patience and kindness we have been shown. We will abide by your sage counsel and hope not to burden you and the others with our problems for the remainder of the journey."

Esther remained standing, glaring down at her husband as if she could not believe what was coming out of his mouth.

Chester had not taken his eyes off the Colonel as he spoke. He never turned around to look at Esther again but closed his eyes with his back to her and said in a firm and frightening voice, "Now, wife!"

Esther flinched but obeyed.

As the Colonel directed the removal of Warren's many belongings, Esther stood watching, her face stricken with grief and horror.

"No," she whispered, "Please, no!" as the barrel with her good china was lifted and placed on the ground.

As her things were removed from her wagon, Esther paled. When the men lifted down her harmonium, she burst into tears and attempted to push it back up into the wagon.

"No!" she screamed. "Everything but that!"

Her feeble attempt to return the instrument to the wagon was ignored. As the keyboard was set on the side of the road, the Colonel jumped down from the Warrens' wagon and helped drag the dead ox to the side of the trail where it would rot and eventually leave nothing but bleached bones to mark its life.

"Let's get moving!" the Colonel shouted.

The train started its slow course toward the Sierras. Chester Warren sat taller and straighter than Olivia had ever seen. Somehow, he looked younger, and she knew Chester was going to be just fine.

As the wagons pulled away from Esther Warren's beloved belongings, Olivia turned back periodically. Esther sat crumpled and weeping, with her arms around her harmonium. For the entire of their journey, Esther never once played the instrument, despite repeated requests. The requests eventually stopped. Now Olivia wondered if Esther regretted her refusals. Few of the others seemed to care whether Esther stayed behind or returned to the group.

Olivia remained at the back of the wagon train, occasionally turning to keep an eye on Esther. She did not want Chester's moment of strength to haunt him. Nor could she allow Esther to die a broken woman left by those she had alienated for so long. She called to Molly.

"I am going back for Esther," she said. "We will catch up with you."

When she reached the still sniffling Esther, who was draped over the harmonium, Olivia put her arm around the older woman's shoulders.

"Come, Esther," she said in a whisper. "It's time to go."

Esther Warren looked up. Olivia saw the heartbreak in her eyes. She also saw something that perhaps no living soul had ever seen in those eyes before—confusion. And the look softened her.

Olivia supported Esther with her arm around the older woman's waist. They walked slowly. Occasionally, Esther's breathing jerked suddenly as if she had forgotten to breathe and suddenly her body remembered for her. Every once in a while, she would sniff and automatically pull a handkerchief from her sleeve to wipe her nose.

They tarried behind the group, walking slowly, Olivia still supporting her around the waist.

After some time, Esther said softly, "I wasn't always so disagreeable, you know?"

Oliva said nothing but gave Esther's waist a tiny squeeze.

"It hasn't been easy for me," Esther continued, almost as if in a trance. "Maybe if I had been able to have children, things would have been different."

It almost seemed as if Esther were talking to herself. Olivia felt a bit like an eavesdropper.

"Five miscarriages in five years," Esther said almost wistfully. "It takes a toll on a soul."

They walked again for some time before Esther said, "So I threw myself into helping Chester with the business. It didn't take long to see how everyone took advantage of him. He did not know how to stand up for himself."

"How did you meet Chester?" Olivia asked.

"Oh, we were arranged through our parents. I didn't meet

Chester until a few days before our wedding when he and his family arrived from some little town in Illinois. Our mothers were distant cousins, but they grew up near each other until my mother's family moved to Iowa."

"How long have you been married?" Olivia asked.

"I'm not sure, maybe sixteen years?" After a long pause Esther continued. "Chester should not have been a businessman. But his parents wanted to set him up to be in business, so they built a storefront like the one they had started in Illinois and left him to run it. By the time I came in and saw how bad things were, I, well, I had to take charge." She shook her head. "Like I said, maybe if I had been able to have children, things would have been different. As it was, running the business and collecting debts from people did not make me a popular woman in our town."

"Sounds like it was very stressful for you," Olivia commented. "Was this journey to be a new start for you both?"

Esther grunted. "Some new start. My husband has lost his leg and I," she stopped and turned to see her belongings in the distance, but they were no longer visible. "I have lost . . . I have lost everything." Esther's voice faded on the word everything.

"You still have Chester," Olivia said softly.

"Do I?" Esther asked quietly.

Olivia took her arm from around Esther's waist and slipped it through her arm. "He may not be the same Chester he was at the beginning of this journey," Olivia said, looking ahead to where they were nearing the end of the wagon train, "but that may not be a bad thing. And, you still have him."

As they were nearing the others, Olivia stopped and turned to look at Esther. "I don't think any of us are the same people who left Council Bluffs, but we still can be here for one another, no matter what lies ahead."

The sun beat down on Olivia and Esther as they trudged through the desert. Olivia said, "My aunt raised me. She is a very wise woman. I hated everything when I got to the shores of this country. I hated the city, hated the voyage that killed my parents. Hated the disease that left me scarred. I was full of so much anger that I was certain I would spend the rest of my life angry and resentful. Life had become a painful existence, and I did not know what would become of me." Olivia let her thoughts drift back to her childhood days when she'd first arrived in America as a lost, sick, orphaned child. Then she smiled a far-away smile and nodded, almost as if she were listening and agreeing with someone or something. "My aunt used to say to me, 'Everyone breaks in this life, bambina. Unless we break, we cannot change. We cannot grow.'

Olivia chuckled and turned to Esther. "You know what else she said to me?"

Esther looked at her and shook her head.

"She said that God must love me very much to break me so hard!" Olivia closed her eyes and smiled. "I spent a very long time being angry at God."

"And how did you get over that anger?" Esther asked.

"Not easily, I admit," Olivia added with a smile. "But another thing my aunt said finally made sense to me one day." She looked ahead and noticed they were almost ready to join the others. She was grateful because she was very thirsty.

"I am afraid to ask," Esther said.

Olivia was nodding to herself as if she understood another layer of her aunt's words. "It isn't the breaking, but how we choose to mend ourselves that makes all the difference." Olivia squinted into the sunlight, but out of the corner of her eye she thought she saw Esther's head nod up and down, too.

Chapter Thirteen

"I do not know how in the world your lone ox made it over miles and miles of desert, Chester," Olivia said as the last fort came into view.

"Perhaps we should look on the poor beast's survival as a bit of a miracle, Miss Olivia," Chester replied.

"You were due for one," Olivia said and laughed.

Chester turned his head over his shoulder and could make out his wife walking with Mary Grover and the three Fowler girls. They seemed to be in lighthearted conversation.

"Looks like the good Lord has blessed me with an abundance of miracles lately," Chester said. His smile was sweet and full of gratitude.

But, Olivia knew, as did everyone in the train, that one more snowy pass lay ahead of them. The Colonel had intended to take them through Donner Pass[9] but changed his mind and opted for the more southern Carson Route that would take them along the Carson River after Fort Churchill.

They were so close to the end of their journey. Some days Olivia could not believe that in a few short weeks she would be in Sacramento and married to a man she loved and had never met. Other days, reality grabbed her by the heart and warned her that there was still a mountain to cross. The mountains had claimed more lives and caused more travails than the long, tedious treks across the plains.

The journey had begun with forty-four hopeful souls nearly

---

9 During the winter of 1846-47, George and Jacob Donner attempted to take a group of immigrants through the pass of the Sierra Nevada Range. The pass was completely blocked by snow and more than half the party died. The remainder of the travelers survived by consuming their dead compatriots.

five months earlier. They'd lost eight of the group, including Brewster, and several wagons. They were weary and much worse for wear, but still hopeful in ways that Olivia had difficulty comprehending.

Olivia left Chester's wagon and walked more quickly to catch up with Molly and Alice.

"Shouldn't be too long before we get to Mormon Station,"[10] Alice said. "Then, there is only one more fort before Sacramento, Olivia," Alice said playfully. "Are you getting cold feet?"

"Hah!" Olivia said with a laugh. "I'm sure my feet will get cold in the mountains, but, no, they won't get cold for fear of marriage."

"I certainly hope we will get a chance to meet this man," Alice said.

Molly tripped over a rock but managed to catch herself before she fell. "Well, Sam and I have no intention of leaving Sacramento until we meet Stewart. Further, we fully intend to be present when you tie the knot."

Again, Olivia laughed. "You are certainly welcome to do both," she said. "In fact, I thought to extend an invitation to the entire wagon train."

The lead wagon was pulling up to Mormon Station. Molly went off to help Sam but shouted over her shoulder, "Well, we are your family now!"

I best go help Bob and gather up the children," Alice said. Before she walked a few steps she turned and said to Olivia, "Molly is right, you know? We have become family on this journey."

Olivia nodded, her eyes misting as she acknowledged Alice's

---

10 Mormon Station is located in Nevada on the eastern side of Lake Tahoe. It was built as a trading post for travelers on the Carson Route of the California Trail. The station was built in 1851, but it burned down in 1910. A museum with original pioneer artifacts was built on the site.

comment.

"Don't know how I ever could have made this trip without you, Olivia," Alice added.

A bloom of tears rose suddenly in Olivia's eyes. She lowered her head to keep Alice from seeing them, but Alice was too quick. She returned, gave Olivia a quick hug, and ran off while Olivia headed for the Warren wagon.

Chapter Fourteen

The Carson Route of the California Trail led them through the Mormon Station at the top of the Sierra Nevada Range. The weather was milder than Olivia anticipated. Perhaps, she thought, it is just that each mile closer to Stewart warms me in surprising new ways.

Sally and Little Deer walked beside the wagons as the trail started to descend on the western slopes of the Sierras. Little Deer was healing and had seemed more relaxed in the past few days. She was more comfortable sitting with the others around the campfires at night. A couple of times she even approached Olivia and her accordion and indicated her desire to press the keys. Her hand was no longer a constant in Sally's hand. The girls often walked with other children, playing skipping games and singing songs, but much of their activity seemed concentrated on learning the different words for everything they encountered.

As they passed the bleached bones of some poor, long dead ox, Olivia saw Little Deer point and say, *Keteuteu!*

Sally responded with, "Bone!"

The girls ran off to find other things at which to point, each repeating the last word learned until they found something new.

As they began this final descent, Olivia noticed that Little Deer seemed more animated. Her whole spirit seemed lighter.

"Is it just me," Alice asked, "or does Little Deer seem particularly happy this morning?"

Olivia nodded. "I was just thinking the same thing," she said.

She and Alice were walking together, keeping an eye on the children.

Alice reached up to adjust her bonnet. "The man you shot," Alice started, "didn't he say that they had kidnapped her in California?"

"He did." Olivia could feel Alice's anxiety. "Alice," she said, "that does not mean he was telling the truth. Part of me hopes that she is just feeling safer and relaxing a bit in our company."

"No, I know it doesn't," Alice responded. They walked in silence for some time after their exchange.

Moving down the mountain was slow going. They made little progress in order to keep control of the wagons. They stopped for the night well before dark as they came across a meadow that seemed perfect for the animals and for keeping the wagons level.

As the group gathered for dinner and the end of the day, Olivia sought out Colonel Dawes. The man was pouring himself a cup of coffee after having finished a hearty bowl of stew. He sat on a log.

"Colonel," Olivia said, "what do you know of the Indians in this area?"

Although he was still no more comfortable speaking with women than he was at the beginning of the trip, the Colonel no longer ignored them as intently as he had. He cleared his throat but avoided eye contact with her. "Not a whole lot," he said. "I believe the tribe on this side of the Sierras might be the Miwoks."[11]

Olivia squatted down to be level with the man. "Have you ever laid eyes on them?"

Dawes thought for a moment. "Maybe. Not sure."

Olivia tried not to become frustrated with the man's short, simple answers. "Please think back to those encounters, sir. Did they have similar features to Little Deer?"

The Colonel took his pipe from his pocket and knocked it against a rock. "Hhmm," he grunted. "Might be, I s'pose."

Olivia waited for him to get his pipe smoking. "I am asking, Colonel, if we might be at risk if the girl is found with us by her own people."

"No way o' knowin'," the Colonel responded, at which point he stood up, nodded, and added, "'Night, Miss."

The trek down the Sierras was slow going, but the group found game to be abundant. There were deer, elk, quail, and all sorts of small game. It was October, so many of the animals were migrating to lower elevations to winter in the warmer foothills. Hunting was easy and the grass plentiful. The livestock and people ate well.

Whether it was the nearness of their destination, the milder weather of the lower elevation, or the fact that every beast and person was well fed and physically content, there was a sense of excitement around the camp the second evening.

They were camped along the South Fork of the Cosumnes

---

11 Barrett, S.A. (1908). The Geography and Dialects of the Miwok Indians. University of California Publications in America Archaeology and Ethnology, Vol. 6, No. 2. The Miwok (or Moquelumnan) are generally believed to have occupied the western slope of the Sierra Nevada mountains from the Cosumnes river on the north to the Fresno River on the south.

River on the second evening of their descent when John Clayton, who still mourned the loss of Mildred, stood up and said, "You folks got me and my son all the way to California. Wish my Mildred was still here, but" he paused, clearly not comfortable with speaking publicly, "we—me and Mark, well, we are mighty appreciative of each and every one of you." He appeared as if he were about to say more, but his eyes glistened in the firelight, and he sat down as quickly as he had stood.

A harmonica started up a tune and pretty soon the instruments all came out. The songs and dancing were full of joy and thankfulness. In spite of the joy of the evening, Olivia observed the losses of so many of those gathered. The sadness was etched in the faces of the Meadows family, the Fowler girls, John and Mark Clayton, and Alice and Bob Whitcomb. She knew their sorrow would always be part of them. Nonetheless, they joined in the celebration, honoring their lost loved ones with careful smiles and silent tears.

Chester and Esther Warren sat at the far end of the circle from Olivia. She looked over at them. Chester grinned large at her, and she saw his remaining foot tapping in time to the music.

Esther nodded and offered Olivia a quick smile as she leaned her head on Chester's shoulder. Chester reached down and grabbed her hand.

Even Little Deer danced around the fires with the other children and laughed when she tripped on her dress and fell down. She still had not become accustomed to wearing the clothing of pioneers, but she had accepted the dress, shoes, and bonnet without complaint. Olivia was fairly certain the child would be far more comfortable in a short hide and moccasins, but Little Deer seemed to be adapting to what she surely considered unusual clothing.

As Olivia's eyes closed that night, she pushed the rosary

beads through her fingers and thanked God for bringing her this far, for helping them through some of the most difficult days most of them would ever know, and for blessing them with each other and Little Deer.

"Thank you especially, Lord, for Little Deer." Olivia thought back to how Little Deer broke open the dam in Alice that so desperately needed breaking. Little Deer seemed to have brought healing to the whole Whitcomb family. "That broken child has been a blessing for all of us. Please keep the children safe and warm tonight. Amen."

Chapter Fifteen

It seemed, as it had since the first day nearly five months ago, as if Olivia had only just dropped off to sleep when the four o'clock gunshot jolted her awake that morning. It didn't matter how long they had been traveling, the morning shot always startled her. She groaned, but her groan was cut short by a scream. Olivia jumped up, stuck her head out of the puckering string to see if there might be any way to tell what had happened. There were no fires lit yet, so she expected it would be difficult to see anything.

"Sam, Molly?" she called into the dark.

"Right here," they both answered.

Several fires seemed to start simultaneously. As soon as she got down from the wagon, Olivia headed straight for the Whitcomb wagon, where the sound of highly agitated crying filled the air.

"Alice?" Olivia called up. "Alice, what is it?"

Alice's head emerged from the wagon. Even in the poor

light, Olivia saw the fear and worry in her face.

"Little Deer," she said. "Gone."

From inside the wagon, Sally could be heard crying. "We have to find her! Someone must have taken her in the night!"

Frantically, Sally climbed down the side of the wagon, still sobbing. She desperately looked around the folks gathering as if hoping that Little Deer might suddenly appear. After scanning the group and not seeing her friend, she took off for the woods.

Her father, trying to get the morning fire going, called after her to no avail. He took off running after Sally, easily caught her, and carried her flailing body back to the camp.

"Sally Martha Whitcomb!" her mother shouted into her face.

Sally startled and became still. Even her hyperventilating and crying was scared silent.

Bob put her down but kept his hands on her shoulders.

"Mama," Sally said softly. "Mama, please help me look for her."

Alice wrapped her daughter in her arms. "Of course, we will look for her," she said, smoothing her daughter's hair. "Of course we will, honey, but there is something you must do for me first."

"What is it?" she asked, wiping her face with her sleeve. Sam had his campfire going strong. Alice looked up, put her arm around her daughter, and walked over to Sam's fire. They sat down on a fallen log.

"Honey, have you noticed how happy Little Deer has been these past days?" Alice asked softly.

Sally nodded.

"Do you think that might be because these woods are familiar to her—that perhaps this might be her home?"

Sally's head shook back and forth. "No." Sally answered firmly. Her mouth turned downward into a pout. "No, because she is happy with us. And, and she would never leave without saying goodbye."

"I don't know. None of us can say what we might do in a similar situation," Alice said. "We will look for her, but I need you to consider that she may have left on her own."

Sally nodded, but tears fell from her cheeks and made tiny divots in the dirt at her feet.

By the time the sun crested, and it was time to move the wagon train, there was still no sign of Little Deer. Everyone available to search was calling for her as the wagon train moved slowly down the mountainside. Parties of two or three ventured into the woods calling her name. There was never an answer.

When the sun was overhead and the day was beginning to warm, Olivia, Molly, and Sally emerged from a stand of trees where they'd been searching for Little Deer. Olivia had her arm around Sally. "You know, Sally," she said, "your mother and I were talking just yesterday about Little Deer's light heartedness since we began down this side of the Sierras. If this were her home, would you want her to find her family?"

They stood in a large meadow. A cloud moved over the sun. Sadly, Sally nodded.

From the other side of the meadow, a thunderous rumble of horse's hooves and the whoops of a multitude of Indians filled the meadow surrounding the slowly moving wagon train.

Colonel Dawes halted the train and rode up to the Indian who had indicated to the others to stay put.

Olivia, Molly, and Sally went over to where Dawes and the Indian, who was sparsely dressed in a type of loincloth and had strips of material tied at intervals around his legs, were looking at each other. The Indian wore no clothing above the waist and was adorned with several strands of beads. His hair was long, graying, and quite thick.

"We are a peaceful group," the Colonial said. "We mean no harm."

"You," the Indian said in English, "take Indian girl."

"Found," the Colonel said, clearly alarmed. "We found her and saved her."

The aging Native did not appear to understand the Colonel. He said again, "You take Indian girl?"

"No," the Colonel said again. "Not take." He was clearly frustrated and concerned at not being understood.

"*Sake-t osa-ti!*" Sally cried out as she stepped toward the Indian. "*Sake-t*!"

The old Indian looked down at Sally—quizzically, at first, then his eyebrows raised. He swung his leg over the front of his horse and slid down. When he knelt in front of Sally, he smiled

"*Sake-t*," he said and placed his fist over his heart.

The line of Indians on horseback just behind where Sally and the Indian were smiling at each other parted. A male Indian strode through the opening on foot. A woman wearing a head band, short hide skirt, and fringed top was with him. Between them was Little Deer. No longer in pioneer garb, she was bedecked in beautiful leather skins, moccasins, and beads.

"Little Deer!" Sally shouted, and she ran into her friend's arms. Little Deer hugged Sally, then turned to the couple with her and said to Sally, "*Upu, Utu.*"

Sally smiled and nodded. She repeated, "*Upu, Utu.*" She turned and said, "These are Little Deer's parents."

Little Deer nodded happily and pointed at her father again, "*Utu*," then pointed at the old Indian with whom Sally had been speaking. "*Utu.*"

Sally looked back and forth between the two men and finally nodded. "Your father's father, your grandfather," she said, pointing to the older of the two Indians.

Little Deer nodded and grinned, then started looking around at all the people from the wagon train, searching. When she finally spotted Alice, she took her parents' hands and pulled them over to the Whitcomb's wagon where Alice stood. As the entire meadow full of pioneers and Indians looked on, Little Deer's mother fell to her knees, grasped Alice's hands, and pressed them to her forehead.

Alice looked around, her face crimson with embarrassment. Little Deer said, "My mother thanks you."

Alice dropped to her knees and embraced Little Deer's mother. "Thank you."

"My family look and look many days," Little Deer said. "Think I die. Think wolf carry me off. Want meet, thank you."

Alice and Little Deer's mother stood. Little Deer grabbed her mother's hand, then her father's and brought them to stand before Olivia.

"Olivia," Little Deer said by way of introduction, then raised her arms as if holding a rifle "shoot bad man."

Little Deer's father looked at his father, who had come to join them. They both looked astonished.

Her grandfather asked, "*Osa?*"

"*Osa.*" Little Deer said as she smiled and nodded.

A murmur of surprise and talk erupted among the Indians, who were all quite astonished that a woman, *Osa*, was the one who shot the kidnapper. Then all turned to make room for the women of the tribe who arrived on foot. Their arms were full of baskets.

"Gifts," Little Deer's grandfather shouted in English.

Colonel Dawes said with more than a little worry in his voice, "We are at the end of our journey, we have nothing left to trade."

Little Deer understood. "Gifts. No trade. To thank for life," she said as she pointed to herself.

Little Deer's family proceeded to present many things to the Whitcombs, Olivia, and others in the wagon train. There were conical baskets, hide blankets, moccasins, dried meats, and beautifully strung beads. When all the gifts were given, Little Deer pulled Olivia and Bob Whitcomb to their feet. The grandfather walked solemnly to stand before them. He held out his hand. Little Deer put a leather strap in her grandfather's hand. He reached up and wound the band around Bob's upper arm.

"You Miwok warrior," he said. A spear was presented to Bob. It was adorned with feathers and matched the spears carried by the other native men.

Olivia watched in awe as Bob blushed, then smiled, and said, "Thank you." He held out his hand instinctively to shake the older Indian's hand. Little Deer said something to her grandfather, who then took Bob's hand in both of his and held it.

The grandfather then turned to Olivia. His smile was mostly in his eyes as he reached for another leather strap. He wrapped it around Olivia's forehead and adorned it with a single feather.

"You Miwok warrior," he said and presented her with a bow and quiver of arrows. "*Osa* warrior. *Sake-t.* Friend."

"*Sake-t,*" Olivia said. "Friend."

Little Deer then led her grandfather to Sally. The dust kicked up by the wagons during their morning travel, combined with Sally's near constant crying, created clean tracks down her dirty face. Little Deer ran off to her mother but returned a moment later. When she arrived at her grandfather's side, she was holding a complete leather Native outfit for Sally. The garments were exquisitely crafted, especially the moccasins. In addition, there was a feathered ceremonial headband, multi-colored beads, and a bow with a quiver pouch filled with arrows.

Little Deer handed the items to Sally, who had begun to cry.

"Sister," Little Deer said to Sally. "Heart sister." She placed her hand over Sally's heart and then her own.

The people of Little Deer's tribe erupted in whoops and cheers, then brought forth a feast of foods. Though there was little ability to communicate, the celebration was an event to remember. Indians and pioneers set up campfires and cooked foods. Feasting, singing, and dancing went on for a couple of hours. Little Deer pantomimed playing the accordion to Olivia, who brought out the instrument and showed many of the native children how to make music on it. Their eyes lit up and opened wide at the first sound.

When the sun indicated it was about midafternoon, it was time to say goodbye. Little Deer embraced Alice and said in English, "Thank you." She had tears in her eyes and lowered her head quickly to hide them, but she could not hold back the flow when she embraced Sally.

Sally, likewise, cried openly as she said goodbye to Little Deer. They held each other for a very long time, then Little Deer walked to her parents' sides and disappeared into the thick trees. The wagon train moved in the opposite direction, continuing the descent down the mountain to Sacramento.

Chapter Sixteen

Stewart

"Slim! Hey, Slim!"

Stewart Anderson stopped his ascent. He was chopping away at the base of a huge Douglas fir that had been topped by his friend, Erik, a high rigger. "Yeah!" he called down.

"Message from town," Burley called up to him, waving the paper in his hand.

Stewart was glad to be high enough up the tree that only one of his fellow loggers were able to see the smile that lit up his face from ear to ear. "Olivia," he said softly. Then he sent up a quick prayer of thanks and started to make his way down the thick trunk. He was probably descending the tree faster than he should have, but his anticipation of the news that Olivia had finally arrived in Sacramento propelled his legs faster than his reason.

Burley laughed out loud. "Spectin' somethin' special there, Slim?"

Stewart's logging outfit had nicknamed him Slim after his first attempt at high rigging. His lanky form and slender build made him a natural, although he opted to work lower to the ground. Everyone had a nickname. Stewart was pleased to be given a nickname so quickly on the job.

Slim's feet hit the ground with a thump. He reached for the paper in Burley's hand.

"No hurry, I guess," Burley teased him as he turned to walk away with Slim's message.

Slim ran up behind Burley, who was nearly six feet tall, and quickly reached for his message, yanking it from Burley's hand.

Burley turned. On his face was a look of mock surprise, which was quickly replaced by a warm smile. "Okay, Mr. Lover Boy. All yours."

Without a moment's hesitation, Stewart ripped open the envelope.

Stewart,

I have arrived in Sacramento and wait for you at the home of Miss Clark. Please come as soon as you are able.

Love, Olivia

There was no hiding Stewart's grin as he read the note.

"I'm guessin' it's a good thing you already got your weddin' duds packed and ready to go," Burley said.

Stewart looked at Burley, his boss, whose real name was Burgess Wilson. "She's arrived," he said with more than a little wonder in his voice. "She's here," he said again, then swallowed hard.

"Well, what you still standin' here for?" Burley shouted, laughing. "Go get 'er, son! And have yerself a right honeymoon!"

Stewart ran down the mountain for his gear, which was, in fact, already packed and had been for some weeks. When he got to the stables, he found Burley had his horse already saddled. He blessed Burley for the foresight to do so before he came up the mountain with the message.

Stewart mounted his horse. It was all he could do to keep from racing all the way to Sacramento. All his restraint was needed to maintain a steady trot so as not to wear the horse out. He had a good two days of travel to get to Sacramento.

"You've waited this long," he said to himself. "Don't kill

your horse for trying to get to your gal in one day."

Stewart let his mind roll around all his plans and hopes and dreams for his life with Olivia. He patted his shirt pocket, where her picture nestled against his heart and smiled.

"She made it, Midnight," he said to his horse. "She made it." Then, because he couldn't help himself, he spurred Midnight into a gallop and let out a whoop as the wind whipped through his hair.

When Stewart reached Sacramento, he went directly to the church his parents built and founded when they arrived in California. Walking through the front doors evoked an emotion for which he was unprepared. He'd been so lost in thought of Olivia, so engrossed in the actual meeting and marrying of her, and so excited to begin his life with a woman he loved that he'd stepped away from his past and the accompanying pain.

The church was empty. He was grateful. Before his eyes adjusted to the dimmer interior from the bright sunlight outside, they filled with tears. The smell of the church—the wood and the lingering smell of incense, the flicker of the candle near the altar—swirled around him and filled him with aching sadness that his parents had not lived to see him marry.

His father was an exceptional pastor. His mother nurtured the parishioners in her role as the minister's wife. Together, his parents raised him with firm, loving guidance, a strong sense of God, and an understanding of the importance of community. He walked toward the front of the church on shaky legs and fell into a pew nearby. Without warning, a sob escaped him.

Stewart Anderson sank to his knees and wept.

When he finished crying, Stewart raised his head and looked at the cross. He pulled his handkerchief from his pocket and mopped his face, taking a deep breath and sighing.

"They're here, you know."

Stewart turned to find Reverend Stevens standing in the aisle behind him. As the minister walked toward him, the soft-spoken man who had taken his father's place as the leader of the church, smiled and said, "Your parents are here."

Stewart pushed himself up from his knees and sat down, still a bit shaken and a little embarrassed at being discovered crying. He looked down at the floor.

Matthew Stevens moved to the pew behind Stewart and sat down. "I heard your gal arrived, and I have been expecting you to come by to make arrangements to marry her. Been waitin' on you. I didn't know you were here. I am sorry if I disturbed you."

Stewart still said nothing and wasn't at all certain he could speak.

"This morning," the Reverend said, "I was here very early. Sun wasn't even up yet. I like to come in to pray before the work of the day." He smiled and looked at the cross. "Couldn't shake the feeling that I was not alone." He got up and ambled toward the altar.

"Do you know when your father built this church?" he asked.

Stewart thought back to that time. "I remember it was in the fall of '45. It opened sometime before All Saint's Day. That was the first service we held in the church. It was kind of a big deal. Why?"

The Reverend walked toward Stewart and looked up at a window over on the eastern side of the church.

"Like I said," Stevens continued, "I had this feeling I wasn't alone. I asked for some help. Prayed for a little enlightenment and reassurance that I wasn't losing my mind." He chuckled a little and looked directly at Stewart for the first time.

"Sun came up while I was praying," he said. "Somethin' told me to turn around, so I did." He walked up to the altar. "I was kneeling here and turned around to see the first ray of morning light shoot through that window," he jutted his chin up at the eastern window, then walked to the west wall near the front of the church.

A ladder leaned against the wall. Stewart hadn't noticed it when he came in.

"The light from the window shone on something up on this wall. Never noticed it before. Couldn't make it out, but I could see there was something there, so I went and got the ladder. Come here, son."

As Stewart got up to walk over to where the minister stood, he felt something he could not quite describe. He was a little anxious but not frightened.

"Climb to where your hands reach the top rung," the minister instructed.

Stewart's brows knit together as he wondered what could possibly be up there. He hesitated briefly, then slowly climbed the ladder. When his hands reached the top rung, he stopped.

"Look to your right," Stevens said softly.

Stewart's eyes scanned the wood to the right of where he was. It was no longer illuminated, but the light within the church was enough that he could make out the heart carved into the beam. Inside the heart were his parents' names, "Lloyd and June."

Stewart stared at the heart for some time, his heart thumping in his chest. When he finally rested his head on the top rung, Reverend Stevens said, "You didn't know it was there, did you?"

Stewart reached his hand to touch the carving. His fingertips traced each letter, then his hand covered the heart momentarily. "I did not know."

When he finally descended the ladder, he looked at Matthew Stevens, shook his head, and said again, "I did not know."

"So," Stevens said, "I believe that God found a way to tell us that your parents are here and that they are happy for you."

Stewart's eyes began to mist, and he swallowed the lump in his throat.

Stevens rescued him. "So, when do I get to meet this lovely gal of yours?"

Stewart laughed. "I haven't even met her yet!" He shook his head. "Came here first to let you know she was here and to make some arrangement with you."

"My wife would never forgive me if I let you meet your gal looking the way you do," Stevens said. "Best come on over to the house and get cleaned up or I will be in a heap of trouble."

Stewart nodded and followed the minister to the front door. But before he left, he turned and looked for the carving. It was not visible from where he stood, but knowing it was there filled him with peace.

Chapter Seventeen

It was a transformed Stewart Anderson who made his way to the home of Miss Clark. He was cleaned up, shaved, and combed and was wearing his Sunday clothes as he and Midnight rode through the gate to the boarding house on the river.

Someday, he thought, maybe me and Olivia will have a pretty little place on a river somewhere.

As he neared the front of the home, he spotted two women heading to the front porch steps from the flower garden. When they reached the porch, one of them, who Stewart knew to be Miss Clark, went into the house. The other turned around and looked out to the road.

"Whoa, Midnight," Stewart said as he stopped the horse and stayed right where he was.

He knew her immediately. She saw him as well. One of her hands reached for a porch post. The other flew to her heart.

Neither of them moved. It was as if they were frozen in time, each needing to believe that the moment had come and not wanting to lose the importance and significance of what certainly had to be a miracle. This gift—seeing each other for the first time after having waited and worried for so long—was sacred. They both knew it.

The porch door squeaked as Miss Clark stepped back outside.

Stewart could see her smile and say something to Olivia. She then gave Olivia a tiny push to propel her down the steps.

Stewart spurred Midnight into a gallop. When he was close enough, he stopped the horse and dismounted. He started to run to Olivia without thinking, just planning to scoop her up in his arms and kiss her, when he stopped short. His face, on which there had been a huge grin, turned crimson, and he suddenly didn't know what to do. He felt his insides turn to jelly. Stewart walked hesitantly, unsure of himself and what to do in this situation. He opened his mouth to say something, but not a sound came out.

He stood there, staring at his betrothed with his mouth agape and could not think of a word to say.

Olivia smiled and held out her hands to him. He looked down at them and slowly reached for them, feeling the tremble in her hands all the way up his arms. At first, he thought it was his own hands shaking, but he soon realized that she was terrified, too. He looked back up into her eyes and smiled.

"I can't believe you are finally here," he said. "I—"

Awkwardly, they moved into each other's arms. Stewart felt as if his soul had arrived home.

It may have been a minute, or an hour, Stewart could not have said how long he held Olivia in his arms. He felt her arms around him. Her head was perfectly nestled against his chest. He held her tightly and did not move. He did not want anything to alter the moment.

Olivia was the one to finally pull away, but just slightly. She looked up into his face.

"You are Stewart, aren't you?" Olivia said with a twinkle in her eye.

Stewart burst into laughter, and Olivia joined him. When the laughter died down, he said, "Beautiful and funny. How lucky can one man get?"

The screen door smacked into the frame, and they both looked up to find Miss Clark standing on the porch with a tray, a pitcher of lemonade, and three glasses. "Come on up here, you two. Some plans need to be made."

When they settled on the porch, Miss Clark said, "Now, I understand you will be married by Reverend Stevens over at the Episcopal Church in town. Has the day been set?"

Olivia looked at Stewart, who was having a very hard time taking his eyes off her and an equally hard time not smiling.

"Yes, Ma'am," he said. I just came from there. It will have to be the day after tomorrow because there is a funeral in the church tomorrow."

"That would be Jess Johnson," she said. "Poor devil."

Stewart nodded. "I didn't know Jess, but Reverend Stevens spoke highly of him. Said they would be waiting on some family to arrive from Oregon, and they didn't know exactly when the family might get into town. Otherwise, we could have married tomorrow. He looked at Olivia again and added, "I am sorry about the delay." Then to Miss Clark he said, "I hope it won't inconvenience you to have Olivia for an extra day."

"Don't be silly," she said. "In fact, that will be perfect. I want to host a little reception here at the house for your wedding."

"Oh, no, Miss Clark!" Olivia blurted out. "We really don't want to put you out any more than you have been. You have already been so generous letting me stay here until Stewart arrived."

"Nonsense," she responded. "It has been a delight having you here, my dear. And I knew Stewart's parents quite well. It would be an honor to have a little party for your wedding. I won't take no for an answer."

Olivia and Stewart both stammered their thanks as the woman continued. "Now, Olivia, I am sure there will be some folks you traveled with on the wagon train who will still be in town.

You must invite them. Stewart, I doubt any of your logging friends would make it in time even if we sent a courier up there this minute. If any are in town, they are welcome. I know several friends of your family who would love to celebrate with you. I'll get word to them."

"What can we do?" Olivia asked.

"You can go wander the town and get to know each other," she said. "Or walk here by the river. Stroll the gardens. You two have hardly said two sentences to each other." She stood up.

"Olivia," before you and Stewart head off, however, I'd like you to have a look at my Aunt Jenny's wedding dress. It might fit you with an adjustment or two. Unless you brought something with you."

Olivia shook her head and looked embarrassed. "I never even gave a thought to a dress. Oh, Miss Clark, you are a marvel."

Once Olivia disappeared into the house, Stewart drank down

the remainder of his lemonade and stood and walked toward the corner of the house. The porch wrapped around the house and had a swing hanging in the perfect spot to watch the Sacramento River. A fish jumped, then another. Off in the distance he watched a hawk circle higher and higher on an updraft. Stewart sat on the swing and thanked God for blessing him with such an abundance of happiness.

Chapter Eighteen

Two days later Stewart stood at the altar with Reverend Stevens. Music filled the little church from the harmonium in the corner where someone Stewart did not know sat happily pumping the pedals.

There was a sprinkling of Sacramento folk in the pews, including Miss Ophelia Jane Clark, who finally divulged her name to Olivia when they finished fitting the wedding dress.

"I guess I was expecting at least a few folks from the wagon train," Stewart whispered to the minister.

Just then the doors to the church opened, and a crowd filled the doorway. Stewart expected Olivia but did not see her anywhere in the crowd. He did not know any of these people, but they all looked at him as if they knew him. Steadily, in procession, they all walked up the aisle of the church. There were children, men, and women. As they reached the front of the church, they parted, spreading out on either side of the aisle. As the last of them separated, there stood Olivia, her arm linked with an older man on crutches, who was missing a leg.

Stewart nodded his head and smiled as he understood that these were the people with whom Olivia had spent the last five months. His grin overtook his face as he looked at Olivia, who was radiant in her borrowed wedding dress.

Although it may have been floor length at one time, it fell above Olivia's ankles. The bodice was of white worked embroidery. The sleeves were fitted at the wrists, with some beadwork, and full sheer to the upper arm where horizontal gathers bunched in rows. The neckline was low and scooped out to the tips of Olivia's shoulders. When Olivia tried it on, Miss Clark saw her face fall in the mirror as Olivia's hand reached up to cover her smallpox scars.

"It is entirely up to you, my dear," Miss Clark had said to her. "It is your wedding day, and as the bride, we want you to feel beautiful."

Olivia dropped her hand and looked at herself. Miss Clark stepped back and gave her a moment to contemplate her decision.

Finally, Olivia turned and examined the dress and herself. "If my aunt were here, I know what she would say—and I know she would be right."

"What would she tell you?" the older womanasked.

"Not to be ashamed, to wear my scars with pride and courage," Olivia said. "I want to," she started, then hesitated, "and the dress is gorgeous, Miss Clark, but—"

"But it is your wedding day, and the attention should focus on your beauty and your happiness, not your painful past," Miss Clark said authoritatively. "Of course, your aunt is right. However, I believe if she were here, she would want you to do what makes you happiest. I have an idea."

Miss Clark returned with a rather sheer piece of lacy material that Olivia was certain she'd spotted adorning a table in the sitting room. Miss Clark draped the material around Olivia's neck and slipped the bottom inside the low neckline. The material reached around to the back.

"That should work just fine," she said. "What do you think?"

Now, as Olivia stood before Stewart and an entire church full of people, she blessed Miss Clark for her understanding and foresight. She felt beautiful, more beautiful than ever in her entire life. While she knew the scars were there, she was happy not to have to display them on her wedding day.

"Who gives this woman to be wed?" Reverend Stevens asked.

As one, every man, woman, and child who traveled the long journey with Olivia shouted, "We do!"

Reverend Stevens laughed. "I do believe that is a record-breaking response to that question," he said. "Excepting the bride and groom, you may all be seated."

The ceremony was short, sweet, and simple. At its conclusion, Reverend Stevens announced that a reception was to be held at the home of Miss Clark. Everyone was welcome.

It was a perfect fall afternoon with full sun and mild temperatures. There were tables set outdoors near the rose garden. Flowers from her garden adorned each of Miss Clark's tables, matching the small bouquet that Olivia carried down the aisle. There was a table filled with all kinds of things to nibble and plenty of lemonade to go around.

Stewart met each and every person from the wagon train, the only exception being Colonel Dawes.

"Can you imagine that poor man trying to be congenial at something as social as a wedding?" Molly asked Olivia as she and Sam explained the man's absence.

"He took off the day after we arrived carrying mail back east," Sam said. "He must make a decent living bringing wagon trains west and mail all back along the route to Iowa."

"Well, I am sorry he is not here," Olivia said. "I would have liked you to meet him, Stewart."

Stewart was pumping Sam's hand up and down. "Thank you so much for bringing Olivia. She has told me such wonderful things about both of you," he said to Sam and Molly. "I am grateful she had you both to travel with."

"Well, we told Olivia," Molly said, "so now we will tell you. We are her family and that makes you family as well."

"Are you planning to settle in the Sacramento area?" Stewart asked.

Sam looked around at the river flowing nearby, the trees, flowers, and the intense blue of the sky. "Seems like as good a place as any to start the hunt for gold."

"And," Molly added, "if the gold digging does not pan out," here she giggled at her own pun, "we can always open another bakery to cater to folks. Seems like opportunity is abundant here."

Sam took a swallow of lemonade and then said, "Maybe I'll

join Stewart and become a lumberjack."

"One thing at a time!" Molly said with a laugh.

The afternoon flew by with Stewart and Olivia chatting with, and meeting, so many new folks. Stewart felt as if he knew so many of the people from the wagon train that after a few introductions, he played a guessing game with himself, naming the individuals in his head before Olivia introduced them. He was right most of the time but had not guessed that it had been Esther Warren playing the harmonium at the church.

A bell started clanging wildly on the front porch. Miss Clark asked for everyone's attention as servers carried trays filled with glasses of champagne to the guests.

"We have," Miss Clark announced, "someone who wishes to address the crowd."

A middle-aged gentleman walked up the steps to the porch and turned to face everyone. His head was balding, and he was somewhat heavyset. He sported a very large moustache and clearly had no problem speaking in front of crowds. He reached up and ran his index finger along one side of his moustache and then along the other.

"Hello," he said. In a voice loud enough for everyone to hear and with a good deal of European accent, he said, "My name is John. I have known Stewart since the day he arrived with his family here, what, about 1845, wasn't it Stewart?"

Stewart nodded. "Yessir, Mr. Sutter."

Stewart and Olivia made their way to the porch amid quite the buzzing of whispers that the actual John Sutter was speaking.

Sutter cleared his throat. "This young man and his parents filled quite a need in this town when they arrived. Weren't many churches around back in the forties, and this fella's father brought his family out from New York to establish the First Episcopal Church where we earlier witnessed the marriage of these two. Now, I know it must have been a hardship for a young boy to leave all he knew to venture across the country to a new land. That is something I know a little about."

A few chuckles rippled through the crowd, for some had heard of Sutter's story of leaving Switzerland to avoid jail because of mounting debts.

"Nevertheless," Sutter continued, "this young man accepted his fate and never complained. In fact, I have known him to be a hard worker—first for his parents and now as a logger. He is as decent a young man as I have ever known, and it is a pleasure to be here to celebrate this day with him. Stewart, your parents would be proud of the man you are.

"I have only just met Stewart's bride today but have spent time speaking with a few of the folks with whom she made her way here from Iowa. From all accounts, she is as kind and decent a woman as can be found."

"And so," he concluded, "I would like to propose that we raise our glasses to salute the marriage of Stewart and Olivia."

"Stewart and Olivia," the crowd responded.

The bell clanged again, and Miss Clark called out to the crowd, "And now a very special surprise. Please turn around, everyone!"

Almost as one, the crowd turned to see two servers holding

a large cloth up, concealing something. When all eyes were upon them, the servers dropped the cloth to reveal a large table filled with sweets.

The children gasped. The adults oohed and marveled at the array.

Olivia's eyes filled with tears. She turned to look at Miss Clark, wondering how the woman had known, but the woman was already headed to her.

"The sweet table is an Italian tradition at weddings," Miss Clark announced to the crowd. "Quite a lovely tradition, I might add. But this one is not provided by me. In fact, it is not provided by anyone here." She turned to the couple. "Olivia, your Aunt Maria and Uncle Michael could not be here today. However, they wanted you to know that they are thinking of you and wishing you all happiness. This table is provided by them with their love and blessing."

Olivia knew that her aunt would have loved to be with her on this day of days. She was so touched by the gesture that tears instantly blurred her vision. She turned and buried her face in Stewart's chest. He held her as she sniffed softly and then whispered in her ear, "What is your favorite? I want to try it before it is gone."

Olivia laughed and hugged him, then scanned the table for the anise cookies and found them dripping with vanilla frosting.

Miss Clark watched her and smiled. "Your aunt informed me those were your favorites. Don't worry, there is a separate batch for you to take with you. By the way, your aunt sent all the recipes, and Sam and Molly worked with my cook to prepare everything. They are a lovely couple."

Olivia and Stewart made it a point to thank them as well as the cook.

Chapter Nineteen

Midnight was used to carrying a mounted rider, but Stewart had worked with him at the camp to practice pulling a wagon. He'd purchased a small wagon that was waiting at Miss Clark's stable. Midnight adapted well to the light harness and wagon.

"Good boy, Midnight," Stewart said to the horse. "You need to get used to this because our gal is here now, and we need you to help out a little more."

Olivia smiled as she listened to Stewart calm Midnight. "He is a beauty," Olivia said as she stroked the horse's neck.

The couple bid their guests farewell. Olivia did not know where they were going for their first night as husband and wife, but she didn't care—as long as they were together.

When they arrived in downtown Sacramento, Stewart pulled up in front of the Orleans Hotel. [12]

"Oh, Stewart," she exclaimed. "It is so grand."

He laughed. "You have definitely been on the trail too long." He helped her out of the wagon and grabbed their bags from the back. Olivia stared at the three-story brick building.

12 The Orleans Hotel was built in 1852 with lumber that was cut and numbered in New Orleans and shipped around Cape Horn. It burned during the Great Fire in 1852 shortly after it was built. It was rebuilt in only twenty days.

She hadn't seen a building this big since she left the east coast at the beginning of the year. As she admired the brickwork, a young porter came, took their bags and arranged to have the horse and wagon stabled nearby.

Once inside, Olivia looked up. "It is even grander on the inside," she said, staring around her in awe.

Stewart pointed out the stairway and said, "You should have seen the original building. It was only open for a short time. It burned down last year."

"Was it brick as well?" she asked.

Stewart shook his head. "In fact," he said, "it was all wood. The wood was shipped around Cape Horn from New Orleans. That's how the hotel got its name. It was built very quickly because all of the lumber was numbered so it could be assembled as fast as possible when it arrived."

"How sad that it burned down. How did the fire start?" she asked.

Stewart thought for a moment. "I don't think anyone ever figured that out," he said.

Olivia was intrigued by the ornate railings and beautiful woodwork detail inside. She looked back at Stewart and smiled. "It is wonderful."

"Let's hope it stays wonderful," he said. As they walked over to the desk to check in, he added in a whisper, "This one flooded the day after it opened."

"Stewart Anderson and Olivia Rus-," he stopped, smiled, and shook his head. "Sorry, this is Mr. and Mrs. Stewart Anderson checking in."

The desk clerk smiled and nodded. "Yes, sir, I have you in the California Suite on the third floor. If you will sign here."

Stewart signed, and the desk clerk popped the ringer on the bell. "Congratulations to you both. Enjoy your stay."

A bell boy arrived. Stewart and Olivia followed him to the staircase.

The room had a small divan, a dining table and chairs for two, a three-panel screen concealing a water table and pitcher, and a four-poster bed. The bell boy accepted a coin from Stewart and left after having shown them around.

Olivia made her way to the dining table, upon which was a bottle of champagne, two fluted glasses, and a card that read, "Mr. and Mrs. Anderson."

"For Slim and Olivia," it read. "From Burley."

"Slim?" Olivia looked at him, her brows knit together in confusion.

"My nickname," he said. "That's the only thing anyone calls me at camp. He looked a bit chagrined. "Sorry, I should have mentioned that in one of my letters."

She reached up and placed a hand on his cheek. "Don't be sorry. There is so much we still don't know about each other." She smiled, then added, "Slim."

He laughed. "I guess that's true."

"And who is Burley?"

Slim picked up the card and smiled as he held it in his hand.

"Burley is Burgess. Burgess Wilson, my boss at the logging camp." He set the card on the table. "He is a good man. You'll meet him soon enough."

Olivia's eyes drifted over to the bed. Her face turned red. Stewart saw the blush and said, "Let's open this, shall we?" He proceeded to open the bottle from Burley.

Olivia let out a breath. She hadn't been aware that she was holding it in until she heard it escape her. "I guess I am more nervous than I thought I'd be," she said timidly.

"Me, too."

Stewart struggled with the cork on the bottle and finally got it to pop. It put a dent in the ceiling. "Oops."

Olivia started to laugh and then saw the champagne begin to bubble up and out of the bottle. "Oh, dear!" she cried as she grabbed the two glasses and Stewart tipped the bottle toward them.

When the glasses were filled and the bottle set back on the table, he held his glass toward her. "To my beautiful wife," he said.

Olivia looked into his eyes and saw the sweetness and strength of the man she just married. It filled her with gratitude. Her heart swelled. "To my beautiful husband," she responded.

Stewart lay silently in the next morning's light, just watching Olivia sleep. Her dark hair spilled over the pillow in gentle waves as the sun slowly moved over it, giving it an impossible luster. He was used to waking early and knew she was, too, but was glad for the time to just watch her. He thought about their first night together and could not help but smile at the memory. They were both awkward and hesitant, but it did not take long for them to begin to feel more at ease. "I definitely have to thank Burley for the champagne," he thought. He remembered Olivia's eyes as he removed the neckpiece from her dress. She had never kept from him the description of her smallpox scars, and he had not really known what to expect.

He hoped they would not matter to him, and he set his mind to make that so. Still, wanting to feel a certain way and feeling that way were sometimes incompatible. He'd removed that material very slowly, praying that his expression would not betray him. His hands shook. Her eyes misted. She swallowed hard and took a breath.

The lace addition pinned at the back of Olivia's neck fell into his hands, and his eyes moved down to her neckline. He let his eyes linger on the pockmarks for only a moment or two, then he lifted his fingers to her face and smiled.

"You are no less beautiful to me now than you were a minute ago," he said. He pulled her to him and kissed her.

He was glad he hadn't had to lie to her. He hadn't been quite sure what to expect, but he'd anticipated angry looking divots. Although he knew there was nothing like that on her face, for he had her photograph, he wasn't exactly sure how bad the pockmarks would be. In fact, they were divots in her skin—nothing more. There was no color to them, they were simply irregularly shaped depressions. They did not bother him at all.

When the sun's rays scooted over her face, her breathing began to change. It wasn't long before she opened her eyes and found him staring at her.

"How long have you been awake?" she asked.

"Long enough to fall in love with you all over again."

He leaned over to kiss her, and they made love in the morning light.

"Shall we order room service for breakfast," he asked, "or go down to eat in the restaurant?"

Olivia stretched and smiled. "Do you have a preference?"

"I am happy either way," he said.

"Room service sounds like such a luxury," she said, "but I am used to so much more activity. Can we go downstairs? The restaurant looked charming. Perhaps we can walk around town a bit more after breakfast."

Stewart and Olivia were finishing their breakfast when a couple of business gentlemen sat at a table near them. They could not help but overhear the men's conversation as it related to San Francisco.

"It is a shame," the older of the two said. He was dressed in the style of a man with money.

"The extreme growth of the past few years, combined with the lack of government," he said as he shook his head, "has created a breeding ground for criminals, corruption, and debauchery."

The younger of the two was about fifty years of age and impeccably dressed. "What with the Chinese arriving in droves and the Australians dumping their penal colonies there, is it any surprise? It does seem to be a bit better since the

Vigilantes[13] instituted their unique form of justice. However, I do try to avoid going to San Francisco if I can help it."

"Still," the older man said, "the opportunity for those of us in banking and mining is too great to avoid. Too much money to be made."

"I agree," said the young man. "I just wish I did not feel that I had to take own my life into my hands to make it."

"Excuse me, gentlemen," Stewart said, stopping at their table as he and Olivia were leaving.

The men looked at him as if he were out of place at such a nice establishment. His suit, though clean, was clearly not in their class. He was uncomfortable approaching the men but had become alarmed at what he'd overheard.

"I do beg your pardon," Stewart proceeded. "I am planning to leave for San Francisco tomorrow. We," he indicated Olivia, "have just married and are planning to honeymoon there."

"Well," the older gentleman replied, "congratulations to you both."

"Thank you," Stewart said. "I could not help but overhear your comments about the city and do not want to take my bride there if it is as dangerous as you seem to think. I would be most grateful for your honest assessment."

The men looked at each other. The younger of the two answered. "Sir, I would not take my wife or my children to San

---

13 (Wikipedia) The San Francisco Committee of Vigilance was a vigilante group formed in 1851. The catalyst for its formation was the criminality of the Sydney Ducks gang. It was revived in 1856 in response to rampant crime and corruption in the municipal government of San Francisco, California.

Francisco at this time. Although better than a few years ago, I would be wary. Now, that is just my opinion, and you must do as you wish. The environment is improving, but it is most unstable at present. Undoubtedly, that will change. But for now, I would not risk taking your lovely bride to such a den of iniquity."

"I must agree," the older man said with a nod. "You would likely be robbed or set upon by thugs without a good knowledge of the city."

Stewart nodded sadly and thanked the gentlemen, then turned and guided Olivia from the restaurant.

"I should have planned this better," he said. "I have not heard any of this before. I am not sure what to do."

When they stepped outside, the morning air was crisp and cool. Olivia breathed deep and smiled.

"Stewart, we don't have to go to San Francisco. I have been traveling for so long that I can think of nothing that would make me happier than to spend a few days here in Sacramento and then see my new home and begin to settle in with you. I don't need a honeymoon. I am perfectly content to abandon the whole idea—especially in light of that conversation."

"Are you certain?" he asked.

"Absolutely." She slipped her arm through his and dropped her head onto his arm. "Are you terribly disappointed?"

"Only about disappointing you," he answered.

"I'm not in the least disappointed. In fact," she said, "I am a tad relieved to avoid any more travel for the time being."

"You are amazing, you know?" Stewart said. "I must be the

luckiest man alive."

They strolled around for a bit and returned to the hotel. The clerk called them over to the desk.

"Miss Clark sent over your wedding gifts," he said. "I have taken the liberty of sending them up to your room."

The table in their room was overflowing with wrapped packages.

"Now that is something!" Stewart said as his eyes surveyed the gifts.

Olivia's eyes opened wide in amazement. With childlike glee, she said, "Let's open them!"

Stewart laughed, dropped his hat on the bed, and untied the chin ribbon that held Olivia's hat in place. He dropped it on the bed as well and said, "You are even more adorable than I imagined." He bent his head to kiss her, loving the feel of her lips on his. He loved the scent of her. He loved the taste of her mouth and the softness of her skin. He pulled back and looked into her eyes and smiled, then kissed her again. His arousal bloomed between them.

"Do you think the gifts might wait just a little bit longer?" he whispered hoarsely into her ear.

She smiled and nodded, secretly hoping that this time she would finally feel the things that she knew women felt when their husbands made love to them. There were times when she could hear the sounds coming from her Aunt Maria and Uncle Michael's room, and it was nearly impossible to block out the sounds that occasionally came from Sam and Molly when she was in the wagon. All of those sounds sounded happier, fun, and more sweetly intimate than Olivia had thus far felt. She hoped that things would eventually help her to look forward to what she had always imagined to be one of the most special things about marriage. She whispered a silent prayer and opened herself to the sweet, gentle loving of her husband. Stewart was so considerate, and she was so eager to try again.

Later, after ordering dinner to be delivered to the room, they opened the presents sent over by Miss Clark.

"Oh, my goodness," Olivia said after opening what felt like a piece of wood. The plaque was a sanded oval with rounded edges. A delicate carved design adorned the edge. Olivia held it up for Stewart to see. The sign said simply, "The Andersons."

"For our home," she said. "How beautiful."

Stewart reached for the plaque and ran his fingers over the carving, remembering how he'd done that just a couple of days ago over his parents' names. "Let me guess," he said. "Hollis, right?"

Olivia nodded.

Each of the gifts from folks on the wagon train were handmade. Most of them had to have been made while they were still traveling. There was a beautifully knit blanket from Abigail Allen and her family and a delicate lace tablecloth from the Whitcombs. Horace and Mary Grover's gift was a King James Bible within which the Fowler girls had pressed wildflowers from all along their journey. Sam and Molly gave them a bread pan and a pie pan with a note that said, "May your home be filled with good bread, sweet pies, and much love." John and Mark Clayton's gift was an exquisite knife, the blade of which was the sharpest Stewart had ever seen. The handle was made from bone and shone to a beautiful luster.

Stewart had far fewer acquaintances at the wedding, but the ones who came all gave very thoughtful and useful gifts. John Sutter's gift made them both gasp. It was a gold nugget "to start your life together."

It was the Warrens' gift that surprised Olivia the most. The package was small but beautifully wrapped in a linen cloth and tied with a cream-colored silk ribbon. Inside was a small, handmade wooden frame that contained a drawing of Olivia. It was a profile of her face. In it, her head was bowed down just a bit. Her hair, although pulled up and gathered on top of her head, had many loose strands that fell across her cheek. Her look was full of intent, concern, compassion, and focus. It was entitled, "My Angel Nurse." It was signed by Chester.

"It is an amazing likeness," Stewart said. "More than that, it captures the depth of your personality in a way that I never would have thought a drawing could. Did you know he was an artist?"

"No," Olivia said. "I don't think anyone did." She opened the letter that came with Chester's drawing. It was in Esther's hand. She read it out loud.

Dearest Olivia,

Chester discovered his talent for drawing while he recovered from his amputation. He did not even tell me he was drawing until we arrived in Sacramento. He seems to have quite a gift for it, don't you think? I believe he captured your beauty and spirit so perfectly.

There is so much Chester and I do not know about each

other—so much that has been lost along the way. However, we have been given a gift, too, and that is the gift of a new beginning.

Without you, dear Olivia, we might not have had this opportunity. I have always considered myself a God-fearing, devout, and holy woman. You taught me what it means to be a Christian woman. Without you, Chester may have died of his wounds, and I might be a pile of bones scattered around a musical instrument whose enjoyment I withheld from all. Thank you for sharing the gift of yourself in spite of our—MY—inability to accept it for so long. Stewart is a lucky man.

Chester and I wish you both a sweet life, full of love.

Olivia was crying as she finished reading the letter. "This," she said as she blotted her eyes with a handkerchief, "this may be the most touching gift of all."

Stewart reached out and placed his hand over hers. "That is," he said, "quite a remarkable thing."

"Her transformation was quite remarkable," Olivia said.

There was a knock on the door. "That must be our dinner." Stewart went to the door, and Olivia cleared the dining table of gifts so that the tray with their food could be set down.

Stewart took a bite of the chicken he'd ordered, chewed it thoughtfully, and swallowed. "My father had to deal with all kinds of people as a minister." He took a sip of wine. "Some of them pleasant, some as ornery as it sounds like your Esther was. I asked him once what made some people so mean and self-righteous."

"What did he say?"

"I didn't really understand his answer until later, but he

said that when people, especially very religious people, couldn't allow themselves to feel weak or vulnerable, then they tended to become quite rigid and extreme in their beliefs. It was his belief that the Crusades and the Inquisition were not only the result of power-hungry leaders but also the response of people afraid of their own humanity. He always encouraged his parishioners to practice patience and acceptance of their neighbors' faults and foibles, while also being gentle with themselves."

"I guess," Olivia said, "being raised a Catholic, I am bit more used to guilt and fear as a motivator to get to heaven. I wish I had known your father—your mother, too."

"They would have loved you," Stewart said. "I wish the same. I do wonder, though, how it is that you seem so comfortable giving up the staunch Catholic religion."

Olivia finished her bite and said, "That would be the influence of my Uncle Michael." She smiled. "I probably would not even be here if it were not for that man. He was in Italy for a summer to study the ruins at Pompeii and spent a few days exploring Sicily. My Aunt Maria was a teacher in Palermo and happened to be guiding a small class of students around town giving them assignments to draw. As she tells the story, she looked up from a student's work and saw Michael sitting at an outdoor café watching her intently. She blushed and tried to pay him no mind, but she thought he was the most handsome man she'd ever seen. My father happened to be Michael's waiter and noticed the interaction. After inquiring after Michael's presence in Italy and learning that he was planning to be a professor, my father invited the man to our home for dinner."

"Your father played matchmaker?" Stewart said with considerable astonishment.

"My father was quite romantic," Olivia said wistfully. "Maria was my mother's youngest sister. She lived with us. And my father knew that Maria needed someone smart and worldly. Maria was bright and curious—always looking for something to read. She was also quite lovely."

"So," Stewart pressed, "I already know the end of the story, but tell me what happened when Michael arrived for dinner."

"Only my father and mother knew Michael was coming. He was introduced to Maria and me as a customer of the café. I was oblivious, of course, but Maria was quick to figure things out and later accused the two of them of matchmaking."

"She was smart," Stewart observed.

Olivia agreed with a nod and then added, "By the end of the evening there were plans for a tour of Palermo that included my mother and me. Michael returned to Pompeii for his studies after a week, but he wrote Maria daily from the mainland. Then, when his studies in Pompeii concluded, instead of returning home to America, he came back to Palermo to continue to court Maria. They married in Palermo and stayed on until after my grandmother died. My grandmother had been ill for some time but died a happy Italian mother after seeing both of her daughters married. They left for America shortly after that."

"It is a wonderful story," Stewart said. "I really hope that someday I get to meet your aunt and uncle. Who knows, with talk about the railroad being built across the entire country, it could happen in our lifetime."

"Wouldn't that be something?" Olivia asked. "Can you imagine how much that will change everything?"

They finished their dinner and started making plans to return to the logging camp where their home awaited them.

Most of the folks who were in Olivia's wagon train were still camped on the outskirts of Sacramento. There was much to do to figure out where there was land upon which to stake a claim to look for gold. The atmosphere was a mixture of discouragement and anticipation. Word had spread that there was very little gold left to find and that Mr. Sutter was leaving the area broke. Available claims were few and far between. The realization that they had arrived at the tail end of the actual gold rush was a huge disappointment to many. A visit from Olivia and Stewart was the perfect antidote to the frustration. They visited for a short while and then made their way to Miss Clark's home to pick up Olivia's belongings and begin the trek to the logging camp. With their wagon full, Midnight rested, fed, and watered; and their goodbyes said, they began the journey up the Sierras to the logging camp.

Chapter Twenty

Shu Jiang

Huge and heavy clouds reflected in the flooded plains of the newly planted rice paddies along the Pearl River Delta. Soon green shoots would sprout from the earth. Before long, there would be terrace upon terrace of green fields of rice, gently bending in the breeze of a pink evening sky. The clouds moved slowly as if the sheer size of them would only allow the speed of a snail's crawl.

Late 1854

Enough!" the gruff shout came. "Back below!"

The memory of her home in Guangdong was quickly replaced by the reality of her situation.These were not reflections on the calm rice paddies where her family had worked for years; these were clouds dancing on the cold, gray waters of the ocean that separated her from her home in China. She was aboard a ship that would deposit her on a shore of unknown possibility and hope. Shu and her cousin, Bao, had left home for the *gum saan*, the gold mountain, and all the possibilities promised in California, America.

The steamer, *Libertad*, left Canton weeks ago. Accommodation was poor. Although she and Bao had paid for their passage, they were forced to stay with the freight. Even with their sleeping pads, there were only seventeen inches between bunks into which each sleeper had to slide. Those who had paid for the cheapest tickets did not even have a bunk.

The food was inedible—not anything identifiable by Chinese standards. The food smelled, the bodies smelled, and disease was rampant in the freight hold. The ship's captain threw dead bodies overboard, although on rare occasions there would be collections by those in the hold to prevent bodies being unceremoniously dumped into the sea. That way the bones could be saved and shipped back for rituals in the homeland.

Shu's family had been desperate for her to earn enough money in America so that she could help them leave their impoverished life in China. They had saved and sold everything to pay for her passage to join her cousin, Bao, on the same voyage. Shu was afraid to leave her family, but she was the oldest of three girls. With no sons, she knew there was no other way to help her family prosper. Her mother's back ached constantly from working the rice paddies. Her father was getting older, and Shu feared what would become of them if he could no longer work. So, Shu bravely announced that she would happily go to the gum saan in America to work for her family.

The memory of the rice paddies was an older one, from when she was a young girl. Shu's parents told her stories of the elite Manchu ruling class and how they created a welfare state for their own people. The government corruption by the Manchu turned them into entitled leaders who only thought of themselves. They lived beyond their means and emptied the coffers of fifty-one million liang[14] of silver. Although China had experienced a long period of peace, the result of that time more than doubled the population to four hundred twenty-one million people.

Shu saw her beautiful rice paddies less and less able to meet the demand for rice. Because her parents were tenants on the land, the landowners raised the rents. When crops failed for reasons beyond their control, Shu's parents were still responsible for paying the rent. Her parents, like so many in Guangdong, chopped down trees to make more room for growing more rice to feed more people.

To make matters worse, British smugglers found a way to get opium into her country. Millions in the population of China became addicted and died from the drug.

And so, to try to save her family, Shu offered to cross the

---

14 A liang is a Chinese method of weight. One liang was the equivalent of 1.33 ounces

ocean to the gum saan, the gold mountain.

Her father cried. Her mother nodded sadly.

"Are you not afraid, daughter?" her mother asked when they were alone.

Shu smiled her bravest smile. "I am honored to serve my family, Muqin. I am not afraid."

Now, as she was herded back into the dark hold of the steamship, she tried not to be afraid. In truth, her cousin, Bao, had not been kind to her since they said their goodbyes to their respective families in Guangdong. He'd barely spoken two words to her since they'd boarded the ship. When she attempted a conversation, he ignored her.

There was almost no light in the ship's hold. If a storm struck, the tiny holes that offered them air and light would be closed. The darkness was absolute then, and the storms would batter the ship so badly that bodies in the hold would slam against each other and the sides of the ship. Shu was grateful that the clouds were not storm clouds as she descended the ladder back to her dark, temporary home.

Shu Jiang was also grateful for Bao, even though he treated her badly. She caught many of the men giving her looks that made her skin crawl. She understood what those looks meant, but the men did not do anything more than look because Bao glared at them when he caught them. Sometimes he cursed at them as well.

She served Bao as best she could, although there was not much she was able to provide except rice with a little bit of pork water when it was offered. She made certain he received the lion's share of their food. On occasion, he grunted his acknowledgment.

They had been on the ocean for weeks. Hopefully, in another few weeks, they would arrive in San Francisco, where she and Bao planned to find work learning how to mine gold. Bao assured Shu and her family that he knew the basics of "panning" for gold and would find other Chinese to teach them the rest.

"What about tools?" Shu's father had asked.

"I have some extra money to purchase equipment," Bao had answered.

"You honor our family, Bao, by protecting our eldest daughter." Shu's father bowed to Bao.

Bao bowed in return and said, "Come, Shu, we must begin our long journey to Canton if we plan to meet our ship."

With a frightened and heavy heart, Shu swallowed her tears and said goodbye to her family.

Just a few more weeks, Shu kept repeating to herself as she tried to take the shallowest of breaths in the ship's hold. Just a few more weeks.

When the steamship finally arrived in San Francisco, Shu hesitated, fearful due to the noise and crowded dock. It smelled bad and so many people were moving so quickly and yelling, most in a language she did not recognize. Although the docks of Canton were frightening and dangerous, at least she understood the language there. She began to tremble.

Bao grabbed her by the hand and pulled her down the gangplank and onto the dock. Once on land, Shu expected to feel steadier on her feet, but she still felt the motion of the ship rocking. It made her a little dizzy. Bao parked her near a large post and told her not to move.

It was difficult for her to keep her eyes on Bao, but she managed to track him despite the crowds. She saw him talking to a tall white man whom she had seen on their ship. The man seemed to communicate well in Chinese. He handed Bao something. She breathed a little easier thinking that Bao had already made a connection for work here in America.

A low rumble of thunder over the water distracted her. She looked at the great storm clouds growing over the ocean and was grateful they were not still on the boat. She looked back to find Bao but could not locate him. Desperately, she looked around but could not see much over the people on the dock. She was very small and looked for something on which to stand but could find nothing.

"Bao," she called out. "Bao!"

Through a part in the crowd, she searched for him, but there were so many Chinese with long hair queues down their backs that she could not tell one from another.

"Bao!" she screamed in terror. "Baaaoooo!"

The white man Bao had been talking to appeared at her side. "Bao has left you," he said in flawless Cantonese.

"No," she said as she looked up at him. Then again, "Bao!"

The man gripped her upper arm causing her to yelp. She tried to pull away, but his grip only tightened.

"Your cousin has sold you to me to pay for his passage," he

said with a sneer. "You are mine now."

He roughly pulled her along without another word. Shu fell into silent shock as she was dragged into an unknown future.

Chapter Twenty-One

Rose

1855

"There is no discussion to be had, young lady. You will marry Frederick Barton and give up any foolish notions about love once and for all. Frederick Barton is wealthy and respected. Frederick Barton is well established in Boston. Frederick Barton will provide well for you. Frederick Barton has chosen you. You should feel honored that of all the eligible girls in Boston, you are his choice. Frederick Barton is a fine match, and I do not want to hear another word from you."

Frederick Barton is a wrinkled, old prude, Rose Wentworth said to herself as she tried to block out the litany of praises sung to the tune of her intended. Her parents had arranged this marriage for her without even considering feelings. Not that that was anything new. As one of the elites of Boston, she was raised to believe that looks are everything and that everything must be finessed toward that belief.

She had long since given up trying to fight the marriage. To be clear, Rose had given up the "look" of fighting the marriage. But Rose had a secret. A very big secret. Her parents were about to discover that she was gone.

Rose had been reading about a man named Asa Mercer.[15] He spoke eloquently about the need for teachers and women, in general, in the northwest where "loggers and gold diggers were waiting for women to marry. The men were rugged, hard-working, and desperately lonely." Anything being better than the life planned for her, Rose paid the $225 for the trip and the promise of a future in which she might have a say.

Mr. Mercer had been speaking in Lowell, Massachusetts. He'd left Lowell with a small group of women planning to be wed to men in the west. The train to New York stopped in Boston. Rose was waiting to board and join the other girls who traveled with Mr. Mercer. Once she boarded the train to New York, she quickly found Mr. Mercer. Off they headed to New York and the steamship, the *Illinois*. Not the adventure, really, she said to herself as she watched the city of New York shrink into the distance, if the truth be told, this is the beginning of my life.

It was cold on the deck of the ship, and soon Rose found her way to her cabin. Rose was a larger girl. She was not heavy, nor was she slender. According to her mother, that was the reason she had no suitors to speak of. Anna Wentworth kept a close eye on her daughter's diet and food intake—to no avail. So, when Frederick Barton asked for Rose's hand in marriage, her parents were ecstatic. Rose, however, was horrified. She had always dreamed of falling in love with a handsome young man—someone who would look past her thick waist and

---

15 Enss, Chris; Hearts West; True Stories of Mail-Order Brides on the Frontier (2005). Asa Mercer was considered a "Bride Entrepreneur." He made two trips via ship from the east coast to the west coast via Aspinwall (now Colon) to bring women to California and the Northwest.

deeply into her brown eyes. Rose did have large, beautiful eyes, long, dark blonde hair, fair skin, and an impetuous and headstrong demeanor. She was seventeen years of age.

Rose was unpacking for the ten-day voyage to Aspinwall, wondering what her frantic parents must be doing as they searched for her. She'd left a note, but all it said was "Don't bother to find me. I will contact you when I am ready." Of course, she knew her father well enough to know that he would stop at nothing to try to find her, but she was certain that she'd been clever in her departure.

On the morning that she planned to leave for New York, she decided to use the name Rose West. She thought her cleverness was quite ingenious. She smiled at the memory of it. Her parents were attending a luncheon function that was to be followed by a matinee of some sort. They would not return home until the evening hour. Following breakfast, she announced her intention to help with a function at the church. Back in her room, she lowered a suitcase from her window (feeling the slightest panic about leaving most of her belongings behind because she could not manage a trunk on her own) and left with a cheery goodbye through the front door. After retrieving her suitcase, she walked all the way to the train station and purchased her ticket. Her parents might only now begin to realize that she was gone. She breathed a sigh of relief as she sat down on her bed to keep the slight dizziness from the rolling of the ship at bay.

"Yoo hoo, Rose," a voice called from the other side of her cabin door. A knock followed."Come play with us. We are starting a game of cards."

Rose recognized the voice. It was Aurelia Coffin from Lowell. Aurelia had instantly latched onto Rose on the train ride from Boston. Not only were they the same age, but also Aurelia seemed the only girl from Lowell who had not known the other girls. Rose was happy for the attachment and eagerly joined Aurelia to head off to the lounge area of the ship.

Some of the girls were looking rather peaked. Although they attempted to play a round of cards, two of them left quickly to head to the rail.

"I hope they haven't caught anything," Aurelia remarked.

Rose smiled and reassured her. "It's motion sickness. Hopefully, they will adjust to the motion of the ship. If not, they will have a difficult time of things."

Just then, Mr. Mercer arrived. "The captain has informed me that dinner will be served promptly at seven, ladies."

Mr. Mercer was a decent-looking gentleman with dark, curly hair that rolled into a large tube around his ears and in a great mound on the crown of his head. He also sported a beard and moustache. His face was kind, but serious, and he had a slender build.

"Mr. Mercer," Lizzie said. "It would appear that some of our group are not comfortable with traveling upon the sea. Is there anything that might be done?" Elizabeth Ordway, or Lizzie, was the oldest of the group at twenty-six and had already taken on the role of the mother hen to the younger girls.

"I will advise the captain to see if there is any remedy that might be afforded them, but I fear they will just need to endure their discomfort," he said apologetically. "Meanwhile, there are no stops until we arrive in Aspinwall where we will journey by train to

Panama City and board the SS America to San Francisco."[16] "How long is the voyage to San Francisco, Mr. Mercer?" Rose asked.

"If all goes according to plan, the voyage is nearly sixteen days. The captain has assured me that he does not anticipate any difficulty on this part of the voyage. The *Illinois* has quite a good record, and we should be in Aspinwall on time.

By the time dinner had ended that evening, Rose was quite ready to retire and excused herself from the group.

That night she dreamt her father had found her and ripped her from her bed. In the dream, she was thrown into a frightful room that was so dingy and dirty, she could not find a suitable place to sit without getting filth on her dress. She cried to be released, begging her father to open the door, but there was only silence in response to her wails.

The next morning at breakfast, Rose found several of the other girls already seated. In all, there were only thirteen girls who had answered Mr. Mercer's ad for brides. Rose was quite certain that she was the only girl who had been a debutante. Her family was wealthy and well known in Boston. The others seemed rather from lower classes, although she wisely did not inquire. At least they were decently dressed and appeared to have reasonable manners.

Not all the girls were present at breakfast. Mr. Mercer arrived at the table and announced that the unaccounted-for ladies were indisposed.

---

16 The total journey, if there were no problems, should have been ten days via ship to Aspinwall (now Colon), a one-day train ride across Panama, and sixteen days via ship from Panama to San Francisco.

"Still struggling with motion sickness?" Rose inquired.

"It would appear so," Mr. Mercer responded. "Perhaps, it would be appreciated if some of you checked in on them periodically."

Lizzie and Aurelia both offered to do so. Aurelia looked at Rose, who avoided the look and began to fuss with her napkin. Several of the other girls agreed to help as well.

Rose was no stranger to ship travel. She had been to Europe twice on luxury liners. Always in first class. She had no intention of being nursemaid to seasick women.

Conversation at the breakfast table was lively and informative. Rose learned some of the Lowell girls' names. Apart from Aurelia and Lizzie, the others at the table were Constance, Annie, two named Mary, Eliza, Phoebe, and Flora. She discovered that Kathleen, Elinor, and Dorothy were the seasick girls. Rose introduced herself and immediately began inquiring about the backgrounds and reasons each girl had for taking on this journey. Only Aurelia, Lizzie, and Phoebe were from Lowell. The rest of the group resided in the countryside outside of Lowell. Most were farm girls who had little education.

"I am actually from Ohio," said Eliza. "I was living with my grandmother, but when she died, I decided I had nothing to lose, so I hopped on a train that took me to Lowell where I supposedly had a cousin. Turns out the cousin left some time ago to join in the search for gold in California. When I read Mr. Mercer's advertisement, it seemed more like an invitation."

Eliza was slender and exuded a very sweet and innocent nature. Her eyes were expressive and intensely blue. "I don't have any other family to speak of, so, here I am." Eliza looked around the table at the others. "Sounds like we all have a fairly similar story," she said. "Rose, what about you?"

Rose had absorbed everyone's story with intense curiosity. "Oh, mine is pretty much the same as everyone else's," she said with a smile. "The only difference is that I was engaged to the love of my life, and my sister stole him from me right out from under my nose." She reached into her pocketbook for a handkerchief to dab away a tear. My parents supported their union because she was older than me. They wanted me to marry a much older widower who had seven children. Can you imagine?"

Aurelia was the first to rush to Rose's side and pat her on the hand. "Poor Rose. How awful!"

"Well," Rose said as she sniffed and put her hankie away, "at least I have all of you now. I feel like we are our only family!"

"Yes, yes!" the girls around the table all cried. "We are family now!"

Three days into the trip saw all but one of the girls well adapted to the rocking ship. Only Dorothy, an outlier from about twenty miles east of Lowell, was still unable to eat anything. She tried to drink water every day, but most of that was rejected by her stomach. Primarily, it was Lizzie, Aurelia, Eliza, and Annie who checked in with Dorothy throughout the day. Their concern grew as Dorothy remained in bed. Her color was a sickly green. Sleep was her only escape from her desperate seasickness.

"Rose, would you like to come check on Dorothy with me?" Eliza asked on the fourth day of the ten-day trip to Aspinwall.

"Oh," Rose responded, squelching her disdain for such an encounter, "thank you so much for the invitation, but I am just on my way to speak with Mr. Mercer. Perhaps another time."

Rose turned and made her way toward Mr. Mercer, who was seated at a table nearby. As soon as Eliza was out of sight, Rose darted off to her room. She was the only one of the girls who had a room of her own. She had paid Mr. Mercer an extra twenty-five dollars to encourage him to pair the other twelve girls, leaving her with a single room all to herself.

At dinner that evening, she purposely sat near Eliza to inquire about Dorothy and her status.

Eliza shook her head sadly. "She really seems to be wasting away. I am concerned that she may not survive the journey."

"Oh, dear!" Rose exclaimed. "Cannot our leader find some way to help the poor girl?"

The leader Rose referred to was Lizzie. All the girls loved Lizzie. She took all the girls under her wing—comforting, consoling, educating, and encouraging them all. Only Rose seemed immune to Lizzie's affections.

Rose was always polite to Lizzie but took every opportunity to illustrate to the others just how ineffective Lizzie's ministrations could be whenever Lizzie was out of earshot.

Eliza, sweet, innocent Eliza, looked horrified at the suggestion that Lizzie was anything but kind and helpful.

"I suppose one could see it that way," Rose commented, her hand patting Eliza's as if she were a small child. "I am afraid I sense an ulterior motive, however."

"What do you mean?" Eliza asked, her eyes full of concern.

"I can't put my finger on it just yet," Rose responded. "I'd be careful, though, Sweet Eliza, she worries me. I will go and visit Dorothy first thing in the morning. Perhaps I might be able to assist the poor child."

"You are so kind, Rose."

"Well," Rose replied, "we are family. We need to look out for one another."

True to her word, the very next morning Rose knocked on the door of Dorothy and Elinor's room.

"Come in," came a voice from inside.

Elinor was trying to get Dorothy to sit up to take some sips of water. Eliza was right. Dorothy looked like death. There were dark circles under her eyes. Her cheeks were sunken.She was drenched in sweat, and the room reeked of vomit and body odor.

"Please, Dot," Elinor begged. "Please just take a sip."

Dorothy took a sip and swallowed. She instantly began to gag. The little bit of water shot out of her mouth, and the poor girl slipped from Elinor's arm and back onto her pillow.

Elinor looked up to see Rose watching from the door. She could not read the look on Rose's face but was surprised to see her there.

"Oh, Rose, I didn't expect to see you here," she exclaimed.

"Why don't you go have breakfast with everyone," Rose suggested. "I will sit with Dorothy for a spell."

"I didn't think you were the caretaking type," Elinor said

with some surprise in her voice.

Rose took a few steps into the small cabin. She tried not to inhale but did take a breath through her mouth. "Well, if we are family, I feel I should try to help in some way."

"Thank you, Rose. I would like to have breakfast with the others." Elinor stood to leave.When she got to the door, she stopped and took a very concerned look back at Dorothy, who seemed to be dwindling on her bed.

"We will be fine," Rose said. She waved her hand in a shooing motion. "Go enjoy your breakfast."

Elinor left and closed the door behind her. She was not quite comfortable about leaving Dorothy with Rose, but she could not, for the life of her, figure out why. Nonetheless, she was happy to be out in the fresh sea air. Suddenly, she realized she was starving.

At the eleven o'clock hour, Eliza arrived at Dorothy and Elinor's room. The door was wide open along with the small window above Dorothy's bed. Dorothy was sitting up and eating a bit of soup and some crackers from a tray. Rose was directing one of the ship's staff to strip down Dorothy's bed and put on fresh linens.

"Dorothy?" Eliza asked. "Are you actually eating?"

Dorothy looked up at Eliza and gave the weakest of smiles. She nodded.

Eliza looked at Rose. "What did you do? I can't believe she is eating."

"Nothing much," Rose responded. "I made her some tea with herbs and next thing I knew she asked for something to eat."

"It's a miracle," Eliza exclaimed. "After five days of such horrid seasickness! I am amazed."

Eliza just stood staring and tried to understand how such a change was even possible.

"Perhaps you might be inclined to help Dorothy wash up and change her clothes?" Rose asked. "It would probably help eliminate some of the sick odor of the room. We are airing it out and changing the bed linens. I'm sure that Dorothy would benefit from a bit of a wash and some clean clothes."

"Yes, of course!" Eliza answered. "First let me get Elinor and tell her the good news. I really can't believe it!" she said as she flew from the room.

Rose smiled as she watched Eliza leave. She turned back to Dorothy who was slurping down the soup as fast as she could. "Not too fast, my dear. You have had nothing for several days. I think it best to take things slow until your strength returns."

Dorothy nodded and gave her a barely perceptible smile. "Thank you, Rose. I believe you have saved my life."

"Nonsense," Rose said. "It was just a simple tea."

Chapter Twenty-Two

A day out from Aspinwall on the *SS America* found Mr. Mercer hiding from his charges.[17] The discord had become too much for the man, and he could take it no more. Several of

17 During his second and last entrepreneurial trip, Mr. Mercer was actually found hiding in a coal bin.

the girls had come to him in tears, complaining that they felt ostracized from the group.

Constance was upset because Flora had informed her that Phoebe couldn't tolerate her. "I thought we were getting along very well, Mr. Mercer, but I've been told thatshe no longer wishes to room with me!"

Annie and Mary, who had quickly become great friends and roommates, were, at best, barely civil to one another anymore.

Jane accused Lizzie of being a dominating witch.

Aurelia had lost her bubbliness and tended to stay to herself.

Lizzie did try to quell the squabbles that seemed to be taking over the whole group, but there was an overwhelming amount of conflict. Eliza, the youngest of them, who was also Lizzie's roommate, was inconsolable.

"I don't understand what's happening, Lizzie," she confided one evening in their cabin."How can there be so much discord? We were all getting along for several days."

Lizzie felt, more than saw, the disintegration of the group from the first. She met with each of the girls to get to the bottom of the acrimony. Only Rose seemed oblivious to the unraveling and stress.

"Whatever are you talking about?" Rose queried when Lizzie caught her alone along the rail one afternoon. "I haven't noticed any trouble. Perhaps you are just too involved in everyone's lives, Lizzie," she said sweetly. "I haven't had any trouble with anyone."

Rose patted Lizzie's hand condescendingly and excused herself. Lizzie stared after her, left with more questions than answers. The interaction with Rose left her unsettled. Something did not feel right about the conversation, but Lizzie could not put her finger on exactly what it was—only that a tiny alarm went off somewhere inside her.

Lizzie was on high alert after her abrupt, seemingly caring conversation with Rose. As she continued to interact with some of the girls, her questions became more pointed about exactly who said what to whom. It did not take Lizzie long to determine that Rose was the source of all the acrimony. Only Dorothy sang Rose's praises. Since her miraculous liberation from seasickness, thanks to Rose and her tea, Dorothy and Rose had breakfast every morning together. And, every morning, Rose put a pinch of the white powder[18] herb into Dorothy's tea to keep her stomach settled.

"Honestly," Dorothy said to the few girls who ate together, "I was absolutely convinced that I would have to get off the ship in Aspinwall."

Days came and went and still there was no sign of Mr. Mercer. The truth was that he was hiding from the women. Most often his hiding place was in the boiler room of the ship. He only slipped out at night to eat and bask in the fresh sea air. He slept in his cabin at night but found numerous hiding places around the ship as soon as morning came. He did begin to wonder if the enterprise he'd undertaken was worth the money or the effort. He could not wait to get to San Francisco to rid himself of these petty women.

Rose assumed that Mr. Mercer abandoned ship at Aspinwall. Certain that he was fed up with his charges and their complaints, she informed the girls as much.

"Certainly, he would not leave us without fulfilling his mission with us," Lizzie stated with some authority.

---

18 Cocaine was sometimes used for seasickness at the time.

"Have any of us seen him?" Rose asked. "Has he been present in the dining hall? Do you think he is just hiding in his room?"

"Perhaps he has fallen ill," Eliza suggested. She looked genuinely worried.

"I am certain he is gone," Rose said. "Don't worry Eliza, I will watch over you when we arrive in San Francisco." Rose leaned over and put her arm protectively around Eliza's shoulder.

"Mr. Mercer did not leave the ship," Lizzie stated firmly. "I was also concerned, Eliza, that he might have fallen ill and asked the captain to check his quarters. I have been assured that Mr. Mercer is still with us aboard the ship."

"Is he avoiding us, then?" asked Dorothy.

"Can you blame him?" Lizzie asked. "We have become a whining gaggle of women. It really is a wonder that he didn't sneak away at Aspinwall!"

Rose departed the morning breakfast table to pace on the deck. She was not at all happy that Lizzie seemed to have the upper hand regarding Mr. Mercer. She formulated a new plan that she hoped would turn all the girls to her for guidance and support.

Five days into the sixteen-day journey on the SS America found only Dorothy, Eliza, Lizzie, Phoebe, and Jane at the breakfast table with Rose. The atmosphere was tense. Surreptitious looks were exchanged between all. Food was pushed around on plates more than it was eaten. Rose, alone, seemed in good spirits and had no trouble eating.

Rumors had spread among the girls that Lizzie had been

taking advantage of Eliza. Specifically, that they were more than friends and that Lizzie was seen kissing Eliza, who did not seem at all comfortable with the situation. Eliza was not aware of the rumor, but Lizzie overheard Elinor telling Kathleen and Flora the horrifying details.

"Why is everyone so quiet this morning?" Eliza asked.She looked around at everyone at the table, but the only one to make eye contact with her was Rose, who shrugged her shoulders.

Rose then looked around the table and asked, "Is everything alright?" She paused and waited for an answer, but none was forthcoming. At that point, Dorothy arrived. Rose issued her a hearty good morning and added the powder to Dorothy's tea.

Morning tea had become a ritual for Dorothy and Rose. As the trip progressed, Dorothy seemed a bit anxious for her morning cup, nearly inhaling it once Rose added her herbal. After her tea was drunk, Dorothy was pleasant and chatty.

"How was everyone's night?" Dorothy inquired of the group.

Almost as one, the group answered, "Fine."

Seemingly oblivious to the mood of the group, Dorothy chatted amiably about her excitement for the landing in San Francisco and her dreams of finding a husband.

"I am as well," Phoebe said. "I do hope we all find dashingly handsome men who are sweet natured and good providers."

"That is the dream," Rose offered. "I suspect that someone as adorable as Eliza with her milky skin, blonde hair, and blue eyes will have no problem."

Phoebe started and looked pointedly at Lizzie as if waiting

for a worried or pained look from her.

Dorothy took up Rose's line of assuring Eliza that she would have nothing but good fortune in finding a perfect husband. She nattered on and on until Lizzie cut her off.

"Rose!"

Dorothy jumped and looked agape at Lizzie, then Rose.

"Can it be that you are the only one, with the possible exception of Eliza," Lizzie demanded, "that has not heard the malicious and untrue rumor being spread about myself and Eliza?"

Eliza gasped with surprise. "What rumor?"

"Eliza, my dear, you know I have nothing but sisterly affection for you, do you not?"

Eliza reached for Lizzie's arm and placed her hand on it tenderly. "Yes, of course I know that, Lizzie. Whatever is the matter?"

"I am sorry to have to tell you this," Lizzie said with concern, "but . . . " Lizzie paused, patted Eliza's hand in a motherly fashion, then glared pointedly at Rose. "Someone has spread a vicious lie that they have seen me forcing kisses on you, on your mouth."

Eliza gasped and drew her hand back from Lizzie's arm. She paled instantly and visibly. Her voice was barely a whisper. "Why?"

"A perfectly logical question," Lizzie responded. "Rose?"

"I am sure I have no idea," Rose responded in abject horror

as if totally surprised by the whole idea of the rumor. "This is the first I've heard such a thing. How revolting."

A server appeared to offer more tea and coffee. Lizzie shooed him away with a stern, "Not now." The poor boy disappeared faster than a fly.

"You can claim innocence all you want, Rose West, if that is even your name. But let me tell you that I know you to be responsible for every rumor spread about every one of us. I care a great deal about these women and have taken it upon myself to interview all of them since the discontent and backbiting began before Aspinwall. You, it seems, are at the root of every lie spread among us." Lizzie stood. "Oh, you were very clever about it, saying that so and so told you, or you heard from this one or that one. But it was you all along—and now everyone knows to avoid you."

It was all Rose could do to remain in her seat and not fly across the table to scratch Lizzie's eyes out. No one, in her whole life, had ever exposed her like that. Instead, she smiled sweetly and repeated, "I am sure I do not know what you are talking about."

The others got up as one, except for Eliza, who remained seated with her mouth gaping open. She was trembling and still pale as a ghost. Phoebe and Lizzie came to her rescue, each taking an elbow and helping her up. Indeed, she looked as if she were about to pass out but managed with help to leave the dining room.

Rose was left sitting alone. Before long, Mr. Mercer appeared at her elbow, along with the Captain of the ship.

"Miss West," he said.

She looked up at him and smiled as if nothing were wrong.

"The captain and I insist that you spend the remainder of this journey in your quarters. Meals will be brought to you."

Rose's smile became a sneer. "I will do no such thing, Mr. Mercer."

At a nod to the captain, two swarthy sailors appeared and escorted Rose to her quarters. One of them always remained outside her door.

Rose was neither seen nor heard from for the remainder of the voyage.

Chapter Twenty-Three

The Logging Camp

1855

Olivia and Mr. Chang were cleaning up the cookhouse after breakfast. It was still dark outside, but the lumber crew was already working their way up the mountain to the most recent cutting area.

Meals were important to sustain loggers for a ten-hour day. The sheer number of calories needed for the men to be able do the work required of them was enormous. Meals generally consisted of eggs, bacon, sausage, biscuits, beans, boiled corned beef, pancakes with syrup, milk, and coffee. The men ate all of it every morning, and each got lunch containers to eat while up on the mountain.

Mr. Chang had been an assistant to the previous cook, who had been lured away by another lumber outfit. The better an outfit's cook, the more likely loggers were to go to work there. Cooks were the primary draw for an outfit, and the competition was fierce.

It was late in 1854 when they lost the last cook. Mr. Chang was a competent enough cook, but his specialties all included rice, which the men tired of quickly. Olivia had been feeling under stimulated during the long days alone without Stewart and offered to help with cooking until a new cook was found. Not only was she an excellent cook, but the men loved her dishes. She slid right into the role of cook and enjoyed working with Mr. Chang. She was learning a little Chinese and teaching Mr. Chang more English as they worked.

While most meals in logging camps were alike, Olivia experimented with different Italian recipes for dinner. The loggers could not get enough of her tomato sauce with ground beef and sausages. Once a week she always made something special for the loggers. That meant more trips down to Sacramento, but word spread about the camp's new cook, and Burley found himself able to hire more men; therefore, Stewart and Olivia were able to make the trips to town a bit more often. Olivia was grateful for that. Although she enjoyed the work at the camp and working with Mr. Chang, the work itself was exhausting. Another benefit of the trips for supplies was that it gave her time away from the men. Most of them were respectful and grateful, but a few of them were rude and made her very uncomfortable.

"Olivia," Stewart said as they made their way down the mountainside to Sacramento. "You amaze me, you know? You have thrown yourself into this life with such grace. You know I plan for us to be here for only another year, right?"

Olivia sighed and smiled. "I know, honey. It's fine. The work is exhausting, but I do love to get away more often."

"You don't have to do the cooking, you know," Stewart said. "Burley can hire someone else."

"I really don't mind the work, and Mr. Chang is very sweet. Besides, the extra money will help us more than meet our goal in the next year. Think of what we will be able to build when you are ready to stop logging."

Stewart slowed Midnight as the wagon maneuvered around some boulders.

"I am looking forward to building a little place near the river and learning another trade," Stewart said.

"Something less physical and tiring, I hope," Olivia said.

Stewart laughed. "For both of us! I am aware, you know, that you are actually putting in longer hours than the loggers."

Olivia rested her head on Stewart's shoulder. "I do have an hour or so most afternoons when Mr. Chang begins the prep for dinner."

She became quiet and pensive. It was obvious that she went somewhere in her mind. She lifted her head from Stewart's shoulder, and her eyes drifted off into some distant place. Since their marriage almost a year ago, Stewart had learned to just let her go there. He sensed her sadness and wished there was a way to help her but knew that he just needed to let her be. She always came back.

When they arrived late the next evening and had checked into the hotel in Sacramento, Stewart slipped up behind Olivia and held her.

"We are both working such long and hard hours that I haven't made love to you in weeks," he whispered into her ear. "I am sorry if you feel ignored."

Olivia felt his erection press up against her and chided herself for her lack of desire. She wanted to want him. She did love him. How could she not? He was sweet, considerate, handsome, and her best friend. She turned in his arms and pulled his head to hers, inviting his kisses—and returning them with as much feeling as she could muster.

After their lovemaking, Stewart fell into a deep sleep. Olivia turned to watch him sleep. He worked hard as a faller, using his ax to make deep cuts into the bottom of trees so big around that several men could not stretch their arms around one. Though slender, Stewart's upper body muscles were well developed and stronger than Olivia thought muscles could be. His hands usually ached from holding the ax for up to ten hours a day—rain or shine. He often worried that the callouses might be too rough on her skin.

She listened to his breath and wondered how he managed to reconcile his spirit to this work. He had confided in her, after a particularly long day, that the longer he worked at his job, the more he felt like an executioner.

"I am determined to finish my contract," he said as they lay in bed at their little cabin, "but the more time I spend in these forests, the more connected I feel to the trees. I find myself offering a prayer each time I begin hacking away at the base of a new tree."

She understood what he meant. On afternoons, when Mr. Chang would tend to the bread rising in giant pans or slice the huge chunks of roast for dinner, she often strolled into the woods outside the camp. One time, she went farther than normal and came upon a small meadow filled with grasses and wildflowers. Though surrounded by trees so tall that she could not see the tops, the sun managed to light a small patch. She often went to that spot to sit and pray and ponder her life. As she watched Stewart sleep now, she thought of that place, her spot beneath the great firs and hemlocks.

The first time she found herself in the tiny meadow, she sat just breathing deeply, taking in the beauty around her. It wasn't more than a minute when she realized that she was weeping. She had no idea why she wept, but the tears became uncontrollable. She allowed herself the luxury of just crying. Sitting and crying. When, finally, her tears stopped flowing, she felt a presence. Thinking an animal might be near, she looked around. Apart from the birds all around, she could find no animal or person. Still, a distinct presence felt unmistakable. She began to pray.

"Olivia." She heard a voice but not with her ears. The voice was distinct, but she heard it within her. Only one other time in her life did she hear that voice. It was on the ship from Italy when she was so sick and realized that her parents were dead. The voice was that of her deceased grandmother.

On the ship the voice simply said, "All will be well, my child. I am watching over you."

In the many years that had passed, she'd filed that memory away as a symptom of her delirium and forgot about it. But now, in the forest, her grandmother's voice was so clear that she could not deny the voice or what it said.

"All will be well, my child. I am watching over you."

Now, as she watched her husband sleeping contentedly, she thought back to the voice and the feeling she had when she heard it. There was a peacefulness that filled and surrounded her. She often went to the meadow after that first time but did not hear the voice again. Olivia never shared her hearing of her grandmother's voice with anyone—not even Stewart.

Olivia felt a kinship with the great trees since she had lived in the forest with Stewart. There was something majestic and regal in the way they reached so high into the sky. She loved the smells of the forest as well and found herself breathing deeply whenever she had a moment to herself.

"I love you, Stewart," she said silently to his softly snoring body. "I wish I knew what was wrong with me."

Something was missing, but she had no idea what it was.

Chapter Twenty-Four

The next morning, there was a light fog over Sacramento. After breakfast, Stewart and Olivia went to the general store with a list of things the camp needed them to bring back. Now that Olivia was cooking, the food items that she needed were slightly different from what the store typically stocked. However, some of her herbs and cooking utensils may have made their way to Sacramento since their last visit. Additionally,

Olivia was always trying to make their little cabin homier, so she had also ordered some material to make a quilt for their bed. While the cabin was too small to work on such a project, she intended to make use of the long tables in the dining hall during non-mealtimes. She hoped that the signs that she and Stewart were posting for extra cook help would allow her a bit more time for herself. Mr. Chang was worth his weight in gold, but the camp was gaining a reputation for the food, and more loggers came seeking work.

A portion of their first day was always spent tracking down those from the wagon train who decided to make their home in Sacramento. If time allowed, they liked to stop in on Reverend Stevens and Miss Clark, both of whom were always happy for a visit. But the slow journey down the mountain took two full days with a wagon. Heading back up could take longer, depending on the weight of their load.

Much to their surprise, a walk down the main street of Sacramento found them staring into a shop that was not there on their last visit. "Clark's Bakery" was a new establishment.

"No," Olivia exclaimed. "It couldn't be, could it?"

As they peered through the window, Olivia squealed with delight. "Molly, Sam!"

Molly and Sam looked up as Olivia opened the door and ran into the shop.

Following hugs and greetings all around, Molly said, "We were just going to close up shop and head to the back for some dinner. Will you join us?"

"Heavens, we would not want to impose," Stewart said.

"No imposition, at all," Molly said. "In fact, we insist."

Over a light dinner, they discovered that both Sam and Molly put all their effort into finding gold. In a full year of digging and panning, they became discouraged and decided to give up that dream.

"I understand now why Mr. Sutter went bankrupt," Sam said. "We only found one small nugget in the whole year."

"And," Molly said as she poured more coffee into everyone's cups, "it was just enough to purchase the lumber and supplies to build everything you see."

Olivia looked around admiringly. "You have built a lovely home and a great future for yourselves."

"How are things up at the logging camp?" Sam asked.

Stewart ran his fingers through his hair and rubbed his chin.

"I won't lie," he said. "It's damn hard work, and I am looking forward to us leaving the camp sooner than we anticipated." Stewart looked at Olivia, and she saw a sadness in him that he'd not shown before.

Stewart continued. "The logging work is hard, but Olivia is working longer hours up there, and we are both exhausted. I guess I had hoped that things would be easier on her."

"Olivia!" Molly scolded, "Please tell me you have not taken up logging!"

Olivia laughed. "I am no logger, Molly. The camp lost their head cook. It seemed like something I could do and, quite honestly, as beautiful as the forest is, I was feeling rather useless. While I have had to learn much about feeding so many hungry men all at once, at least I feel like I am doing something helpful."

"She is more than helpful," Stewart said as he beamed with pride. "Word of Olivia's cooking has spread, and more and more loggers are leaving their situations with other camps to join ours."

Olivia lowered her head. She was never comfortable with praise. Her grandmother once heard her boasting to a friend, and she got quite the talking to about humility. She felt, more than heard, the lesson.

"With your cooking skills and our baking," Molly said, "maybe when you are done at the camp, we should open a fine restaurant!"

They all laughed, and Stewart said, "That is something you don't want me anywhere near!" he said.

By the time they left the company of Sam and Molly, it was dark. They went back to the hotel and settled in for the night. When the lantern was turned down, Olivia snuggled next to Stewart with her head nestled into his shoulder.

"I am sorry that I brought you all the way across the country on a dangerous journey to have you live with me in a logging camp," Stewart said softly. "I guess I just fell so much in love with you through your letters that I just didn't think it through very clearly. Can you forgive me?"

Olivia heard the sadness in his voice. "There is nothing to forgive, Stewart. I fell just as much in love from your letters. I would have been beside myself to have to wait to come to you."

"I love you, Olivia. You have no idea how much I love you."

"I love you, too, Stewart. Good night."

The next day dawned without fog or clouds in the sky. Olivia and Stewart had breakfast early, hitched Midnight to the wagon, and set about loading all the supplies from the general store. The wagon was about three-quarters loaded with barrels of flour, rice, herbs, spices, and several crates of tomatoes, eggs, and oranges. Someone else from the camp would come down in a week or so to do it all over again. The camp raised their own cows and sheep for beef and made cheese, butter, and milk. Olivia and Mr. Chang struggled to grow a garden at the camp, but it did not produce enough to feed so many men. The altitude and the cold nights made growing much of anything fairly impossible.

Stewart was helping to load the wagon with a young boy who worked at the store. They were nearing the end when a lavishly dressed and perfumed woman entered the store with another woman and what looked to be a young Asian girl. The second woman was equally dressed and perfumed and seemed to hold the young girl with an iron grip. The young girl held her head down but looked up briefly when they entered the store to see where they were. Her eyes met Olivia's for the briefest of moments, but Olivia saw fear in her eyes and wondered how she came to be with these women. Stewart stepped in behind the trio and noticed the commotion the new customers were creating. He walked over to Olivia, guided her to a secluded corner of the store, and pretended he was interested in something there.

"That is the local madam," he whispered. He noticed the confusion in Olivia's eyes.

"She runs the only whorehouse in Sacramento," he added. "Just be polite and go about your business. They will not bother you."

Olivia nodded but said nothing. She had never laid eyes on women like these, and she failed to understand why they had a young girl with them.

The Madam grabbed the girl by the arm and held up a ready-made dress in front of the girl, who could not have been more than fifteen.

"Take her to the back room and have her try this on," she said to the other woman with them.

The Madam then walked over to where Olivia was perusing bolts of material. The perfume threatened to overpower Olivia, but she remained where she was, slowly feeling and holding up the corners of several fabrics.

Olivia took a couple of the bolts to the owner's wife and requested several yards of each. While the material was being cut, the other woman came out front with the ready-made dress.

"It is far too large on her," she said.

The Madam pulled a dress from the children's section. "Try this one—and don't leave her alone again," she said sternly.

Olivia watched as her materials were being wrapped in paper. The merchant's wife handed them to her.

As Olivia was preparing to pay for the fabric, the woman who had gone back to bring the new dress to the girl, came to the front of the store, her face pale and full of fear.

"She's gone, Ma'am."

"What do you mean, gone?" the Madam demanded. "There is no place for her to go!"

The Madam marched toward the entrance to the back room, shoving the other woman out of the way.

Stewart and the boy had just come back in the front door of the store, when the Madam stormed out of the back room.

"When did you install a window back there?" she demanded.

The owner shrugged his shoulders. "I don't know, couple months ago? It's very small and rather high up. We needed more light back there."

"What are you standing around for?" the Madam demanded of her cohort. "Start searching for her! She can't be far."

Both women headed for the front door, exited, and disappeared in different directions.

Finally, the owner said, "I apologize for the drama."

Olivia smiled and said, "I imagine her money is no different than anyone else's."

The owner's wife came to the counter. "You are very understanding, Olivia. Most women are very upset when they see that we do not turn away the whores."

"The only thing that upset me was the young girl—who seemed not to be here of her own will. I do hope she gets as far from those women as possible," said Olivia with a little catch in her throat.

"Please, Olivia, take the material. The logging camp helps us make ends meet and feeds our family well enough. Please, it is a gift."

"That isn't necessary, Mrs. Campbell," Olivia said shaking her head.

"We insist, please."

"That is very kind of you. Thank you," Olivia said.

Stewart nodded, placed his hand on the small of Olivia's back, and together they left the store and climbed into the wagon. Before long, they were on their way up the mountain to the logging camp.

"It's been a lovely respite," Olivia said. She sighed and let out a long, "Mmmmmm."

Stewart nodded and maneuvered the wagon up the side of the mountain for the trek back to the logging camp.

Chapter Twenty-Five

A light drizzle was just beginning as Stewart pulled the wagon to the door of the dining hall. Olivia went inside to let Mr. Chang know they were back. Mr. Chang went out to help unload the supplies. Olivia remained in the kitchen to direct them where to place the supplies as they were unloaded. When, after a period of time neither of them came to the kitchen, Olivia went out to see what the holdup might be. She found both men staring into the front of the wagon, just behind the bench seat. There, sitting up and looking quite frightened was the small Asian girl who had escaped at the general store.

Olivia ran to the wagon and reached her hand up to the girl. "Come," she said.

The girl's eyes were opened wide. She had not moved since Olivia came out.

"Mr. Chang, please try reassuring her," Olivia said. "She might understand you."

Mr. Chang was still gaping at the vision before him.

"Mr. Chang," Olivia said with a little more force.

After a blink of his eyes, Mr. Chang said something in Cantonese to the girl, who nodded to him. Still, she remained where she was.

Olivia held her hand out to the girl again. This time she took it and climbed out of the wagon. Olivia brought her into the dining room, which was empty. She led the girl to a bench next to one of the tables and sat down with her. Stewart and Mr. Chang followed but stood off to the side.

"Mr. Chang, please bring her something to drink and a bite to eat," Olivia said.

A few moments later, Mr. Chang arrived with a glass of water and a bowl of stew that was still warm from the afternoon meal. He set them before the girl and, again, said something to her.

The girl gulped down the water and picked up the spoon and began to eat the stew.

Olivia told Mr. Chang about the incident at the general store in Sacramento. He nodded, and a look of great sadness came over him.

"Very common," he said. "Sell women for money to buy tools. Look for gold." He shook his head.

When the girl finished eating, she said something to Mr. Chang.

"Ask her name and how she came to be with the women from the whorehouse," Stewart said.

Mr. Chang and the girl exchanged words for some time. At one point, the girl started crying. Olivia put her hand on the girl's shoulder until her tears subsided. She continued to speak to Mr. Chang. When she seemed finished, she hung her head.

Mr. Chang related the story he had been told. The girl's name was Shu Jiang. Her cousin brought her across the sea so that they could find work and she could help her family back home in China. As soon as they landed, her cousin sold her to a man who brought her to Sacramento from San Francisco. Once there, the man sold her to the Madam. Another Chinese there told her she would be the newest virgin, demanding a very high price.

Olivia was both horrified and heartbroken by the ordeal suffered by the girl. She had Mr. Chang assure her that it would be safe to go with Olivia.

Olivia took Shu to Stewart's and her little cabin. She motioned for Shu to climb under the covers Olivia pulled back for her. The poor girl cried herself to sleep.

Erik Johansson was Stewart's best friend in the logging camp. Like many of the loggers, he was of Scandinavian descent. Many Scandinavians had come across the ocean and settled in Minnesota. Erik was quite young when he migrated with his family. When he was older, his family moved west to Oregon to resettle. Erik's father was an accountant. When word got back to Minnesota that big logging outfits were looking for men of his profession, Erik's father packed up the family, and they joined a wagon train from Council Bluffs a few years back. There were more logging outfits in Oregon and Washington. Erik's family settled in southwest Oregon.

Erik joined Burley's outfit right around the same time that Stewart did. They connected on many topics during conversations in the bunkhouse and had similar personalities and senses of humor. They often talked about their families. Eric's father was still living in southern Oregon. His mother had died a few months back from a serious bout of cancer. His sister, Hannah, never married and lived at home, taking care of his father who continued to manage the books for several mills in Oregon.

Erik often talked of his sister, whom he adored and worried about. Sometimes Stewart could tell that he felt guilty about leaving Hannah to care for his parents. He and his sister corresponded regularly.

Erik was happy for Stewart as he watched the love between Stewart and Olivia bloom through correspondence and Olivia's arrival. Olivia was grateful that Erik had been there for Stewart and that he remained a good friend to both of them.

"Good morning, Erik!" Olivia called out several days after Shu had arrived.

"Good morning, Olivia, Shu!" Erik called out as she and Shu entered the dining hall from the kitchen.

It had taken Shu a few days to recover from her ordeal. Burley agreed to hire Shu to help with all the chores in the kitchen and the animal yards. As the camp was growing, he knew he would have to hire more help anyway. They were building a little add-on to the kitchen where Shu would have her own place to sleep. It would be ready soon.

Olivia appreciated Erik's pleasant, lighthearted nature. She trusted him and was glad that he was there for Stewart in the bunkhouse until Shu was able to sleep in her little room.

Erik smiled and waved to Shu, who gave him a curt nod back.

As the rest of the camp filed in for the morning meal, Olivia, Shu, and Mr. Chang got to work setting all the bowls and platters of food on the tables. At first Shu was in disbelief at the amount of food the men could consume, but she was a hard worker and a fast learner. It helped that Mr. Chang was able to communicate with her. He and Olivia were working to teach her English, and Olivia was learning a bit of Chinese as well.

Olivia was careful to keep an eye on Shu whenever she was in the hall with all the loggers. Most of them were just decent, kind-hearted men who kept to themselves. One of the men, however, always gave Olivia a bad feeling. He spoke very little, but when he did, it was usually something derogatory. She saw him eyeing Shu the first morning Shu began helping, and the look in his eyes was downright chilling. She'd mentioned her concern to both Stewart and Erik and asked them to stay alert and protect Shu from Burt, who always stared at her in a creepy way. He was unkempt, and his scraggly, long beard and moustache always held the remains of his recent meals.

Burt was last to sit at the table where Olivia was serving. He nodded a greeting to Olivia but said nothing.

When the little room was ready for Shu, Stewart moved back into the cabin with Olivia. Although exhausted from a long, hard day, Stewart climbed into bed with Olivia for the first time in several weeks.

"I am glad for Shu's help for you but must confess I rarely slept well in the bunkhouse. Seems I can't get used to all the snoring and farting anymore," Stewart said as he snuggled up to Olivia. "I missed the soft, gentle feel of you next to me at night. I missed the smell of you. I missed talking to you. And I missed . . . ," his voice drifted into breath, quickening as he reached under her nightgown for her breast.

His calloused hands moved gently over her body, breasts, stomach, and thighs and then back up to breasts. Olivia sighed, more resigning herself to his lovemaking than loving his lovemaking. She loved him. Of that she had no doubt. But she hadn't missed the lovemaking. That made her sad.

Stewart's hand slipped slowly between her legs. It always surprised her when he touched her there. It wasn't unpleasant. In fact, his fingers seemed to turn a key that unlocked her sexuality in a way that always made her think that she would love the rest of the experience. She gave herself to his loving as best as she could. She could see herself being with Stewart for the rest of her life. If only this one smallest part of their lives together brought her as much joy as it seemed to bring him.

"It makes him so happy," she thought. "I am glad to make him happy."

Chapter Twenty-Six

A few weeks after Shu moved into her new sleeping room, Burt requested some time off. He offered to stop in Sacramento and pick up supplies for the camp on his way back from an unknown destination. Burley was hesitant but gave in when Olivia told Burley she had enough to get through for an extra week.

"Are you certain you can trust him to come back with everything?" Olivia asked. "I can manage an extra week, but if he is later, we could be in trouble—especially since he is taking the camp wagon."

"He has taken off before and always comes back on time," Burley said. "I don't see any reason not to trust him."

"I'm sure you're right, Burley," Olivia said. "I'm probably just being overly concerned."

There was a chill in the air. Winter wasn't far off for the Sierras. Olivia and Shu were tallying up the supplies left. Burt had been gone thirteen days. She was starting to get worried. It was late afternoon, and the men would be down wanting supper soon. Mr. Chang was boiling the last of the beef. Bread was in the oven. There were no vegetables left from the garden, but plenty of bread was baking.

Olivia heard a commotion outside the kitchen. She went outside to find the horse and wagon pulled up to a stop at the kitchen door. A handsome man with a couple of days growth of beard was jumping down from the wagon.

"Woman!" he hollered. "We are here. Wake your sorry ass up and come greet your new boss!"

When she heard the voice, and the contempt in it, Olivia realized this was Burt. She hadn't recognized him without his longish beard. He was also rather nicely dressed—not his usual logging duds.

Olivia was surprised when a woman sat up in the back of the wagon. She was clearly worse for wear, with dark circles under her eyes and her hair in disarray and tangled. Clearly, her clothing was of a higher quality than Olivia was used to seeing, but it certainly was not the kind of clothing meant for camping out or life in a logging camp. She had a frightened look about her—one that alarmed Olivia.

Burt reached up to pull the woman out of the back of the wagon.

Meanwhile, Mr. Chang came out from the kitchen, anxious to hear what the commotion was about. A few of the loggers were wandering and came to see what was going on as well.

Burt turned to the other men. "Boys," he said, "meet the wife."

Olivia could only stare while the men congratulated Burt. How, in the name of God, could that man have been able to find this woman. She looked as if she did not understand what had happened to her. She had a lovely face and smooth and fair skin. Her eyes were large and dark brown although filled with confusion. Her hair looked to be blonde but was too dirty to really tell. She looked healthy enough—though "sturdy" is the word normally used for women of her build. Olivia instantly felt sorry for her.

"Hello," Olivia said as she walked to the woman and held out her hand. "I'm Olivia. My husband is one of the loggers in the camp. How nice to have another woman join us."

The woman just stood and stared at Olivia as if she did not understand the language.

"Do you speak English?" Olivia asked.

"Of course, she speaks English," Burt said as he whirled around from talking to the other men.

"Perhaps I can show her where to clean up a bit," Olivia offered. "She looks a little worse for wear."

"She's fine," Burt said in a tone indicating that this was none of her business. "She's going to help you unload the wagon with your two coolie friends. I gotta go find Burley about hiring her on as help."

Olivia watched Burt stroll proudly towards the bunkhouse. She realized in that moment that she detested Burt. She turned to his wife. "Please, come with me. We'll give you a place to clean up a bit, but first, would you like a cup of tea?"

The woman nodded, and Olivia took her by the arm and led her into the kitchen while Mr. Chang and Shu started to unload the wagon.

Once the woman was cleaned up a bit and had some food, she seemed a little less frazzled.

Olivia sat across from her at the long dining table. "What is your name?"

After a long pause, almost as if she couldn't remember, the woman said, "Rose."

"How did you come to marry Burt?" Olivia asked. "We didn't even know there was a woman in his life."

Rose hung her head. She had been used to being able to control everything in her life—if not through money or status, then through manipulation. For perhaps the first time, she resorted to the truth.

"I ran away from home because my parents wanted me to marry an old man just because he offered. There was an ad in a paper out east about a man who intended to bring women to the west to marry gold diggers and loggers. It seemed like the answer to a prayer." Rose stopped and looked Olivia in the eyes.

Olivia held her gaze and after a bit said, "I take it this is not what you had in mind."

Rose's eyes filled with tears. She pulled a handkerchief from her bosom and blew her nose. She began again.

"It has been a nightmare." She took a huge breath as if she needed courage from the air to continue. "We were on the sea for nearly thirty days from Boston. When we finally reached San Francisco, all the other girls were let off first." Rose did not think it important to explain that she had been quarantined in her cabin for her outrageous behavior. "By the time I was allowed to disembark, there were about twenty-five men still hoping to find a wife. Most of them were slovenly, with long beards and dirty clothes. I . . . my prospects looked quite dismal. But then I saw him . . . " Rose's voice trailed off, and she closed her eyes.

"Burt?" Olivia asked.

Rose nodded and began to cry again. When she could speak, she said, "He was so handsome. I suddenly thought my dreams had come true. He smiled at me and came to my rescue from all the others. He was, well, almost chivalrous. He was clean shaven, with beautifully combed blonde hair and tall. He wore clean clothes and—and I went with him without hesitation. I was certain that I was the luckiest girl alive."

Olivia sighed a large knowing sigh that indicated she could predict what came next. She closed her eyes and when she opened them, she spoke softly.

"Tell me," Olivia said.

"He took me to his horse, and we walked to where there was a preacher to marry all the happy couples," Rose said.

What Rose did not say was that the other girls who'd traveled with her were already in the process of marrying, except for Eliza. Eliza had fallen in love with one of the ship stewards and opted to stay aboard the ship. The captain married them just prior to their arrival in San Francisco. Rose had been excluded from the occasion.

"The other girls from the ship were there, all giddy with excitement about getting married," Rose continued. "I was happy, too. I seemed to have the cream of the crop. The most handsome of all of the men."

"Burt is quite good looking when he cleans up," Olivia said. "I suspect you have since found that looks are not everything?"

Rose broke down in fresh tears. "It was awful," she sobbed. "He pulled me up onto his horse the minute we were declared man and wife and started out on the long journey here. I'd never ridden a horse in such a manner and had to cling for my life. After riding all afternoon, I was raw and achy. I could barely walk."

"Did you talk to each other at all?" Olivia asked.

"I kept trying to talk to him. After he said "I do," he didn't say another word until we stopped for the night. He offered me water from a bag and dried meat for dinner, then he made a fire and laid out a blanket for sleeping. I was horrified. This was to be my wedding night. I couldn't even tolerate sitting on a log I was so sore! Do you know what he said?"

"I'm afraid to ask."

"He looked at the fire and the blanket and said, 'well, this is mighty romantic,' and unbuttoned his breeches. I tried to tell him that I was too sore from riding to enjoy our first night together, but he just laughed and said that I was his wife and threw me onto the blanket! It seemed forever until we reached Sacramento. He'd stored the wagon there. At least it was easier to travel once we had the wagon."

"Oh, Rose. I am so sorry things turned out like this for you. Has he told you where you are going to live?"

"I am afraid to ask. I assumed he would have taken care of that, but . . . " Rose's voice trailed off.

Olivia was about to ask another question, but Burt walked into the dining hall with Burley.

Burt strolled over like a proud peacock and rather roughly pulled Rose to her feet.

"Wife," he said, "this here's Burley. He heads this outfit, and he makes all the decisions. Tell him what you can do to make yourself useful."

Burley was clearly uncomfortable with the situation.

Nevertheless, he took off his hat and said, "Pleased to meet you, ma'am."

An uncomfortable silence ensued until Olivia said, "We can always use more help in the kitchen, Burley. Would it be alright if we took her on as an additional helper."

"Course, Olivia," Burley said, grateful to be saved.

"Burt," Olivia added, "I wonder where you and your bride plan to sleep?" She could not imagine that he had given that an ounce of thought but sincerely hoped she was wrong.

"No reason she can't sleep with me in the bunkhouse," he said with a matter-of-fact tone.

Olivia looked at him in horror. "You cannot be serious!" she exploded.

He drew himself up and glared at her. "Ain't none of your business, now, is it Mrs. Anderson? She is my wife, and she will do as I say."

It was Burley's turn to save Olivia. "Now, Burt, you know there's a rule that no women can be in the bunkhouse. You will have to think of something else for you and, I am sorry, what is your name?"

Rose was still gaping at her husband and aghast at his suggestion that she sleep with him in the bunkhouse.

"WIFE!" Burt shouted at her. "He asked you a question."

Rose shook her head to come back to the present. "I'm sorry, Mr. Burley?"

Burley cleared his throat, clearly embarrassed by the

uncomfortable situation. "I only asked your name, honey."

"Oh," she said. "My name is Rose, Mr. Burley."

"Well, Rose, I am sorry to say that I don't know where you might be sleeping tonight, but I'm sure you understand that I can't allow you to sleep with all the men."

Burt's nostrils were flaring. Olivia couldn't tell if he was more upset with Burley, Rose, her, or the situation. She could feel him seething.

"Of course, I understand, Mr. Burley," Rose said softly.

Following another uncomfortable silence during which Olivia was sure that Burt wanted nothing more than to start beating the hell out of all three of them, Olivia suggested that perhaps Rose might be able to sleep with Shu in her little addition until such time as Burt created a home for them.

Burt, working exceedingly hard to control himself, finally smiled. It was such an evil smile that Olivia almost found herself shriveling.

"As I recall, Olivia," he said, "it seems not so long ago that Stewart volunteered to sleep in the bunkhouse while you stayed in your little cabin with that chink. I think it would be quite hospitable for you to let me and my bride use your cabin until I can build one."

Olivia said a quick prayer and looked at Burt with all the determination she could muster. "That was an entirely different situation, Burt. If you recall, my husband had our cabin ready before I arrived. We will not give up our home because you failed to think of accommodating your own wife."

The dining hall was beginning to fill with hungry men wanting their supper.

Erik entered and started over to say hello to Olivia and Burley. Before he reached them, he sensed the tension. He turned on his heel and returned a moment later with Stewart.

Olivia saw Erik come into the hall again. This time he had Stewart with him, and he nodded to where she and Burley were standing. Stewart walked over, clearly alert to the tension.

"Hello, beautiful," he said to Olivia and kissed her on the cheek. "Hey Burt, Burley, Ma'am," he nodded to Rose as he addressed her.

"Stewart," Olivia said, "this is Rose. She married Burt a few days ago. Burt thinks we should give up our cabin because women aren't allowed in the bunkhouse."

Stewart burst out laughing. "Good one, Burt!" When he stopped laughing, he ignored the glare from Burt and continued. "Seriously, though, congratulations!" Stewart clapped him on the back, then turned to Rose.

"Congratulations to you as well, Miss Rose," he said. "Burt is a character; you know you got your hands full?"

Rose forced a smile and said, "Thank you, Stewart."

"You will all have to excuse me," Olivia said. "These men are starving, and I need to help get food on the table. Rose, we can talk more after you settle in about how you might help in the kitchen." She was never more grateful to escape a conversation than she was that one.

When dinner was over and the majority of the men were

back at the bunkhouse, Burt, Rose, and Stewart appeared in the kitchen where Mr. Chang, Shu, and Olivia were cleaning up. Olivia had already communicated to Shu about the sleeping problem.

The room Shu slept in was small, maybe twice as big as her sleeping mat. Erik had brought another mat to the room right after his supper.

"Shu, let's show Rose where she will be sleeping," Olivia said, ignoring the searing looks from Burt.

Shu, still very formal in her manners, bowed slightly and said, "Come, come. I show."

Olivia and Burt both followed. Stewart stayed behind, but close enough to monitor the situation.

"Thank you so much, Olivia, Shu. I am most grateful for your hospitality."

"This is only temporary, woman. I'll not have my wife sleeping with a filthy chink for long."

Rose nodded but avoided eye contact with him. She made a step into the room she would share with Shu.

"Not so fast," Burt said as he grabbed her forearm and yanked her toward him. "Let's go for a little walk." He paused briefly and smiled menacingly before he added, "Honey."

Olivia was helpless to do anything as she watched Burt pull Rose from the kitchen. She closed her eyes, imagining what awaited the poor woman. When she felt Stewart come up behind her and place his hands on her shoulders, she nearly collapsed back into him.

"Mr. Chang, Shu," Stewart said softly, "thank you for your kindness to that poor woman."

When Stewart and Olivia left the kitchen to head back to their cabin, they both saw and heard Rose crying and Burt grunting. Oblivious to their presence, Burt had Rose bent over a tree stump going at her like an animal.

Stewart steered Olivia away as quietly as possible.

Rose approached her kitchen chores with about as much enthusiasm as the wet dishrag with which she mopped up the dining room tables. Her melancholy followed her like a dark rain cloud and everywhere she went others could feel the heaviness. Olivia saw the overwhelming sadness of the woman as well as the bruises.

"Rose," Olivia said one day when they were setting up the dining room for dinner, "have you considered leaving?"

Rose looked at Olivia with a look that said, simply, "I am empty—there is nothing left of me."

Olivia had seen the life ebb from the woman over the many weeks since she'd arrived. She had no idea what Rose's life had been before the fateful voyage that brought her to this loveless life. Olivia had tried many, many times to engage Rose in some sort of friendship. Nothing worked. So, sadly, Olivia watched whatever spirit that had been there drip from her like water from a cracked pot.

Olivia tried again now.

"Rose, please sit here next to me," Olivia pleaded.

Rose sat, obediently. Her shoulders slumped, and her eyes drifted off at nothing in particular.

"You cannot go on like this. You must do something to get yourself out of here—away from him."

Rose turned her head to look at Olivia, and a small snort escaped her.

"You think I have not tried to think of a way of escaping? I have nothing—not a penny to my name. I would die in the woods. Believe me, dying would be better than this life with this . . . this . . . "

Rose's words trailed off, and her eyes again drifted off. There was nothing there.

"Does he take all of the money from Burley?" Olivia asked.

Rose nodded.

"Do you have family somewhere?"

Again, Rose snorted in derision. "I humiliated them by running away. I was to marry an old man with status and money. My parents were pillars of the community. Elite, powerful, wealthy. I was their only child and the hope of their future. The marriage was one arranged by them. I simply left. I am certain they would not be happy to hear from me."

"Have you tried contacting them?"

"From this desolation? How?" Rose shook her head back and forth.

"Rose, it is worth a try, don't you think?"

"Sometimes I think now that even a life with ancient

Frederick Barton would be heaven compared to this. If I'd known this is what my life would look like, I'd have married that codger in a heartbeat."

Olivia put her hand on Rose's shoulder. "Rose, will you let me help you?"

"How? You see how he is."

"I do," Olivia said, "but I have an idea. First, I think you need to, at the very least, write a letter to your parents. Find out if they will have you back. I cannot imagine they won't. Can you do that?"

"And get it to them how?"

"Don't worry about that. You just write the letter and leave the rest to me. Okay?"

Rose nodded.

Chapter Twenty-Seven

Hannah

It had been weeks since their father died. She had no idea how long it would take for her letter to arrive at the logging camp. From the dates on previous letters they'd written to each other, it seemed that he wrote back as soon as he'd received her letter. His dates always indicated that it was somewhere between three and four weeks until her letter had arrived at the camp.

She ached for her sweet brother and watched for him from

the porch of the house. Although she had taken care of burying their father and cleaned out the house of his clothing and other things, the smell of his pipe tobacco still clung to the curtains and walls. Before she rid herself of his pipes and tobacco, she tried lighting up one of them because she always loved the smell. After a significant bout of coughing, she put the thing out and chuckled at herself, wondering why anyone would attempt to smoke in the first place.

As she sat on the porch, she silently wished, "Please come soon. I am so lonely and sadder than I ever imagined I could be."

As morning passed into early afternoon, she went inside to make herself some eggs. If and when he came, they would have much to do. Sell the house or keep it? What about the furniture?

The more she thought about these things, the more she realized that she did not want to stay in Linkville.[19] She'd never really fit in. The little schoolhouse that she'd attended only had about twelve students. Most of them were girls. She desperately wanted them to like her, but mostly they made fun of her because she never wanted to play the games they wanted to play. While she always wanted them to climb trees or fish and swim near the falls, they preferred to sew or learn how to cook or figure out new ways to make themselves pretty with ribbons and bows in their hair. They also acted ridiculously helpless around boys.

One day, when she was around ten years old, she had decided to cut her hair off to look more like her brother. Of course, she was sternly reprimanded by both of her parents, and she knew she had made a disaster of her hair. After a second dressing down by her mother, she went to her room as commanded and was

19 Linkville, OR, was not actually named until 1867. In 1893, the name was changed to Klamath Falls, OR.

sitting in front of a small mirror looking at herself. She hadn't heard him slip up to the door of her room. His chuckling from the doorway was both welcome and embarrassing.

"What were you thinking, Hannah?" he asked, unable to keep the smile from his face.

She turned to him and started sobbing.

He went to her and pulled her up into his arms. He just let her cry until she was finished.

Finally, she sniffed and pulled away from him. Turning toward the window in her room, she said softly, "I was trying to look more like you. Boys get to do all the fun things that I want to do. I hate being a girl."

"Oh, Han," he said softly. "It's not so great being a boy. Really, and I love having a little sister."

"Why?" she asked.

"You make me laugh," he said. "And I can't imagine not having you around."

She turned toward him. "Even looking like this?" she said pointing to her hair.

He covered his mouth with his hand but could not help letting the laugh escape. "Especially with you looking like that!"

At that, they both started laughing and could not stop.

These were the memories of him that she cherished most. He always made her feel better, and she really needed him now to make her laugh. It had been so long since she had a good laugh.

The next day dawned cloudy with a healthy drizzle. Hannah sat on the covered porch sipping her coffee and wondering what the rest of her life might look like. Instinctively, she knew that she never wanted to marry. She was quite happy living at home with her family. After her brother left for the logging camp and her mother got sick, her purpose became clear. Unlike the fastidious girls she grew up with, she never shied away from bugs or blood or exceedingly hard work.

She went inside to get herself a second cup of coffee. Even though she wasn't hungry, she cut a piece of bread, spread some butter on it, and sat at the kitchen table to eat it. When she was finished with her bread and coffee, she pushed the plates out of her way and simply rested her head on her arms. It wasn't long before she found herself weeping uncontrollably.

Crying wasn't something Hannah did often. In fact, it was quite rare. Even when her mother got so sick and needed constant care, she handled everything that needed to be done without shedding a tear.

She thought back to when her mother first got sick. It came on gradually. Her mother never complained, but Hannah saw the blood stains her mother had tried to scrub from her clothes and bed sheets. When Hannah asked her about it, her mother said it was just her monthlies.

"They are coming much more often than monthly, Mother," Hannah said with concern. "Have you called Dr. Jacobson?"

"I'm fine, Hannah."

But her mother wasn't fine. It was clear she was losing weight. Her color was slightly yellowish, and she had very little energy.

By the time her father sent for Dr. Jacobson, her cancer was too far along to do anything, and the doctor suggested that anyone who told her otherwise would be lying.

"The hospital here has a very bad record of losing patients with any kind of cancer," he said. "There are very few women who survive uterine cancer. Best to just take care of her at home and keep her comfortable."

Hannah took up the task without question. As her mother became weaker and stayed in bed, Hannah learned how to change the sheets without taking her mother out of the bed. She cleaned her mother several times a day when the blood flowed. She bathed her mother and lifted her by herself when her mother cried and wished to sit by the window to watch the birds or the clouds. Hannah did all of this to help her mother maintain her dignity—and so her father would not have to deal with these womanly issues.

When her mother seemed to have nothing left, she suddenly woke Hannah who was sitting in the rocking chair dosing.

"Hannah, I have a taste for a fried egg and a piece of bacon," her mother said almost brightly.

Surprised by the surge of energy, Hannah smiled and ran down to the kitchen to make the meager meal. Her mother ate the egg and one piece of bacon, then sighed.

"Hannah, my sweet, capable, hard-working child," her mother said with a smile. "Come here and nap with me. You must be exhausted."

Hannah climbed into bed and into her mother's arms. They fell asleep in the glow of the late afternoon sun. When she woke up it was dark, and her mother was dead.

Hannah had never had time to grieve for her mother. When her father became ill and was unable to speak or move half of his body, Dr. Jacobson came on his horse, examined her father, and diagnosed him with apoplexy. Hannah helped the doctor when he made the incisions for the bloodletting. Her father fought as the doctor started the incisions. Hannah was strong enough to hold him as he tried to pull away.

Hannah questioned the amount of blood the doctor allowed to drain from her father's arm.

"That seems like a lot of blood to lose," she commented.

Dr. Jacobson didn't respond until he was satisfied that enough blood had been let.

"It is the only known treatment for apoplexy, child. The more bad blood we let out, the more likely your father's recovery."

Hannah never called for Dr. Jacobson again. "How can he know if he is getting good blood or bad blood," she wondered. Her father looked worse after the bloodletting. She opted to take care of her father on her own. With no medical training, she worked daily on her father's hand and foot, which appeared to be stiffening and curling. Uncurling and massaging the extremities seemed to ease his pain, and he often fell into a comfortable sleep when she was finished.

Grinding up her father's food was the only way she could get any food into him. He was unable to manage regular food, but when she noticed that things like mashed potatoes were easier for him to swallow, she simply began mashing foods up for him.

Gradually, he began to be able to sit up in a chair. He tried to talk, but it was difficult and frustrating for both of them. Eventually, he gave up and fell into despondence. As with her mother, Hannah kept him clean, changed his sheets when necessary, and tried to keep him fed. He began to refuse food and was unconscious at the end. He remained that way for three days before he finally died. Hannah was more relieved than sad, and she felt guilty for that.

She wrote to her brother, but always worried that he might not receive her letters. So, she waited. Alone. Sad.

Chapter Twenty-Eight

Stewart and Olivia pulled into the camp and drove the wagon around to the back of the kitchen.As usual, it was piled high with supplies all covered with an oil cloth. As Stewart untied the oil cloth, Olivia ran in to find Rose.

Since Olivia's plan had been in place, Rose found that place where hope used to be, and she clung to it with all her might. She still dreaded the near nightly abuses by Burt, but she found a way to go elsewhere in her mind while he satisfied himself. She realized she wasn't a wife, just a receptacle for Burt's rage against everything—especially women. She saw how Stewart and Olivia were. That, to her, was love and so much more. She witnessed their tenderness, compassion, and affection for each other. As her hope started to return, so did her desire for what Stewart and Olivia had—and that was what she thought marriage should be. She even saw the respect and love in Mr. Chang and

Shu's budding relationship. It was the little things—Mr. Chang rushing to pick up a utensil Shu dropped when preparing food, or the way that Shu asked him to taste whatever she was cooking and always saved a special bowl for him.

"I could be happy with almost anyone if he just treated me with a little respect," Rose thought.

Olivia came hurriedly into the kitchen. "Mr. Chang, Shu, could you please help Stewart to unload everything, please? I need to speak with Rose."

Both of them bowed slightly and disappeared.

"Rose," Olivia said as she sidled up next to her and slipped her a letter that had been waiting at the Post Office in Sacramento.

Rose looked at the letter, then up at Olivia. It could only be from her parents. No one else in the world knew where she was.

With trembling hands, Rose looked back down at the unopened letter.

"What if they want nothing to do with me?" she asked. "I wouldn't blame them, you know? I was a truly horrid daughter."

Olivia reached up and placed a hand on Rose's cheek. "I do not have children, Rose, but I can't imagine them rejecting you by letter. They could have just ignored responding if they wanted nothing to do with you."

"But I left them with only a letter—telling them not to try to find me!" Rose cried.

"Open the letter, honey. We will deal with whatever is in it."

What Rose didn't know was that Olivia and Stewart had

been putting aside a little bit of their own money to help Rose escape regardless of whether she heard from her parents or not. Olivia prayed daily for both Rose and her parents. She even prayed for that bastard, Burt, but she wasn't even sure there was any saving him. He had even begun to garner support for his hatred of Shu and Mr. Chang. What Olivia didn't know was that when he'd been in San Francisco to find a wife, Burt ran into several groups of men in the saloons who complained that the Chinese were taking jobs from Americans. Always eager to find a new way to vent his angry nature at anyone but himself, he joined several mobs to find and beat poor, unsuspecting Chinese, sometimes to death.

Rose retreated to the opening of the little bedroom she shared with Shu and sat on her little mat. After just staring at her mother's handwriting on the envelope for a bit, she finally tore it open and began to read:

Dearest Rose,

We thought you were gone forever. Receiving your letter seemed a miracle to us.

Of course, we were angry and frantic when you disappeared, but after all this time, to finally hear from you—and hear about what you have endured—are enduring—we were more sick at heart than ever.

Come home, Rose. Come home. All is forgiven. Please, come home.

Love,

Mother and Father

PS. Your father has taken care of getting money to the only bank in San Francisco. It is in Portsmouth Square.[20]

Olivia was helping to unload the supplies when she heard Rose sobbing. Thinking the worst, she ran over to console the poor thing. "Rose, Rose, please don't worry. Stewart and I will help you. I'm so sorry!"

Rose looked up and smiled the most genuine smile of her whole life. She shook her head. "No, Olivia, no. It's okay. Read it."

She thrust the letter into Olivia's hands and waited.

"Oh, Rose," Olivia said. When she looked up at Rose, Olivia began weeping, too. "I am so happy for you."

Together they wept, arms around each other, still sitting on the little mat.

"I don't deserve any of this," Rose cried. "I was an ungrateful and meanspirited child and only grew worse as I got older. How will I make things up to them?"

Olivia wiped her eyes and nose with her kerchief and said, "You'll find a way, Rose. You will find a way."

Chapter Twenty-Nine

20 From The Museum of the City of San Francisco: Henry M. Naglee opened the first bank in San Francisco in Portsmouth Square on January 9, 1849.

The same mail delivery that brought the letter for Rose brought another letter.

Olivia found Stewart and Erik still sitting in the dining hall well after nearly all the other loggers had departed. It was clear Erik had been crying.

"What is it?" she asked.

Stewart answered her. "It's from Erik's sister, Hannah. Their father passed away a few weeks ago."

"Oh, Erik, I am so sorry," Olivia said as she sat and reached for his hands. "I am so, so sorry.

"Thank you, Olivia. He was not well, but I thought he'd still be there when I came back. My poor sister had to deal with everything all alone."

The three of them sat together in silence for a spell.

"I am going to head back to Oregon and get Hannah," Erik said. "Think I'll bring her back up here until the season is over. Between that and what my father left us I think we might just start us a little farm. Hannah always loved the outdoors. I think she might really like being in the mountains for a bit. Change of place might do her some good."

"Anything we can do?" Olivia asked, knowing there was nothing.

"Maybe think of a way she can do some work around the camp?" Erik said. "She is strong and quite capable. She could use a friend, Olivia, if I might ask."

"Oh, Erik," Olivia responded, "she will have two friends as soon as she arrives. Stewart and I will welcome her with open arms."

"Absolutely we will," Stewart added. "And I know the bunkhouse could use a woman's touch. That place gets more disgusting every time I have to go in there! I'll talk to Burley while you head home to get your sister."

"You are good friends," Erik said. He rose quickly before his tears started up again. "I'll leave right after breakfast," he added as he made for the door. He turned back before he got to the door. "If there is a way to figure out where she might sleep, that would be a big help."

"We will think of something, Erik. You just go get her and tell her she has friends waiting here," Stewart said.

Erik nodded his appreciation and left to find Burley to tell him the news.

"Poor Erik," Olivia said.

Stewart nodded, and they headed to the kitchen to help finish cleaning up.

Erik saddled his horse the next morning and started his ride home to Linkville, Oregon. He hadn't left camp much since coming up. He did ride home to be with his family when his mother died late last year.

His mother was a sweet, loving soul. Erik always dreamed of making her happy by finding a wife who would love to cook, quilt, and garden with his mother. He knew his mother loved his sister, but Hannah wasn't much for womanly activities. His mother did not push it, though his father was always on Hannah about her lack of feminine virtues.

Poor Hannah. Sometimes he worried that she would die alone. He understood her because she was more like him than anyone he'd ever known. She was also smarter than anyone he'd ever known—even the doctors who had been called for both of his parents.

Hannah read everything she could get her hands on. When she woke up early, she would read her father's paper before he got up.

"Why don't you do something useful," their father would yell at her. "Perhaps prepare breakfast like a normal woman?"

Hannah would just smile and nod. She gave up trying to get her father to understand that she was more than a housemaid. She began to clear away the breakfast dishes and always made sure that her mother knew how much she appreciated all of the things that she did.

"You know, Mom, that I don't mean anything against you."

Their mother would always smile and embrace Hannah. "You, my daughter, are destined for greater things. Pay your father no mind."

"Are you happy, Mom?"

Erik happened into the kitchen to hear the answer to that question.

Anna Johansson looked at her son and daughter, sighed, and then smiled her most loving smile. "I have, without a doubt, the two smartest, sweetest, and most loving children any mother could hope for," she said. "I am happy enough."

Now, as Erik rode the long journey home with nothing but

his own thoughts and memories of his mother, he wondered what his future would look like. His father tried to interest him in accounting, but the work was far too sedentary for him. If he had a dream at all, it was to make enough money working at logging to be able to find a wife and settle down to start a small farm. His dream always included taking care of Hannah. He knew she would enjoy a farming life. She was so good at creating and building things that made their mother's life in the kitchen easier—from creating a pulley system for heavy pots and pans, to raising the garden bed so that it was easier to look after the plants and keep an eye out for hornworms on the tomatoes.

Erik knew that Hannah was not like other girls. Now he knew that she was not like other women. His heart hurt for his sister, whom he suspected would live her life alone. He was not about to let that happen. She would always have him.

He wondered if she knew that he often stood up for her against their father.

"Why don't you encourage her to dress more like a girl?" their father would say.

"Why don't you let her be herself?" Erik would answer.

"Because she is going to be a woman someday. How will she ever find a decent husband if she cannot make herself more attractive?"

"If she can't be herself, she will never find a man who could make her happy. She is smarter than all of the men I know!"

His father glared at him.

Erik continued. "It would take a very smart man to love Hannah for who she is. If I find one as smart as she, I will personally introduce them."

Lars Johansson was a harsh, demanding, and very particular man. Erik supposed that those traits are what made him a good accountant. But it wasn't just numbers that made him so disagreeable. Any little thing out of place could set him off. His mother worked hard to make certain things were always tidy and where they belonged.

Erik noticed that his father's pickiness had greatly increased once Hannah started to talk and walk and refused to dress like other girls her age. Erik would often tease his sister by telling her that it was her fault that their father was the way he was. "He can't control you and make you do what he thinks you need to do—so he gets more and more finicky about everything else in his world."

"I know you think you are kidding, but there is truth to what you say, you know. And don't think I don't see it," she replied with a raised eyebrow.

"Promise me, Han, that you will never change just to make him happy. Watching him press you to change and knowing it is a losing battle for him is becoming my greatest form of entertainment. I love the way you just nod and then ignore him instead of arguing."

Hannah smiled and punched him in the arm.

Now that Lars Johansson was dead, Erik wondered what kind of effect his death might have on Hannah. He wondered if it would change their relationship and how that might look.

He was nearing Linkville. Nothing much had changed since he left the town after his mother died. Yet, everything was different.

The nearest neighbors to their family home were a mile away. As he drew closer, he wondered what the house would feel like without either of his parents there. He slowed his horse to try to gain control over his feelings.

Erik was hoping to find Hannah on the front porch, but she was not there. From the living room window, he could see that she had her head down on the kitchen table. He tapped lightly on the window so he wouldn't frighten her. When there was no response, he assumed she was dozing. In spite of his attempt to enter quietly, the porch door squeaked when he came in. By the time he got to the kitchen, Hannah had managed to grab a very large kitchen knife. As she turned, readying herself to use it, Erik walked in.

His work had made him bigger and stronger than the brother she knew. She did not recognize him.

"Are you planning to kill me?" he asked.

She recognized his voice, dropped the knife, and ran into his arms. "You're here. You came," she sobbed.

"Of course, I came. I left as soon as I got your letter."

"I worried that maybe something had happened to you, too," she said. "I thought I was alone in the world."

"Never, Han. I promise I will never leave you alone. Okay?"

"You can't make a promise like that," she said. "Everyone dies."

He sighed. "Well, that's true, but I intend to be around until I am really old, wrinkly, and grumpy."

She hugged him. "You had better be," she said and punched him in the arm. "I mean it."

Two weeks later, Hannah and Eric left for the trip to the logging camp. They came in from the north as it was a shorter ride up the Sierras from Oregon. Once they hit Goose Lake, they followed the Pit River up to where the log flume ran down the other side of the Sierra mountain range to Redding. The mill that took all the wood from their camp was in Redding.

"Is that a flume?" Hannah asked.

"How do you know that?" Erik asked with surprise.

"When you left to log, I found everything I could find about logging so I could imagine what you were doing," she said.

"Huh," Erik responded. "Everything is interesting to you," he laughed. "Was there ever anything you didn't want to learn more about?"

"Other than marriage?" she quipped.

Erik looked at her and shook his head. "I worry about you, you know? I wish you could find someone whose company you enjoy. I hate the thought of you being lonely. And don't tell me you were perfectly happy being the only one to take care of our sick parents!"

Hannah was quiet for a time. The only sound was that of their horses clomping up the mountain. When they stopped to water the horses and have a bite to eat themselves, Hannah said, "You know, sweet brother, I really didn't mind caring for them. In a way, I guess it gave me purpose. I can't quite describe it, but it reminded me of saints who heard the call of God and followed that calling to a convent or a monastery. Not that I think of myself as a saint!" she added quickly. "Nothing like that, but" she paused again, "but there seemed to be something more to my just being a daughter and fulfilling an expected role. It was almost holy."

Erik was silent. It wasn't that he didn't understand or thought she was odd, he was processing what she said.

"I think I know what you mean," he finally offered. "I guess I kind of feel that way about logging. I love being a high rigger. There is a certain feeling when I get to the top of an enormously tall tree. The closer I get to where I know I am going to stop to top the tree, the more excited I get. Once I top the tree and it is flat on the top, I often clamber up to sit there. It feels, I don't know, it feels sacred."

Hannah smiled. "That's it, Erik. Sacred," she repeated. "There was something very sacred in knowing that I was sitting so close to death—almost like I was witness to the birth of something sacred."

"Hmmm," Erik said and nodded.

Neither of them spoke for some time. They mounted their horses in silence and rode without speaking for a long time.

Erik did worry about Hannah being at the camp and prayed that she might find some happiness there. Among all those men, he worried that she might be the brunt of many jokes. He knew that in no time she could do whatever they did, and do it happily, but wanted so much more for her. He worried she would want to become a logger. And he knew the men would hate that. He also knew that there were some of the men who would love to have fun at her expense. It had been all he could do to keep from punching Burt, who never missed an opportunity to insult something or someone. In the bunkhouse when Erik told a couple of his buddies that he was going to get his sister because his father had passed, Burt said, just loud enough for Eric to hear, "I guess we'll finally get a look at the spinster sister. Bet she's uglier than sin!"

Just thinking about the likes of Burt made his blood boil. He'd have to find a way to deal with that.

As they approached the camp, Eric noticed that Hannah slowed her horse. He knew she was nervous. She'd never been used to lots of people. She was the smartest person he ever knew but was more of a loner—which was not helped by her reluctance to marry. He thought she was really quite lovely. She had long, beautiful blond hair and large brown eyes. She'd always been strong, stronger than any woman he'd ever known. She was capable of figuring out just about anything. Smart, she was really smart. She was just, well, she was just Hannah, and he loved her dearly.

"Please, God," he silently prayed, "let her find happiness."

Chapter Thirty

It was just after the dinner meal was finished when they arrived at the camp. Most of the men had wandered back to the bunk house for a game or two of cards. A few of them were hanging around and talking about heading to Redding for some drinking on Sunday. Erik popped his head into the kitchen where

Mr. Chang, Shu, Olivia, and Stewart were finishing up dishes and prepping what they could for breakfast.

Any chance a couple of lost souls might get a little something to eat?" Erik said.

"Erik!" Olivia cried and ran over to hug him. "Where is your sister? Is she with you? I can't wait to meet her."

Erik laughed, took a step back, and opened the door all the way. "Olivia, me . . . "

"Hannah!" Olivia interrupted as she rushed to embrace the woman with a warm, welcoming hug.

Erik caught the look on Hannah's face. Clearly, she was surprised and a tad overwhelmed by Olivia's greeting. But as he watched, Hannah's face relaxed, and she smiled and hugged Olivia back.

"And I am Stewart," Stewart said stepping through the door and extending his hand. "We are so happy to have you here, Hannah. Erik has told us so many wonderful things about you."

"Thank you both," Hannah said with a smile. But as she finally looked at Olivia, her smile disappeared and she paled a bit.

"Han, you okay?" Erik asked with concern.

Hannah shook her head as if she'd been in a trance. "Sorry, I guess I am just a little weary from the long ride."

"Let's get some food in you, and I will show you where you can sleep." Olivia said.

"I've been thinking about that," Erik said. "We can continue to sleep outdoors. It worked just fine on the trail."

"Actually," Stewart said, "we took it upon ourselves to

build Hannah a little hut of her own while you were gone. It'll be getting cold soon, and she will need something a little more protective once the snow arrives."

"You didn't," Erik said, quite aghast at the generous gesture.

"We did," Stewart said with a smile. "And it has a simple structure for a small fire to keep you warm as well, Hannah. It's not what you are used to, I'm sure, but I do hope you will be comfortable."

"I don't know what to say," Hannah said. Her eyes filled with tears.

"Don't say anything, then," Olivia said as she put her arm around Hannah. "Just come, and I will show you what we might have for you to eat. You must be starving."

Hannah let herself be guided into the kitchen where she was introduced to Mr. Chang and Shu who both bowed to her and smiled.

After they'd eaten, Olivia could tell that Hannah was exhausted. "You two chat if you want to," she said to Stewart and Erik, "I am going to show Hannah to her sleeping quarters and let the poor thing get a good night's sleep."

If Olivia was surprised that Hannah wore pants, boots, and a flannel shirt, she didn't show it. Again, she put her arm around Hannah and guided her to the little structure, which was next to the one that Stewart built for him and Olivia.

"No way we are going to let Burt anywhere near her without us being close enough to hear her," Stewart had said.

The next morning, Hannah was up and already helping out in the kitchen when Olivia arrived. It was still dark.

"Hannah!" Olivia exclaimed. "What are you doing here? You should still be sleeping."

Hannah smiled. "I've not had a full night's sleep since I began taking care of my parents. I expect I will continue to wake up several times a night. Thought I'd just come and see what I could do to help. Looks like there are a whole lot of hungry mouths to feed."

Olivia's eyebrows shot up. "You are amazing. Erik said you were a wonder to behold, now I know what he meant. Oh, and I am sorry about the loss of your father—and your mother, too. I can't imagine how hard that must have been."

"Thank you, Olivia."

When all the men arrived for breakfast, Stewart took it upon himself to introduce Hannah.

"Hey, Erik, looks like we know who wore the pants in your family!" someone called out from a far table. It sounded like Burt, but it was hard to tell.

Burley came over to introduce himself to Hannah. Then he turned to the men and said, "This, here, is our friend Erik's sister. You men will all treat her as if she is your own sister."

"She looks more like our brother!" It was definitely Burt.

Olivia whispered something to Hannah who replied, "I have been warned. Don't worry, it doesn't bother me."

After the men were gone and breakfast cleaned up, Olivia grabbed Hannah's hand and said, "C'mon, I will show you the most beautiful spot where I try to spend some time every day."

The women walked a worn path up the mountain a short way then turned into a dense part of the woods. A few moments later they emerged into the sunlight that lit up the meadow where Olivia often heard her grandmother speak to her. It wasn't a real voice; it was something she heard inside of her head, and she could not explain it. The voice was as real to her as if her grandmother was standing directly in front of her.

Hannah gaped in wonder. It was nearing the end of summer, so the grass was beginning to turn golden. There were huge boulders throughout the meadow that looked as if each one had been placed with consideration and intention. There were some wildflowers still in bloom. The meadow was small, but perfect. Hannah grinned from ear to ear.

Olivia was so happy to see Hannah's reaction. She felt a kinship with this woman she had just met. Perhaps it was just that she was so hungry for female companionship. The time she was able to spend with Molly was really time with Molly, Sam, and Stewart. Shu was very sweet, but communication was difficult and the cultural differences were larger than she had anticipated. She really missed her aunt Maria, and letters were insufficient. She guessed that she was just happy for some female companionship. Somehow, she could feel her energy level ramp up a notch the moment Hannah arrived. Even though Hannah dressed differently than any woman she had ever known, she knew in an instant that they would be great friends.

"Feel free to wander wherever you like," Olivia said. "For me, this is the closest thing to heaven. I try to come whenever I feel I can take the time. There is something about the solitude, the birds and bees buzzing around, just lying here and watching the clouds float by. I just love my time here."

Hannah looked at Olivia and smiled. When she did, Olivia felt a surge of happiness so large that it made her blush.

"Thank you for sharing such a special place with me. You have made me feel so welcome. I didn't expect any of what you have done—you and Stewart, I mean. In some way I feel like, well, I can't explain it but it feels like I am home . . . like I have found what I have been wanting all of my life. Thank you, Olivia."

Olivia smiled and nodded, then found a place to lay on the grass to stare up at the heavens. Hannah wandered the field, sat on a boulder, and relished an unfamiliar feeling. She was happy. She wasn't sure why she was so happy, but happy was the only word she could use to describe the wonder and the hope that enveloped her as she took in her surroundings. When her eyes fell on Olivia, who seemed to have dozed off, she could not help but smile. Happiness was not a feeling she was used to, but she could most assuredly get used to it here.

Chapter Thirty-One

Olivia and Hannah went every day to the meadow. The weather was getting chillier. It was nearing the end of August, but the sun was usually over the meadow providing warmth so that they were able to relax and chat.

The women shared their life stories over the weeks. Each memory, every pain and trauma, all the grief they each had seemed to flow out and be absorbed by the breeze.

"Liv," Hannah started, "I have never had a woman friend. I am noticing that talking about my life with you feels like a burden has been lifted." She smiled at Olivia, a gentle, peaceful smile. "You are not like other women. There is something about you that makes me feel like I can share anything with you."

Olivia was smiling back at Hannah, whom she had been calling "Han" since the second day Hannah arrived. At the time, she commented that Erik always referred to her by that name. Hannah had been delighted.

"I do feel the same, Han. I have had friends but none like you." Olivia paused and had a puzzled look on her face.

"What is it, Liv?"

Olivia looked up at a cloud that was passing in front of the sun. She sighed. "Remember the night you arrived?"

Hannah nodded.

"When you looked at me, I saw something in your face. I don't know what it was, but I remember it startling me, because, well, you looked like you had seen a ghost. I thought it was just because you were exhausted from your journey, but I can't stop thinking about it."

Hannah looked down. Her hands were in her lap, and she knit her fingers together. When she looked up, she looked worried. "I am afraid you will think me quite mad," Hannah began then stopped.

Olivia reached for Hannah's hands, held them up, and kissed them. "I will think no such thing, sweet friend. Tell me."

Now it was Hannah's turn to release a great sigh. "Three

times in my whole life I have had the same dream. Well, it is not exactly what I would call a dream, but it always came in my sleep. The first time was when Erik left for the logging camp. The second time was as my mother lay dying. The third was when I waited all those weeks for Erik to come home after our father died." She paused and was not able to maintain eye contact with Olivia. She looked down at their hands clasped together on her lap. "Like I said, it wasn't really a dream." She stopped again. Olivia squeezed her hands. "It was a face. A face just staring at me. I did not know whose face it was, but it always showed up when I was so sad that I wasn't sure I could go on. If I looked like I had seen a ghost that night, it was because that was how I felt. The face in my dream was yours."

Olivia said nothing. She wanted to say something but was reeling from what she had heard. She didn't move. She did not release Hannah's hands. They sat without words for what seemed an eternity.

Finally, Hannah said, "Please, Liv, say something."

Olivia pulled her right hand from Hannah's and lifted Hannah's chin so that she could see her eyes. Olivia's eyes were full of tears. As a tear spilled onto her cheek and slid down to her chin she said, "Han, I believe that there is so much more out there." She looked up at the sky as she said, "so much we cannot possibly know or understand," she looked back down into Hannah's eyes. "There have been times in my life that I know something else has taken over in me and guided me. Is it God? Is it my ancestors? Is it an angel? Is it just me opening up into my own soul? I don't know the answers. But I know that things happen. I do not think you have gone mad. I don't know why you dreamed of me before we met. But it does seem vital to me that you have. That is all I know."

"Thank you, Liv. Thank you."

"I could stay here all day with you, but we should head back."

Hannah stood up and pulled Olivia to her feet. Arm in arm they started back to camp.

Chapter Thirty-Two

Two days before Stewart and Olivia planned to take the next trip to Sacramento for supplies, Olivia was in the dining hall with Rose.

Olivia moved close to Rose and whispered to her.

"Tomorrow morning, after the men have left for the mountaintop after breakfast, you need to disappear. I don't want Burt to make any connection between your disappearance and our leaving for town."

Rose looked at her. "Where will I go?"

"Keep wiping tables, Rose. I don't want anyone to suspect that you, or we, are planning anything," Olivia said quietly. "Go to our cabin. You will stay with us tomorrow night. When the men get back for dinner, we will ask Burt if he knows where you are. If necessary, we will all go looking for you."

"What if someone comes to search your cabin?"

Olivia smiled. "No one knows this, but Stewart dug a small,

underground pit for me to store vegetables, in case I wanted a small garden for myself. We always planned on using it for storage. It is big enough for you to hide in, if necessary," Olivia said. "Next morning, when all the men have headed out again after breakfast, we will be taking sacks and barrels back to town and the wagon will be covered with oilcloth. You will hide there until such time as we are far enough away that it is safe for you."

"Do you think it will work?" Rose asked.

"It worked for Shu," Olivia said with a smile. "How do you think I got the idea?"

"You don't think he will come looking for me?" Rose asked with concern. "I am so afraid of him."

"You will stay with me and Stewart until we put you on the stagecoach to San Francisco.You'll be on your own after that. You will have to find the bank office and make your own arrangement for the ship, though.

They were still wiping tables as they spoke in hushed tones. Through sniffles, Rose managed to whisper, "I don't know how to thank you, Olivia. No one in my life has ever been so kind—not that I ever deserved anyone's kindness."

"We all deserve kindness, Rose. Sometimes it takes horrifying pain to create a soul open enough to receive kindness. I am glad we can help. I am even more glad about you reuniting with your parents."

The next morning, just after breakfast, Rose finished her morning chores.

"I think I'll go for a walk this morning," she announced to Olivia, Mr. Chang, and Shu.

It was unusual for Rose to do much of anything except her daily chores. On occasion, she would sit on a log behind the kitchen, but she'd never done more than that.

Shu looked at her with a quizzical look on her face. Though they slept together every night, conversation was limited because of the language difficulty. Nonetheless, Shu continued to stare at Rose. Without saying a word, Shu went over to Rose, placed her hand over her own heart, then reached to place it over Rose's heart. Rose lowered her head as her eyes quickly filled with tears. She blinked them away as fast as she could.

Mr. Chang seemed oblivious to the exchange, engaged as he was with hanging the last of the pots and pans from breakfast.

Olivia shouted, "Good for you, Rose. Enjoy your stroll!"

Shu caught Olivia's eyes, but Olivia quickly turned and busied herself. She had seen the exchange between Shu and Rose and did not want to give anything away with a look.

When it was time to begin preparing dinner, Rose was nowhere to be found. Olivia made a point of heading out the kitchen door and calling for her.

"Mr. Chang," she said when she came back to the kitchen. "Have you seen Rose?"

He shook his head and asked Shu. She told him she hadn't and looked directly at Olivia.

"Rose gone?" Shu asked.

"I haven't seen her," Olivia answered. "Have you seen her?"

"Think Rose run away," Shu said. "Good for Rose. Get far from bad husband."

"Maybe she will turn up," Olivia said. "She could get lost in these woods."

Shu smiled. "She okay."

When the men filed in for supper, Olivia was more anxious than she'd been in a long time. She waited for Burt to notice that his wife was not to be seen. She and Stewart watched him closely, but he did not appear to be at all aware that Rose was not serving.

As the men were leaving after dinner, Stewart left with them. He wanted to make sure that Rose was safely hidden. He knew Burt would begin his hunt for his nightly assault on his poor wife.

Olivia was busily cleaning tables when it seemed Burt finally noticed that Rose was not helping. He went into the kitchen. Olivia followed.

"Where is my woman?" Burt demanded.

Mr. Chang shrugged his shoulders and returned to his task.

Burt towered over Shu. He went over to stand directly in front of her in the most intimidating manner possible.

"Where is Rose?" he said with a snarl.

It was the first time Olivia, or anyone, heard Burt refer to her by her name.

"Burt!" Olivia shouted from the doorway of the dining room. "We don't know where she is. We were hoping you might.

She left for a walk earlier and did not show up to help prepare dinner."

"How the hell would I know where she was?" Burt yelled. "I been cutting wood all day. You're supposed to keep an eye on her!"

Olivia looked at him and simply said, "I am not her babysitter. She's your wife, go find her."

He looked as if he would like to lift her up and throw her across the kitchen. He probably could, too. To his credit, he turned on his heel and stalked off out the back door. She stood where she was, waiting for the trembling to cease. Before long, she heard him off in the woods calling her name.

When the kitchen was clean, Olivia headed for her cabin. When she was just about there, Burt appeared out of nowhere.

"You know something, you bitch," Burt spat at her. "I know you conniving women. Where is she?"

Olivia moved closer to her cabin hoping that Stewart could hear him.

"I don't know where your wife is, Burt. For all I know she ran away to get away from you. You treat her like a piece of trash. I guess you'll have to abuse a tree tonight instead of your wife."

He took two long strides toward Olivia, but Stewart was quickly between them and stopped Burt.

"Burt!" Stewart yelled into his face as he pushed him hard to keep him from hitting Olivia or himself.

Burt fell to the ground but was up quickly and ready for a fight. He put his fists up but realized that it was Stewart he was confronting. He was comfortable enough to treat women roughly, but Stewart was another matter. And he did not want to lose his job. He managed to calm himself somewhat.

"What the hell is going on, Burt?" Stewart demanded.

"Your wife has something to do with this!" Burt shouted.

"With what?" Stewart asked.

"My wife is gone! She knows something!"

Stewart turned toward Olivia. "Do you know what he is talking about?"

Olivia nodded. "Rose went for a walk earlier when the morning meal was over. I didn't think anything of it. She never came back, but I have no idea where she is. I was just coming to ask you to help look for her. I'm afraid she might have gotten lost in the woods."

"It'd be easy enough to do," Stewart replied. "Burt, go get some men and horses, we need to try to find her before it gets any darker."

Burt stood there as if he was weighing whether it was worth the effort.

"Stewart," Olivia pleaded, "please find her."

"Let's go, Burt," Stewart said. "Even if you don't care about her, she is a human being and could be in danger."

As the men walked off, Olivia shouted, "Please be careful!"

A little after dark, the men returned without Rose. Olivia was keeping a sharp ear out for them. When she heard them, Rose slipped into the storage space again. She was afraid that with

Burt's suspicion of her that he might insist upon looking in their tiny cabin. There was only one window in the cabin. The curtain was drawn but she did not put it past Burt to try to see in during the night. There was a lock on the cabin door, so once the camp seemed settled down, she and Stewart let Rose up from the hole.

"We still need to keep our voices very low," Stewart cautioned. "Rose, I think it's safe enough for you to sleep with Olivia. I'll sit up tonight and keep watch."

"You and Olivia are so sweet with each other," Rose whispered. "That is what I'd hoped to find when I came west."

"Don't give up hope, Rose." Stewart said. He smiled and said, "Goodnight."

After breakfast the next morning, Stewart asked Burt if there had been any sign of Rose in the night. Though he knew the answer, he thought that playing the game until the very end was the best approach.

Burt shook his head, but the look on his face was one of pure rage.

"Olivia and I are heading to Sacramento for the supply run," Stewart said. "We will keep an eye out for Rose on our way."

"Humph," Burt grunted as he turned and walked away.

Stewart watched until he saw Burt go up the mountain with the other loggers. When they were out of sight, he went to fetch the wagon, which had been loaded with empty sacks and barrels to return to the dry goods store. Then they drove off with only a quick stop at the cabin to let Rose under the oilcloth. Silently, they made their way down the mountainside for the two-day journey to Sacramento.

Stewart knew the stagecoach schedule from when he'd been planning to take Olivia there on their honeymoon. He didn't want to take any chances that Rose would be seen, so they stopped at Reverend Stevens before they rode full into town. There they were able to let Rose clean up. Olivia had a dress that she was able to alter for Rose, and she gave it to her when they arrived at the Stevenses'. The dress did not need much in the way of alteration as Rose had lost considerable weight since she'd boarded that first ship in Boston.

Stewart also asked Reverend Stevens to make his way up to the camp sometime during the next month.

"I might be able to make it next week—middle of the week, of course. Can't miss Sundays, you know," Reverend Stevens said with a smile.

"Next week would be perfect," Stewart said.

When they left the Stevenses', Stewart drove directly to the office of the stagecoach line. Rose remained hidden in the wagon. After Stewart and Olivia made certain no one was watching, they pulled her up to the driving seat and lowered her to the ground right in front of the door. All three of them entered, and Stewart paid for Rose's passage to San Francisco.

"Stage should be here any minute," the man behind the counter said as he pulled his pocket watch from his vest pocket.

The stagecoach pulled up a few minutes later. Rose, it seemed, would be the only rider.

Stewart and Olivia said their good-byes.

Rose said, "I truly do not have the words to thank you both. I am beyond grateful." There were tears in her eyes.

Olivia hugged her. Stewart shook her hand and wished her luck on her journey.

As they assisted her into the stagecoach, Olivia said, "If possible, please write and tell us when you get home, Rose."

Rose could only nod for holding back her tears.

Stewart and Olivia went to their wagon and unloaded the empty barrels and sacks at the general store. They delivered the horse and wagon to the livery before proceeding on foot to check in at the hotel.

The next morning, they went to get breakfast at Clark's Bakery. Sam and Molly brought sweets and coffee to their table and chatted for a minute before more customers arrived. Stewart and Olivia finished their coffee and sweets and told Molly they'd be back after closing and invited them to dinner at the hotel that evening.

"Looks like you have plenty to keep you busy," Stewart said. "We don't wish to keep you from your work."

The next morning upon their return to the general store to load the needed supplies, Olivia asked Mrs. Campbell if there was any news about the escaped Chinese girl.

"No one ever did find her!" Mrs. Campbell said with more than a little surprise. "They hunted for that girl for days—even had a couple of fellas search the woods. I tell you, I never seen that madam more fired up than she was when that little gal escaped."

"I wonder where she went," Olivia said, glad to hear that perhaps they'd given up looking for Shu. Sometimes she still worried that someone might have said something about Shu working at the logging camp.

Once they were loaded up and on their way back to camp, Olivia said, "Stewart, what did you think of the dinner conversation with Sam and Molly last night? That's the second time they have suggested the joint restaurant idea. Have you given any thought to it?"

"I don't see what possible help I could be in such a venture," Stewart said. His brow wrinkled up as he looked at Olivia. "Is that something you would really like to do after all the cooking and cleaning at the camp?"

"Oh, I think it would be much, much different than that," she said. "For one, I wouldn't be serving sixty plus men all three meals every day. And for another, I'm not sure that what I do would be considered any special culinary effort. It is pretty much the same menu every week. There is little variety or creativity involved when it comes right down to it."

"You like the idea, do you?" Stewart said.

Olivia lay her head on Stewart's shoulder. "I'm not sure," she said. "I do find myself wondering about it. I'd love to work with Sam and Molly. They're good people."

"That, they are, honey," Stewart said and kissed the top of her head. "How do you see my role in this grand scheme? I can't cook to save my soul."

Olivia laughed and lifted her head up. "You? Why who do you think would build us our restaurant and help us maintain it?" She laughed and looked up at him.

"Woman, you are dangerous. You have given this more thought than I imagined!" He shook his head and smiled. "Let me think on it for a while. You know I'd do anything to make you happy—especially in light of what you've had to put up with all this time."

They rode in silence for quite a while after that—each lost in their own thoughts. But no matter how much Olivia tried to think about the restaurant with her friends and husband, her thoughts kept returning to Hannah. She was surprised at how much she missed Hannah and was excited to get back to camp—perhaps for the first time ever.

Now that Rose was safely away, there would be a little less time for the meadow. Hannah mainly kept the bunkhouse clean then came to help in the kitchen as soon as she was free, but more and more men came to Burley's outfit as they heard about the great meals. Olivia was so exhausted at the end of her workdays that she fell instantly to sleep, grateful that Stewart was equally exhausted. They cuddled in bed, wrapped in each other's arms, and fell instantly into sleep. Sometimes after dinner had been served and eaten, Stewart would come to the kitchen to help with all the cleaning and preparation for breakfast. That gave them some time to chat at least.

"I've been thinking about your idea for a restaurant with Sam and Molly," Stewart said after one long and particularly difficult day of logging.

"Oh?" Olivia looked at him and waited.

"I realize that we both cannot keep up this pace or this labor without it making us both miserable." Stewart stopped and tried to hide the tears that were forming in his eyes as they both continued to wipe down the tables in the dining hall.

"I fear it might be the end of us," Stewart continued. "That is something I cannot even bear to think about."

He was silent for a moment. Olivia waited patiently.

"I'd like to give our notice to Burley that we will be leaving before the end of the year. Does that suit you to build a restaurant in town?" Stewart dropped his cloth and turned to look at Olivia.

Olivia did not move. She was facing away from him and simply stopped wiping the tables. Her head dropped.

"Olivia?" Stewart went over to her. "Honey, what is it?"

She stood up, turned toward him, and stepped into his embrace. She was crying.

"Wait," Stewart said hurriedly, "what is it? Do you want to stay here? Do you want to leave? I'm not sure what this means."

Olivia looked up at him. She was smiling through her tears. "Thank you, Stewart. I have been wondering how much longer I could do this but did not want to rush you," she sniffed. "I am so tired. I am tired all the time."

He held her and rocked a bit. "Me, too, Olivia. I have nothing left to give you at the end of the day. Can you forgive me?"

She pulled a handkerchief from her bosom and wiped her nose. "We don't have to do the restaurant. It just seemed so much easier than what we were both doing. I think I just thought of it as a way out of this logging life. We can do whatever you want. I just need to rest and be with you for a while."

"Think you can make it a few more months?" he asked. "Burley will have to replace both of us, and I don't want to leave him high and dry."

She laughed. "Just knowing there is an end in sight helps. I can do this a while longer knowing that our time is limited. Fall is my favorite time up here anyway."

She hugged him hard. "Thank you, sweet man."

He lifted her chin and kissed her so tenderly that she thought she might weep. Only later, as she started to drift off to sleep, did she jolt awake, realizing that leaving camp meant leaving Hannah.

Chapter Thirty-Three

Reverend Stevens rolled into the camp around midday of the next day. Only Burley, Erik, and Hannah knew that he was coming. Stewart and Olivia had stopped to accompany him on the way back from Sacramento. He followed them to camp on his horse. Olivia sat with him in the dining hall and chatted about the reason for his visit as he ate. When he finished his plate, he told Olivia he'd like to wander around nearby in the woods.

"Always loved the smell of the woods," he said to her.

"Somethin' kinda like heaven far as I'm concerned."

Olivia directed him toward her favorite meadow and left him to roam.

Reverend Stevens was back and helping the kitchen staff to prepare dinner when the loggers returned to camp that evening.

When the meal was served, Olivia came out to sit and eat with Stewart, Hannah, Erik, and Reverend Stevens at the long table where they were sitting. She was accompanied by Mr. Chang and Shu, who looked perplexed to be invited to eat in the dining hall. They much preferred eating in the kitchen alone.

Olivia introduced them to the reverend. They bowed and sat in the places Stewart had reserved for them.

"Mr. Chang, Shu," Stewart said, "I've known Reverend Stewart for many years."

Both of them nodded and smiled. Mr. Chang translated for Shu when necessary.

"I understand," Reverend Stevens said, "that you would like to be married. Is that right?"

Mr. Chang's eyes opened wide as he realized what the reverend was asking. He nodded and translated for Shu whose eyes opened equally wide.

"Now I know," Stevens continued, "that you probably have different ways of marrying in China. I am happy to do what I can, but let's get you married and all legal for now."

Mr. Chang was explaining to Shu, who was nodding happily. Shu said something, and Mr. Chang turned to Reverend Stevens.

"Shu ask when," he said.

Reverend Stevens laughed. "That's why I'm here," he said jovially. "How about now?"

Mr. Chang's eyes opened wide, and he nodded vigorously. "Yes, yes. Now."

Olivia clapped her hands and hugged Shu, who was crying with happiness.

Stewart and Olivia knew that the loggers would not be very interested in the marriage of the two Chinese kitchen workers. Not that they did not appreciate them, just that their own exhaustion drained them of enthusiasm for anything other than sleep or a little card playing and drinking. Nonetheless, Stewart stood up on the table to announce that Mr. Chang and Shu were going to be married.

"Just in case," he shouted above the din of the crowded room, "any of you tired fellows might be interested, "our cooks, Mr. Chang and Shu are about to be married by Reverend Stevens. It'd be real nice if you could cart your dirty dishes and serving bowls to the kitchen. Me and Olivia will clean everything up after the ceremony. Any of you wanting to stay, you are welcome. No one has to stay, of course. We just thought we'd let you know what's happening."

A few whoops followed. Several of the men got up and carried dishes to the kitchen. Many of them got up and left without doing a thing. Stewart and the others ignored the anti-Chinese sentiment that seemed to be spreading.

Olivia told Mr. Chang and Shu to take some time if they needed it.

"No, no," Shu said. "Now good."

Erik was clearing tables. Stewart called to him. "We are going to head outside, Erik."

Erik threw his rag down and ran over to join the group as they headed outside. Olivia called Hannah from the kitchen. There was still light in the sky. The clouds overhead were a vast array of oranges, reds, and pinks. The group headed over to a little stand of trees where the last remnants of light still lingered. A few of the loggers tagged along.

When the little ceremony was concluded, Mr. Chang and Shu thanked the reverend and Stewart and Olivia. They turned to head back into the kitchen to finish their daily chores.

"No, no," Olivia said. "You go by yourselves. We will finish everything."

The newlyweds looked astonished and shook their heads.

"Go," Olivia commanded.

"Hold up, Olivia," Erik called as he was jogging up to them. "Some of the men took up a little collection for the newlyweds." He handed Mr. Chang a handful of coins. "A gift from some of the men," he said.

"Hold on," Stewart said, dashing off for his and Olivia's cabin. A few minutes later he came running back.

"Congratulations," he said to Mr. Chang and Shu. "This is from Olivia and me." He handed Shu a beautifully made blanket that Olivia had been working on in the few moments of freedom she could find.

"And this," Stewart gave them an envelope with a few

dollars in it.

"Now go," Olivia said. "You do not want to waste your wedding night with us."

The couple turned to leave, but Shu turned back. "Thank you, friends."

Mr. Chang beamed and added his thanks.

Chapter Thirty-Four

Olivia and Stewart talked about their future plans on the way to Sacramento during their next visit to town for supplies. Molly and Sam were very excited, and the two couples talked at length over dinner for the one night that they were able to spend together. Stewart and Sam started creating a design for the restaurant while Olivia and Molly talked about menus and décor.

"I can't believe this is going to happen," Molly said bubbling with enthusiasm.

Olivia smiled. "I can't believe that the kind of work this will entail will be so much easier than what Stewart and I are doing now!"

On the way back to the logging camp, Stewart was so excited that he let Olivia drive the wagon so that he could begin sketching drawings for the restaurant. He showed them to Olivia that evening as they sat around their campfire.

"Stewart, these are wonderful drawings," Olivia said as she

looked at them.

"Any of them stand out as one you like best?" he asked.

She went through them all again. Finally, she put one on top of the others.

"This one is intimate enough to be able to be a cute breakfast café and a nicer dinner place," she said. "And all it would take is changing tablecloths and putting some candles on the table for dinner. I really think Sam and Molly will like this one, too. But let's get their opinions next visit, okay?"

"Sounds good," Stewart said as he put his arm around her and pulled her toward him. His excitement about the new venture made him more amorous than usual. "God, I love you," he whispered hoarsely.

Olivia was so happy that as he pulled her on top of him beneath the stars and felt his erection between them, she laughed, slid off to the side of him, and undid the buttons on his pants. Reaching inside, she pulled him out and began stroking gently. It wasn't until later, as they lay side by side, that she found herself wondering what it must feel like to be able to feel what seemed to be the ecstatic response that he felt when he came inside her. "It must be extraordinary," she thought. And for the first time in their marriage, she felt jealous of men—and Stewart. As she tried to fall asleep, her excitement about returning to Hannah kept her awake. She did not understand why most of her waking thoughts these days were consumed with her desire to be close to Han. When she finally fell asleep, she dreamed of kissing Hannah.

When they got back to the logging camp and helped unload the wagon, Olivia got right to work in the kitchen. She knew that her trips to Sacramento meant a lot of extra work for Mr. Chang and Shu. Olivia found herself scanning the area for Hannah and felt disappointment that her friend was nowhere near the kitchen area.

"How did it go?" she asked Shu. Although Shu was really good at picking up English, she was sensitive enough to speak slowly and with as few words as possible.

"Good," Shu responded. "Fine."

Olivia smiled. "Are you and Mr. Chang happy?"

Shu blushed, nodded, and did not look up at Olivia.

Mr. Chang and Shu fixed up her little room for themselves. He had always slept on the kitchen floor on a straw mat, but not once they married.

Olivia reached out for Shu and hugged her. "I am so happy for you both!"

"Oh, I almost forgot," Olivia said. "There was mail for you in Sacramento!" She handed Shu a letter that had English writing with Shu's name and the logging camp name on it, but only Chinese characters elsewhere.

Shu gave a little shout as she looked at the letter. "Family!" she exclaimed and ran off to read the letter.

Olivia knew it was the first time she'd heard from her family since she'd written to them about how her cousin Bao had abandoned her. Now Shu would be able to write to tell them she was married.

Olivia smiled as she watched Shu run off, then pitched right in to prepare for dinner.

As Olivia was setting the tables, Shu appeared to help.

"Did you read your letter already?" Olivia asked.

"I wait. Later," Shu said, but she could not hide her happiness about hearing from her family.

Olivia knew that Shu agonized over telling her family about what Bao had done. She struggled with telling them everything, concerned that they might think that she had been violated at the whore house. At the time, Olivia encouraged her to just say that he had sold her but that she escaped and found work. Shu was concerned about bringing shame to Bao's family and causing a rift between her uncle and father.

"Bao not care about bringing dishonor to you or your family," Mr. Chang had said at the time.

So Shu wrote to her family but always worried that she would not hear anything back. It was a concern about which she never spoke, but carried in the sadness of her eyes as time went on and she heard nothing.

Now she had a letter, and that alone erased the sadness from her face. Olivia was genuinely happy for her.

As the men trooped in for dinner and Stewart returned from unhitching Midnight and settling him, Eric greeted them happily.

"No troubles this trip?" he asked.

Stewart sat next to him and shared about their upcoming plans with Sam and Molly.

"I'm a little jealous, Slim," Eric said. "Sounds like a mighty nice opportunity for you all."

"What about you, Eric?" Olivia asked as she set his plate in front of him. "I know you don't want to log forever, but what would you like to do?"

"Oh, I don't know yet," he said.

Hannah came over to sit for dinner with them. "What don't you know yet?"

"What you and I might want to do after the logging camp," Erik answered.

Hannah paled. "What do you mean?"

"We are not staying here forever, you know?" Erik said.

Hannah sat down with her plate. She kept her eyes down. "I know," she said. But she said it so softly that only Olivia heard her.

Olivia felt, more than heard, the sadness in Hannah's voice. Olivia resisted the urge to lean over and embrace Hannah.

Chapter Thirty-Five

A few days later Hannah and Olivia were walking toward the meadow for the short time they were able to take. A crashing sound came from the top of the mountain.

Hannah stopped and looked up. "What was that noise? There are no clouds, but it sounded a little like thunder?"

Olivia smiled and said, "Oh, you'll get used to that. When the wind blows from just the right direction, we can hear the trees crashing from where Eric and the other high riggers chop them off near the tops of the old pines."

Hannah waited, still listening, but only the breeze blew through the trees. Olivia reached for her hand to pull her forward, and they continued toward their little sanctuary.

"It is as if this is a little outdoor church," Hannah said.

"Exactly how I felt the first time I found it. I call it my sanctuary." Olivia had replied. "I guess it's our sanctuary now."

Hannah never had a good friend. She learned, over the years, that she could live without one. She'd found most girls to be tedious, and the boys just made fun of her because she wanted so desperately to be included with them. Eric was the only one she felt close to, and she missed him desperately when he left to work in the logging camp. It was only after her mother got sick that she stopped nagging Hannah about dressing and behaving in a more feminine manner. Hannah knew her mother loved her, but she also knew how much of a disappointment she was to both her parents.

It was different with Olivia.

Now, as Olivia pulled her by the hand, she felt her heart soar. "This must be what friendship feels like," Hannah thought.

"Come on, Han," Olivia said as she tugged on Hannah's hand. "I want to spend as much time relishing the meadow as possible."

Hannah allowed herself to be pulled along happily. She loved their time there. They spent their time in the meadow sharing their life stories with one another. Hannah found herself memorizing every detail of Olivia's story. She was amazed at how much of the world Olivia had seen and lived through. She still thought about it when they weren't together.

"I can't imagine how horrible it must have been to be so sick on that ship," Hannah said as they walked to the meadow. "To wake up and find both of your parents dead! You were too little to have to deal with such a dreadful thing as death." Hannah's eyes filled with tears as she expressed her dismay over what Olivia had been through.

"There is a part of me, I suppose," Olivia offered, "that has learned so much more about the world and people that has been more teacher to me than anything."

"How so?" Hannah asked.

Olivia looked at Hannah and smiled. "I don't think I would be nearly as compassionate for others if I hadn't endured some of the hardships I've been through." Olivia paused and seemed to be lost in her own thoughts for a bit. "We never know what others have been through. I try to remember that and not be as judgmental as I know I can be."

"It's hard to imagine you judging anyone," Hannah said.

Olivia laughed. "Well, Han, you haven't seen me dealing with Burt yet. I have a really hard time being civil to him. He is, by far, the worst human being I have ever known!"

Hannah laughed, too. And it felt so good to laugh. "Erik warned me about him—I just try to keep my distance." After a brief pause, she added, "I love that you call me Han. It . . . it makes me feel special."

"You are special, Han," Olivia said as they entered the meadow.

They no longer kept their initial separate routines of Hannah wandering and Olivia sitting. Now, they always sat together and chatted, but lately they were so exhausted that often Hannah sat against a boulder and Olivia would fall asleep with her head on Hannah's lap. Hannah cherished those moments as she gently ran her hands through Olivia's dark hair. Olivia dozed off quickly, and Hannah just stared at Olivia as she slept, her hand still lightly stroking Olivia's head.

Chapter Thirty-Six

The last few weeks of September meant things were slowing around the camp. Men who had worked all spring and summer were beginning to leave for the winter. They'd made enough money to keep themselves going and headed down the mountain for fairer weather or to head back to their families. Very few stayed during the cold months. This helped ease things for the camp crew.

The Changs took advantage of the opportunity to create more rice meals. They seemed very excited to share the cooking of their homeland with Stewart and Olivia. Hannah and Erik seemed to enjoy them as well.

"You like?" Shu asked Olivia after each of the meals.

Olivia did love the different spices and combinations of rice dishes and soups that the Changs made. She always nodded her appreciation and asked for more.

Hannah, who always helped in the kitchen—mostly to be near Olivia—still liked to keep the bunkhouse clean. It was a disaster when she first arrived, but that didn't bother her. After her first attempt to clean the place, however, it was a little easier. Now that there were fewer men, it took her no time at all.

She remembered the first time she attempted the bunkhouse. "Erik," she said while rolling her eyes at him, "how can you stand the smell in there?"

Erik laughed. "What smell?"

She gaped at him in horror. "Tell me you are kidding, please."

He started to laugh, then said, "It took some getting used to at first, Han, but after a few days of working so hard, I only went in to sleep. I have never spent more time in the bunkhouse than I had to."

The smell, it turned out, was from men taking off their sweaty clothes, dunking them in a barrel of water, and hanging them all over the ropes strung from one side of the house to the other to dry. Once Hannah took a scrub brush and some lye soap to the floors and took the men's bedding to wash and dry outdoors, things started to look—and smell—better.

Stewart and Olivia talked about their upcoming departure to build a restaurant with the Clarks. Stewart didn't say anything but sensed that Olivia might be having second thoughts.

"Honey," he asked one night when they climbed into bed, "everything okay?"

"Of course, Stewart, why do you ask?"

He couldn't see her face in the dark, but he felt something that he'd never felt from her before. It was a kind of distance, but one he could not read—especially not in the dark.

"You seem different lately. It's almost like you don't want to do the restaurant."

Olivia was quiet in the dark. She was trying to figure out what had changed. He was right, but she didn't know how to tell him that it would be hard to leave Hannah. The two had become close, and Olivia could not tell him that she would miss Hannah's company so much that her feelings even confused her.

"I'm sorry if it seems that way, Stewart. I am looking forward to our new adventure. I think I may just be nervous about making a change. I've gotten used to things around here. Plus, I will miss Eric and Hannah. Won't you?"

"I guess I don't see them staying either," Stewart said. "Eric has told me that they made a little money from selling his parents' house and furnishings. With that and what he's made here the last two seasons, he feels like he and Hannah might be moving on. Besides, there is a gal in Linkville he once knew. He wants to try to find her. I think he might like to see where that goes."

"Really!" Olivia said, hoping he hadn't heard the tiny gasp that escaped her when he mentioned that Eric and Hannah might be leaving. "Does Hannah know this?"

"I'm guessing they've discussed it," he said.

Olivia found herself trembling and willed herself to be still. Before long, Stewart's snoring filled the little cabin, and Olivia vacillated between anger and hurt until she finally fell asleep.

The next morning when the few men who were left departed for the mountaintop and the kitchen was clean, Olivia started up the trail to the meadow. She did not wait for Hannah. She needed time to herself to figure out what was bothering her.

As she lay in the golden grass, staring up at the sky, she prayed. It had been a while since she'd spent time alone there, and she missed that daily connection.

Her mind swirled. It was hard to keep focus on anything—and no matter what she did to try to keep herself open to the divine, her thoughts kept going back to Hannah. She had never had this problem before. Even when she was traveling across the country and looking forward to marrying Stewart, she did not struggle as she struggled now. She felt as if God was absent from her, as if she'd been left alone—as alone as she'd been on the ship when both her parents died.

"I don't understand," she said. She got up and knelt in front of a boulder as if it were an altar. "Where are you? I'm scared and sad, and I shouldn't be. I am about to get what I want, but now I'm not even certain I want it. Please help me understand," she prayed and before long she found herself weeping.

Olivia didn't just cry, she broke down and started outright sobbing. It was as if all the world's grief just welled up inside of her and finally found a way out. She wept for the loss of her parents and her grandparents, for the loss of Italy, for her Aunt Maria and Uncle Michael, and for New York. She wept for all of the losses on the trail—so many she lost count. She wept and didn't really understand why she was weeping, only that she was overcome with grief—a grief so sudden and huge that it remained a mystery to her. She wept so loudly that she did not hear Hannah come up behind her.

"Liv?" Hannah called softly. "Liv, what is it? You are breaking my heart."

Olivia pulled herself away from the boulder but continued kneeling. "I can't do this. I just can't," she howled.

Hannah fell beside her and pulled Olivia into her arms. "Whatever it is, Liv, we will figure it out."

Olivia let herself be comforted by Hannah, still not understanding what exactly she was feeling. When her tears finally stopped, she let Hannah continue to hold her. She made no effort to move.

"Just hold me, Han," she said softly. "Please, just hold me."

"Forever," Hannah mouthed, but did not say it aloud.

When Olivia finally sat up and pulled herself from Hannah's embrace, she said, "Thank you, Han. I don't know what came over me, I was just so overwhelmed by sadness. Nothing like that has ever happened to me before."

"Sometimes we don't need a reason," Hannah offered. "I honestly believe that a good cry is our way of cleansing some part of us, I don't know, maybe our souls? Don't ever apologize for your tears, Liv, not to me anyway."

Olivia stood up. "We should be getting back, I suppose."

Hannah stood and took Olivia's hand, and they started back toward the camp. The breeze was driving the sounds of the falling trees down toward them again.

"Think that was Eric or Stewart's work that time?" Hannah asked.

Olivia chuckled. “I thought I was the only one who heard those sounds and comforted myself with the fact that if the men were felling the trees that meant all was okay up there.”

They walked in silence the rest of the way back.

When they arrived back at the camp, Olivia went to the kitchen to help prepare dinner. She felt exhausted but better.

“You not look so good,” Shu said. “You go rest. We cook.”

Olivia smiled at this sweet person whom she had come to feel was a friend. They still struggled to understand each other, but it was always worth the effort. “Thank you, Shu. I’m fine, just a little tired.”

Chapter Thirty-Seven

The next day Olivia and Hannah walked together to the meadow. Olivia walked more slowly than usual and when Hannah reached for her hand, Olivia pulled it away.

“Liv? What is it? Have I done something?” Hannah asked as she stopped and looked at Olivia with a look of both horror and concern.

Olivia turned and glared at her. “When did you plan to tell me you were moving back to Linkville with Erik?”

“What?”

“You heard me, when were you going to tell me about going to back to Linkville?” Olivia repeated, not bothering to hide the anger and sadness in her voice.

Hannah lowered her head and shook it back and forth slowly. "I didn't tell you because I hadn't decided that I was going with him." She looked at Olivia, begging her to see that the thought of leaving her was more than she could bear.

Olivia turned back to the trail and continued walking toward the meadow.

Hannah followed. "Did you hear me?" she asked. "I said I didn't know if I was even going to go with him."

"I know how much you love your brother, Han. And it is clear he loves you as well. I don't expect he will leave you on your own."

The only sound for the remainder of the walk to the meadow was the sound of grasshoppers leaping out of their way and the crunch of their shoes on the gravelly path.

When they arrived at the meadow Olivia sat on a fallen log. Hannah knelt in front of her.

"Liv," she paused and closed her eyes considering if what she wanted to say to Olivia should be said at all. "Liv," she said even softer, "I know my brother expects me to join him, but he has someone there that he wishes to pursue. I . . . I may join him, but I don't want to . . . " Her voice trailed off, and she sunk down until she could sink no more. Her eyes started to mist over, and a single drop fell from each closed eyelid. "I was thinking of maybe moving to Sacramento." Her voice quivered. Her hands were shaking. She was hoping for something from Olivia that might encourage her to move with her.

Olivia saw the tears, heard the fear in her voice, and dropped to her knees in front of Hannah.

"What is it, Han? Tell me."

Hannah shook her head, forcefully. "I can't."

"We have not kept any secrets from one another, Han. Whatever it is, you can tell me."

A huge sob escaped from Hannah, and she crumbled to the earth.

"Han, oh, Han," Olivia said, her voice full of concern and pain. "Tell me what it is."

Hannah stopped crying and took a kerchief from her pocket. She pushed herself back up to her knees and looked at Olivia, hoping to see what she needed to see. All she saw was pure love.

"I love you, Liv."

"I know you do, Han. And I hope you know that I love you, too. Why do you think I am so upset at the thought of you leaving?"

Hannah shook her head. "No, Liv. You do not understand me. I don't just love you . . . I, I am in love with you."

Olivia stopped breathing. Now her eyes filled with tears. Insight filled her in a flash. She held Hannah's gaze as she understood, at lightning speed, all of the fear, sadness, and desire that she had been feeling these past weeks.

"Han," she finally said. "I believe I am in love with you as well."

Then Olivia did the one thing she instantly realized she had wanted to do more than anything for the past several days. She reached both of her hands out to Hannah's face, pulled it to her own, and kissed Hannah long and tenderly. Her whole body began to tingle and vibrate. She thought she might faint from the desire that coursed through her. This was what she expected to feel with Stewart and never did.

When the women finally parted, they both fell back onto their heels.

Olivia began to cry. "I can't want this, Han, and yet I am not sure I can live without you." She reached up and ran her fingers through her own hair, grabbing large chunks of it. "I am married, Han! I'm married!"

"I know," Hannah whispered. She closed her eyes and lowered her head.

"Han, I can't hurt Stewart. I just can't. I love him so much." She sniffed, blew her nose, and looked at Hannah. "What are we going to do?"

"I don't know, Liv. I tried so hard not to want you, but you are impossible not to want. You are all I think about night and day. I have never felt this way about anyone. I always expected to be alone."

"I always thought I'd feel like this about Stewart. All the way here I was so excited to marry him and feel what I feel for you. I never understood why I didn't feel it. Now . . . well, now that I understand I, I feel like I cannot do anything about it. I am so sorry, Han."

Hannah took Olivia's hands and held them. "Don't be sorry, Liv. It makes me happy just to know that you feel the same. I didn't want to go with Erik because I could not stand the thought of not seeing you, being with you, talking to you, and touching you every day. I wanted more. God knows I want all of you. You haunt my every waking hour and my dreams. There are times I feel like my desire for you could start a fire."

"Oh, Han, it is taking every ounce of my strength not to make love to you right here and now. I just can't hurt Stewart like that even though my body is screaming for you."

The afternoon sun slipped behind a cloud. "We should head back," Olivia said, "before I lose my resolve."

Hannah groaned, more of a moan of pain, really. "I know . . . I know."

They got up slowly. Olivia took Hannah's hand, and they started back down the mountain with a heaviness neither had ever experienced.

Part way down the trail Hannah said, "I wanted to tell you something else. I saw something last night that disturbed me to my very core."

Olivia stopped. "What is it?"

"You told me about how Burt treated his wife, Rose. Have you heard from her?"

"Yes, why? I got a letter from her last week."

"Was she okay?"

"Hannah, what is this about? Tell me right now."

Hannah took a big breath. "Last night after supper, Erik and I stayed out a while and talked a bit. He was a little upset that I expressed the idea that I might not go with him. Anyway, it was pretty late. I think you were already back at your cabin. As I was passing the animal pens, I heard this weird noise and stopped to check it out. I was afraid maybe a wolf or something had gotten into the pens."

Hannah stopped and shook her head. "I still can't believe what I saw."

"Tell me," Olivia insisted.

"Well, Burt was with one of the sheep." She waited for Olivia to understand.

"What do you mean?" Olivia said, not coming close to comprehending.

"He was, well, he was mating with it." Hannah said.

Olivia's jaw dropped. She didn't move a muscle. Then suddenly exclaimed, "Oh, my God!"

"I know," Hannah said. "It made me think about poor Rose. I wondered if something like that could make her sick."

"I don't know, Han, but I will tell you that he probably treated the sheep better than he ever did Rose."

"Maybe don't mention this to her. If she seems okay, then don't alarm her."

Olivia nodded and shook her head in disbelief again.

That night Olivia could not sleep. She tossed and turned until Stewart finally asked her if she was okay.

"I'm sorry, Stewart. I'm just restless tonight. I'll sit up in the rocker."

He reached out to grab her hand before she got out of bed. "What is making you so restless? Do you want to talk about it? I know something is bothering you. I've been waiting for you to tell me what it is."

She sighed. So many things were on her mind, the biggest of which was the intense desire she had for Hannah, but she wasn't about to tell him that. Instead, she lay back down next to him, grateful for being able to ask him about diseases that might come about from having sex with animals.

"I've heard about men getting syphilis from woman . . . whores," she said.

Stewart rose on his elbow. He could see her face in the moonlight. He waited.

"Can something like that happen with animals?" she asked softly.

"Olivia, why are you asking?"

"I'm just wondering," she said a tad too defensively.

"Why?" he asked. "Why in the world would that be keeping you up? Are you worried that I've had sex with a whore, or worse yet, an animal?"

"No! Oh, heavens no, Stewart!" she said quickly to reassure him. "No, honey. It's just that, well, I heard something today that worries me."

"Tell me."

"Do you know that Burt does it with sheep at night?"

"Sex?"

She didn't say anything. She didn't think she could say it again.

"Holy shit!" Stewart said as he lay back down on the bed. "Holy shit."

She had never heard Stewart swear before. The other loggers all cussed up a storm like it was just normal language. She was used to that, but to hear Stewart use strong language? That was a first.

"That pig!" he exclaimed. "That disgusting, filthy pig!"

She had never seen Stewart get angry. She worried that maybe she shouldn't have said anything.

"Stewart, he has always been a pig. The thing that really worries me is Rose. I mean, I do feel sorry for the sheep, but Rose had to put up with him the whole time they were together. Do you think she is okay?"

Now it was Stewart's turn to sigh. After a minute or two of silence, he said, "He does seem to be a worse human being than normal. I've heard that syphilis can make people go crazy, but he's always been such a wicked man that it's hard to tell. If you don't mind, how did you find this out?"

The mere thought of Hannah made her body come alive. She shoved it down. "Hannah was up late with Eric last night. On her way back to her cabin, she heard some commotion in the sheep pen and went to investigate. She saw him."

"Did he see her?"

"I don't think so, but it disturbed her so that she told

me today."

"I know she means a lot to you, Olivia. Is that why you feel so far away? You're going to miss her, aren't you?"

"More than I thought possible, Stewart."

He turned his head and saw a tear slip from her eye. "I know, honey. I know."

"You know," Stewart said so sweetly and innocently, "Hannah could come with us to Sacramento. Maybe if we get the restaurant doing well, she could be a help there. Erik always said she could figure out about anything she put her mind to."

Panic filled Olivia, but also awareness of the gift Stewart just offered her. She knew that being anywhere near Hannah would be more temptation than she could bear. Stewart finding a way to help her stay near her friend was so sweet that she was determined never to hurt him. That would be a betrayal with which she simply could not live.

All she could think of to say was, "Thank you, Stewart."

Chapter Thirty-Eight

It took every ounce of strength to slip out when breakfast was finished. Olivia did not even help clean up, telling Shu that she needed a little time for herself.

"If anyone asks, Shu, please just say I went to have time alone."

Shu looked at her in a most unusual way. "Anyone?" she asked. "Hannah?"

Something in the way she looked at her and specifically asked about Hannah startled Olivia. It was as is if Shu knew something was happening between them and wanted to be sure that Olivia was specifically including Hannah in the request.

Olivia lowered her head and took a breath. "Yes, Shu. Hannah, too." Then she bolted for the door and practically ran up the trail to the meadow both wanting Hannah to follow and willing her not to.

The grasses were tall and golden in the fall. They whispered in the breeze. Olivia went to the far side of the meadow and lay flat on her back and stare up at the clouds. She forced her mind to try to think about what was about to happen: how she was about to leave the mountain with the man she married and loved but leave behind the love of her life. She understood that she would live with that choice and endure the heartbreak for the rest of her life.

She whispered to the clouds and the trees and whatever divine being who might be listening, "I don't understand why this had to happen. How could something that feels like what I have waited for all my life come when I cannot have it? How can my heart not break? I would have happily stayed with Stewart all my days and never knew that there was something more. Why? Why?"

She fell asleep in the grass, hearing no answer from the trees or clouds or her inner self. When she woke and sat up, she saw Hannah at the opposite end of the meadow. She was leaning against a tree and just watching her. She did not make a move toward Olivia. She just stood and waited, watching.

Olivia rose and walked slowly toward Hannah. Both her thrill and dread at seeing Hannah threatened to undo her. When she drew close to Hannah, she asked, "How long have you been waiting here?"

"For a while."

"I needed some time."

"I know."

"Oh, Han, this is tearing me apart."

"I know. It's killing me too."

With a sob, Olivia fell into Hannah's arms. "How can this be, Han? It is just not fair!" she sobbed.

Hannah held her, and they wept together. When the crying subsided, Hannah took Olivia's face in her hands. She kissed both of Olivia's eyes, then her cheeks and ears and neck. She moved her hands down Olivia's sides and around to her back, continuing to kiss her until she came to Olivia's full, beautiful lips. There, she paused as if she were waiting for permission to continue. Olivia pulled Hannah's face to hers and kissed her deeply, passionately, and with a fury she did not know she possessed.

They fell to the ground. Hannah was on top of Olivia, her hands roaming every curve of Olivia's body. She undid the buttons on the front of Olivia's dress and exposed her breasts, groaning as her hand cupped the left one, then again as her mouth found the erect areola.

Olivia writhed beneath this woman she had fallen so deeply

in love with. Her hips moved up and down and her thigh pressed between Hannah's legs. Hannah opened and began to move in rhythm with Olivia's body. Hannah reached down to pull up Olivia's dress and slid her own thigh between Olivia's legs. They moved as one, groaning with pleasure as they continued to kiss and their hands continued to explore.

Olivia pushed Hannah up and rolled her over then straddled Hannah and ripped her shirt open. She dove into the ocean of body and kisses and yearning like a drowning woman gasping for air. Her mouth explored every part of Hannah that was exposed, and when she finished with Hannah's upper body, she reached down to undo Hannah's pants and slipped her hand inside.

Hannah gasped and moaned with delirious pleasure. "Oh, my god, Liv. Oh, my god."

"I love you, Han."

Hannah's left arm encircled Olivia's waist. Hannah pulled her more to the side to be able to reach her right hand into Olivia's underwear.

Now it was Olivia's turn to gasp. "Don't stop, Han. Don't ever stop."

They were a knot of lips, legs, arms, and hands searching, stroking, writhing. They were lost in the pleasure and perfection of the moment. When Hannah finally cried out, her back arching and her body pressing against Olivia's, she momentarily stopped breathing then reached down to pull Olivia's hand from between her legs. Then she rolled Olivia onto her back and continued the rhythmic stroking and probing of Olivia's wet opening, while simultaneously running her tongue around her nipple.

"Oooooooohhh!" Olivia finally gasped, and her hips thrust upward several times before the tension in her body released and she became limp in Hannah's arms with a long sensual moan.

They lay silently for a while, still tangled together.

"Please don't leave me, Liv. I don't want to live without you."

Olivia did not respond except to cling tighter to Hannah until it was time to head back to camp.

Olivia's guilt was overpowering. It threatened to undo her. When she returned to the kitchen to help with dinner, she could not look Shu or Mr. Chang in the eyes. She went about her work without a word. At one point Shu passed behind her and patted her on the back. Olivia could only wonder what the pat meant, but she was not about to ask.

She wondered how she would be able to greet Stewart normally. She felt anything but normal. How she would manage her marriage after what she found in the meadow with Hannah tortured her. Oh, how she hoped that giving in to her desire for Hannah would prove to be something less than it was—something she might be able to walk away from and not give another thought to. Far from it. She wanted more, and she knew that anything less than Hannah would never be enough: Hannah's lips, Hannah's scent, the taste of Hannah, the feel of her long blond hair, her silky skin, the way her huge brown eyes looked at her, the way Hannah touched her so lightly and sensually.

"Stop it right now, Olivia!" she reprimanded herself.

Although she did try to stop thinking about Hannah, it was

an impossible task.

When the logging crew started arriving for dinner, Olivia did not think she would be able to look Stewart in the eyes or greet him with her usual kiss. And when Hannah arrived, she was sure she would turn crimson with the memory of their afternoon tryst.

"Shu, would you mind doing the serving this evening. I'd like to stay in the kitchen."

Again, Shu reached out and patted Olivia—this time on the arm. "Okay," she said.

Olivia again had the feeling that Shu knew or understood what had happened. The thought horrified her. If Shu figured it out, how much more likely would others see through her and Hannah's attempt to hide their feelings for one another. Did Stewart see it? Erik?

As Olivia filled plates and bowls for the men she began to tremble. "What have I done? What on earth was I thinking? I wasn't thinking. I just lost myself in the heat of the moment and betrayed Stewart. I am an ass," she reprimanded herself. "I will make it up to Stewart. And I will never mention his invitation to bring Hannah to Sacramento to her. I can never allow this to happen again. What if someone had seen us?"

When dinner was finished, Stewart popped into the kitchen. He slipped up behind Olivia and kissed her neck. She jumped.

"Oh, Stewart, you startled me."

"Lost in thoughts of leaving?"

"I guess so," she said, not turning to look at him. "Only two more days," she said, trying to muster enthusiasm in her voice.

Stewart reached for a dishtowel and started drying dishes.

"I have it, honey. Why don't you head to the cabin and relax. You must be tired," Olivia suggested.

"And you're not?" he asked. "I enjoy helping you so that we can walk back together. You know that. And I don't like you being alone in the camp with Burt anywhere in the vicinity."

He kissed her on the cheek. "I love you too much to take any risks."

If she could have climbed into the deepest hole on earth, she'd have done so right then. "Ass, ass, ass, Olivia!" she chided herself again. Then she was able to say, "I love you, too, Stewart. Thank you."

Chapter Thirty-Nine

Stewart and Olivia had been in bed for over an hour. He was snoring softly, but Olivia was wide awake trying to talk herself out of love with Hannah. She could not close her eyes without remembering the feel and touch of Hannah and their lovemaking earlier. At one point, she even considered sneaking over to Hannah's cabin to talk about things, but even she knew that was an excuse to just be with Hannah and let things take over as they did earlier.

"Stay put and try to sleep!" she kept telling herself over and over.

She was just finally drifting off when she heard something that startled her awake. She bolted upright in bed. There it was again—a muffled cry and thump outside.

"Stewart!" she shook him and whispered. "Stewart, wake up. I think it's Hannah!"

Stewart heard a thump from outside and jumped out of bed. They both ran outside and over to Hannah's cabin. The door was open, and Burt was inside grappling with Hannah.

Hannah wrestled out from under him and screamed. Stewart was inside in a flash, grabbed hold of Burt, and wrestled him to the ground just outside of the little hut.

"Leave me alone, you son of a bitch!" Burt yelled.

"What the hell do you think you're doing, Burt?" Stewart demanded.

"None o' yer goddamn business!" Burt hurled back.

Hannah was with Olivia who put a protective arm around her. "Are you okay?" she whispered.

Hannah nodded and clung to Olivia.

The men stood up, and Burt yanked himself from Stewart's grasp.

"I am going to say this just once, Burt," Stewart said through his teeth. "You need to leave, now, and never come back here."

"I ain't goin' anywhere," Burt said with a sneer. "Anyways, looks like that bitch," he said indicating Hannah, "ain't never had the taste of a man. Thought she might appreciate it."

"Except you are no man, Burt," Olivia spat. "You are even worse than an animal."

"You will leave now," Stewart said more firmly. "And you will leave because Burley will not tolerate you attacking a camp woman in the middle of the night. And he'll likely be mighty pissed that you've been having your way with the sheep as well."

Burt flinched and looked like he was ready to fight but thought better of it and finally said, "Fine, I'll leave first thing in the morning."

"You'll leave right now. If I so much as catch a glimpse of you in the morning, I'll tell the whole camp about your nightly activities."

"It's dark!" Burt lamented.

"That hasn't stopped you from doing anything else you have wanted to do," Stewart said sternly. "Now get out before I wake up this whole damn camp and tell them what a disgusting pig you are!"

"You ain't heard the last of me, Slim," Burt said with a snarl, but he did turn and start down the mountain trail without another word.

"Hannah," Stewart said when Burt was out of earshot, "are you okay?"

"I think so, Stewart. More shaken than anything. Thank you," she said, but she was still trembling.

"You spend the rest of the night with Olivia. I'll stay in your cabin just in case Burt decides to come back."

"Stewart, no," Olivia said. "I'd feel better if we all stayed together."

"It's fine, Olivia. I'm not going to sleep anyway. I don't trust Burt as far as I can throw him."

"But I . . . " Olivia started.

"I want you two to put the chair up against the door handle. I expect I might doze on and off, but if I do and he tries to get in I'll hear him struggle with the door. You two go ahead now. Get some sleep. Try to calm down."

Olivia looked at Stewart in the moonlight. He mistook the look in her eyes as fear. He walked over to her and pulled her into an embrace. "I won't let him hurt you—either of you," he said. Then he kissed Olivia on the top of her head and shooed them into the cabin.

Dutifully, Olivia slid the chair under the doorknob. She stood facing the door and leaned her forehead against the doorframe and groaned.

Hannah walked up behind her, slipped her arms around Olivia's waist, and rested her head on Olivia's shoulder. "What is it, my love?"

"Oooh, Han," she whispered, "this is too hard for me."

"What's too hard?" Hannah said as she placed her lips on Olivia's exposed shoulder.

"The temptation to ravish you. Do you know how guilty I felt after we . . . we . . . " She couldn't even finish the sentence. The thought of what they did and what the knowledge of that would do to Stewart seemed to shred her insides.

Hannah's lips continued to kiss her gently, so gently. Then Hannah turned her around. "I am so sorry, Liv. I never dreamed I would ever fall in love with anyone. More than that, I never dreamed anyone would fall in love with me. You are the single most extraordinary thing that has ever happened to me, and I don't expect I will ever find this again. I so wish this were easier for you . . . for us." Hannah paused for a moment and just held Olivia's head and stared into her eyes. Then she added, "When you leave in two days, I will be devastated. The deaths of my parents were easier than this. Losing you now that I have found you? That will be worse than any hell I could imagine. You brought me to life. Anything after you will feel like dying . . . I . . . " She couldn't speak anymore for the tears she was choking back.

"Han, oh, Han," Olivia said with so much sadness that the room seemed weighed down by grief. Grief seeped from the walls and made the air heavy. "I don't want to lose you, Hannah, I don't. But I cannot live with the guilt of betraying Stewart—and I cannot leave Stewart."

"I know," Hannah sniffed. "Just give me tonight, then, please. Let tonight be just for us, and I will carry it with me for the rest of my life."

The curtains were closed, and the door barred. Olivia looked around at the room. Just the moonlight filtered through the curtains, other than that it was dark. She didn't move.

Hannah waited for Olivia to say something or do something, but she remained standing at the door as if her feet were mired in the grief that muddied the floor.

"It's okay, Liv. I understand." Hannah moved to the bed

alone and climbed under the covers.She turned onto her side and wept silently, her back to Olivia.

Hannah had no concept of how much time passed before she felt Olivia climb into the bed.

"Come here," Olivia whispered hoarsely. "I need you one last time."

Hannah turned and wrapped herself in Olivia's arms. For the second time that day, their passion overcame them.

Each was wearing a nightgown. Neither had anything underneath. Olivia kissed Hannah's body everywhere—neck, lips, breasts, and then moved down into the wetness between her legs. Without realizing that she was doing it, she turned her body around and straddled Hannah with her head between Hannah's legs, kissing and using her tongue to pleasure Hannah. Hannah found Olivia's folds with her mouth, and together they melded into one, undulating in unison until silent orgasms found them simultaneously.

As they lay together afterwards, Hannah asked, "How did you think of what you just did to me?"

"I don't know," Olivia said softly. "It was just something I suddenly knew I wanted to do. Was it okay?"

"Oh, Liv," she whispered in her ear, "it was more than okay."

It was still dark when Hannah woke Olivia with soft, sweet kisses. Olivia felt Hannah's body pressing against her and remembered their lovemaking.

"Good morning, love of my life," Hannah whispered.

Olivia let Hannah kiss her tenderly and slowly opened her eyes.

"We should get ready, Han. Stewart may already be up. You need your clothes from your cabin, and he needs his, too."

Hannah gave her one more kiss and scooted to the bottom of the bed to get up. "Liv?"

"Hmm." Olivia's sadness could be heard in her response.

"Nothing," Hannah said, her voice cracking.

Olivia lit a candle. It spilled light off the table. She stared at the candle, afraid to even look at Hannah for fear that her resolve about leaving with Stewart would melt in Hannah's eyes. She found her clothes and dressed quickly.

Olivia turned and pulled Hannah to her. She pressed her mouth against Hannah's to keep from crying. She knew this was the last time they would be together.

The rap on the door finally separated the lovers.

"Olivia, Hannah," Stewart called through the door. "Time to get going."

Olivia pulled the chair from the door and opened it.

"I need to dress," Stewart said.

"Hannah needs to get her clothes, too. I'll keep watch," Olivia said.

It didn't take more than a couple of minutes for everyone to be ready. The trio walked to the kitchen together. Olivia greeted

Shu. Mr. Chang was outside getting water. Stewart went off to find Burley. He intended to tell Burley about what happened last night. Hannah started to get the lunch buckets ready for the loggers.

Shu went out to set the tables.

Olivia turned to ask Hannah a question about the lunches, but Hannah was gone. She had run out the back door, which was open.

Olivia went to the back door and ran into Mr. Chang. "Oh, Mr. Chang, have you seen Hannah?"

"She run away. Up trail," he said and pointed. "Look like she cry."

Olivia looked at the trail to the meadow. She would not go there again. With a heart so heavy that her chest ached with pain, Olivia went back into the kitchen and finished preparing breakfast and lunch buckets for the men. She moved with memorized motions as if she were not present in her body. Her arms and legs were heavy with sadness. She barely knew what she was doing, only that she felt her heart cracking into a million pieces.

Stewart and Erik came into the kitchen.

"Slim told me what happened last night," Erik said while looking quickly around the kitchen. "Where is Han?"

Olivia was focused on scrambling a stove full of eggs. She heard Erik but did not dare turn around.

Mr. Chang saved her. "She run up hill. Look like she cry."

Eric took off after Hannah.

Stewart sensed that Olivia purposefully avoided looking at him. He went over and gently put his hands on her shoulders. "Have you asked Hannah to join us? I know you two are having a hard time thinking about leaving one another. At least you'll have Molly again," he said, trying to brighten her spirits.

"You're right, Stewart. I'll be fine. It's just going to be hard for a bit." She didn't answer his question about asking Hannah to come with them. She prayed he would let it drop.

"I'm sorry," he said. "Try to think of this as our last day of working so darned hard. Okay?"

"Okay," she said, but she still hadn't turned to look at him.

When Stewart was gone, her tears dripped into the eggs she was mixing. She could not stop them from flowing.

Chapter Forty

Stewart bought poles, ropes, sleeping pads, and blankets when they arrived in Sacramento. He set up a tent for them near Clark's shop. He and Sam finalized the plans for building the addition to the bakery for the restaurant. They purchased the wood needed, and it was to be delivered soon.

Olivia tried to keep her spirits up, but she found that even just conversing was exhausting. She stayed sleeping in the tent while Stewart started his day early. She didn't seem to have the energy for anything. Late on their fifth morning in Sacramento, she got up with Stewart and went to help at the bakery, but Molly noticed that she moved slowly and didn't really talk much.

She and Olivia never ran out of things to talk about as they crossed the country in the wagon train.

"Olivia, are you feeling well?"

"Just a little tired, I guess."

"Perhaps the hard work you did for those couple of years is finally catching up with you?"

Olivia sat down at one of the tables and dropped her head in her hands.

Molly took a good look at her. "My god, Olivia, there are dark circles under your eyes. You really look like hell."

It was hard to keep things clean in the tent and even harder to sleep there. The noises of the town usually died down at night, but many things woke her, not least of which were her dreams of Hannah. When those woke her, Olivia could only cry herself back to sleep with the hope that she might never wake up.

Relentlessly, morning came, and she dragged herself out of the tent.

Sometimes she would hear a voice on the street and turn, thinking it was Hannah's voice. When customers walked through the door of the bakery, she always hoped to turn and find Hannah there. But it was always someone else.

"I think," Molly said, bringing Olivia back from wherever she was, "that you should see a doctor."

"I'm not sick, Molly. I really just think it is the change. I'll be fine. Truly I will. Thank you for being so sweet."

"Olivia, if you are tired, please go to the back and rest on our bed. You can't be sleeping very well in that tent. Stewart will have a place built soon."

"Thank you, Molly. I think I will take you up on your offer. Will you tell Stewart when he comes back? He went to the general store to get a few supplies."

"Of course, I will. You go and sleep as long as you need to."

The sun was blazing through the western window of Molly and Sam's bedroom. With a start, Olivia realized she had slept nearly the entire day away. She got up and went up front to the café. Sam and Molly were sitting at one of the tables with someone she did not recognize. They were talking in hushed tones.

Olivia coughed so that they knew she was there. All three turned to look at her.

"I am so sorry to have slept so long, Molly," Olivia said. Then she saw the looks on their faces.

"What is it? What's wrong?" she asked as she made her way over to the table. "Where is Stewart?"

"Ma'am, I'm Sheriff Connelly. Would you have a seat, please?"

Olivia did not move a muscle. She felt fear grip her insides. Calmly, too calmly, she again asked, "Where is my husband?"

The sheriff pulled a chair out. "Please, Mrs. Anderson, won't you sit?"

Olivia still did not move. Molly got up and went to her. She wrapped her arms around Olivia and said softly, "Stewart is dead, Olivia. He was attacked as he was leaving the general store."

Molly held Olivia tightly, and that is what prevented her from collapsing on the floor. Sam was up in a flash and helped catch Olivia as she slipped from Molly's arms.

"Carry her to the bed, Sam. I'll be there in a minute."

Olivia came to with Molly patting her head with a cool cloth. It was dark, and there were two lanterns lit beside the bed. Sam was standing nearby. At first, Olivia was bewildered, then she remembered Molly telling her that Stewart was dead and thought it was a dream.

"Please tell me I have had a bad dream," she said.

Molly took her hand between both of hers. Sam took a step forward, his face full of concern. "It was no dream, honey. I am so sorry." Molly picked up a glass of water and held it for Olivia. "Sit up and have a drink."

Olivia did as she was told. When Molly put the glass back down, Olivia looked at Sam. "How? What happened?"

Sam shook his head and began. "Stewart had just come out of the general store, his arms full of supplies. Some stranger ran up behind him and stabbed him. He turned to see what had happened and tried to fight the fellow, but he collapsed in the street. The Campbells saw the whole thing from the store window and ran out to help Stewart, but the injury was too bad. The doc said the knife must have got his liver because the blood was black." Sam stopped, afraid that maybe that was too much information too quickly. "I am so sorry, Olivia."

"Where is he?" Olivia asked.

"He is at the undertakers. I can take you if you feel up to it." Molly offered.

Olivia stared up at the ceiling. Her eyes were dry. Where she went in her mind, Molly and Sam did not know.

Olivia blinked rapidly and asked. "Did they catch whoever did this? Do we know who this stranger is?"

"They did catch him," Sam said. "He seemed to be a drifter. They come through here when they are done rail building or gold digging. They are usually pretty harmless, though. Maybe this one was just crazy. Stewart didn't do anything to cause the man to attack him."

"Take me to see Stewart, please," Olivia said as she got up from bed.

"Please, Olivia, have a bite to eat first, you haven't eaten all day!" Molly begged.

"I don't deserve to eat, Molly."

It was an odd thing to say. Molly looked confused for a moment, then said, "This is not your fault, Olivia. You are not guilty of anything!"

"Take me to him," Olivia said firmly.

Sam and Molly walked with Olivia to the undertaker's building. Once there, Olivia asked if they would wait outside.

"Of course," Molly said. They sat on a bench outside the building and soon the undertaker came out to join them.

"She sent you out?" Sam asked.

"Not uncommon," the undertaker said. "Everyone has a different reaction to death. I don't take it personal."

Stewart's body lay on a long table. Olivia stood near the door to the room where he lay. She stood for a long time before she finally approached him.

She lifted his calloused, hard-working hand and held it in her right hand. With her left hand she pushed back the hair that had fallen over his forehead. She kissed his hand and held it to her cheek.

"I am so sorry, Stewart. No woman on earth could have asked for a more perfect husband or best friend. You deserved so much more than I was able to give you, and in the end, I gave you so little. I betrayed you. I gave in to my desire for someone else and pulled away from you. This is my fault, my sin, that killed you! My sin, Stewart. I may as well have stabbed you with that knife. It was my sin. I hoped that leaving Hannah and staying with you would be the answer. It wasn't, and I am not sure I would have ever gotten over her. I wanted to. I wanted to let go of her and find my way back to you. I am so sorry. I don't deserve your forgiveness. And know that I will never forgive myself for the damage I caused. I hurt you. I could see it, but I couldn't stop it. I wanted to talk to you about it. You were always so understanding about everything. You were my best friend. Something happened to me when Erik brought Hannah to the camp. I never saw it coming, and I couldn't stop it. I tried to. Maybe I didn't try hard enough."

Olivia realized she was crying. She bent over Stewart and lay her head on his chest. "I am so sorry. So sorry, so sorry."

When she stood up and looked down at his face, his

handsome face, and remembered how happy she was to finally see it in person when he arrived at Miss Clark's house, she leaned over and kissed his lips. "You deserved so much more than I was able to give you, sweet man. I will miss you . . . and I did love you."

Olivia wiped her face with her kerchief and left the room. When she stepped outside, Sam and Molly stood. The undertaker was already standing, leaning against a post. He turned.

"I'd like to go to the sheriff's office," Olivia said firmly.

Sam nodded, but Molly asked why. "What good will it do you to see a crazy man. He'll be hung and gone soon enough."

Olivia looked at Molly, and no one would mistake the determined look on Olivia's face.

"Okay, let's go," Molly said sadly.

"Ma'am, er, Mrs. Anderson," the undertaker called. "When do you want the funeral?"

The question startled Olivia; she hadn't even thought about burying Stewart. Suddenly she realized that others would want to say goodbye.

"There are some folks I need to contact first," she said. "I will let you know tomorrow."

"Yes, Mrs. Anderson," he replied with a nod and went back inside where he was most comfortable. He never had to converse with the dead.

The sheriff's office was around the corner in the next block. When they entered the building, Olivia saw the sheriff sitting at his desk talking to someone. As she began to walk over to the desk, she heard a familiar voice.

"I told him he didn't see the last of me," the voice sneered. "You think I didn't hear that you two were here?"

Olivia spun around. Burt was grinning at her from behind the bars that contained him. The second she heard his raspy voice, she knew it was him. She was not surprised. Stewart didn't have an enemy anywhere on this earth.

She walked over to the cell slowly, almost as if she were in a trance. She glared at Burt.

"You did tell him," Olivia began in a voice so low and threatening that he took a step back. The smile he wore disappeared. As she got right up to the cell, she glared at him with such hate in her eyes that he took another step back. "You told him, Burt. And you killed him. All he ever did was try to be your friend. But the day you brought poor Rose to the camp, he saw you for who you really are. We all did. You are a freak of nature, Burt. A misfit. Stewart was the sweetest, most generous man you will ever know in your whole evil life. You showed him, didn't you? You showed all of us just what a demented animal you are. You sure must be happy with yourself. And you are all you have now. When they hang you, and they will hang you, it will just be you swinging from that rope. Don't worry, Burt, I'm certain you will be happy in hell. Hell was made for the likes of you. I hope you burn for eternity."

Olivia turned and bumped right into Sam and Molly, who wanted to protect her from the man in the cell and stayed close as she moved toward Burt. They were stunned at the menacing voice and slow words that came out of her mouth. They jumped out of her way and followed her out of the door.

Molly and Sam both had to hurry to catch up with Olivia, whose demeanor was one of purpose.

"Olivia!" Molly finally called. "Slow down."

Olivia stopped and turned to her friends. "I'm sorry," she said. "I'm sorry Molly. I am suddenly aware that there is so much to do. I have to ride up to Reverend Stevens to ask him to do Stewart's funeral. I should also stop to tell Miss Clark. Someone needs to let the camp know. They will definitely need to know about Burt. Where should I bury Stewart? How . . . "

"Olivia, stop!" Molly demanded. "You do not have to do everything by yourself. We are here. We will help."

"Oh! Oh," Olivia shook her head, again, as if she were coming out of a trance.

"I'll ride up to talk to Reverend Stevens and Miss Clark, Olivia," Sam said putting a hand on her shoulder. "I will do that first thing in the morning."

"Thank you, Sam."

Olivia looked at Molly. "You must think I have gone quite mad, my friend. For days I can do nothing but sleep, and now I am marching around trying to manage everything. Forgive me, Molly. I don't even know who I am anymore."

"Nothing to forgive, sweet Olivia. Let's go home and get some food in you. You can tell me what all you think needs to be done, and we will do whatever we can. You have always taken care of everyone and everything. It is time to let others help you now."

Olivia hung her head and began to weep. Molly embraced

her until she finished. It didn't matter that they were in public. Sam put his arms around both of them. Molly had begun to cry as well. Sam tried very hard not to cry, but a tear slipped down his cheek.

Two days later, Sam, Molly, and Olivia picked up the coffin with Stewart's body from the undertaker. Sam got a wagon from the livery, and they rode up to the church Stewart's parents built. Reverend Stevens and his wife were waiting outside the church. The day was overcast and cool, but Olivia didn't notice.

Reverend Stevens called inside the church for the pallbearers to come out. Sam helped Olivia and Molly down from the wagon. They greeted the reverend and his wife. Sam stayed outside because he was one of the pallbearers, but Mrs. Stevens took Molly and Olivia inside.

Olivia's head was bowed as she entered the church. She didn't lift her head or look around. She did not feel much of anything. She was going through the motions and just wanted this ordeal over. Molly led her to the front of the church and saw several of the people from the wagon train. She smiled a sad smile when she spotted them but kept walking Olivia forward.

John and Mark Clayton were there. The Warrens closed their shop by Capitol Park on the other side of Sacramento.

Mary and Horace Grover started their own farm just to the west of Sacramento. They still had the Fowler girls, Betsy, Jane, and Mary. All five of them sat in one of the pews.

Miss Clark came up to Olivia before she sat down and reached for her hands. "Dear Olivia, there is nothing I can say that will make any difference. I am so sorry this happened."

Olivia squeezed her hands and thanked her.

Everyone stood behind her. She heard them and turned to see Reverend Stevens walking ahead of the coffin. Olivia heard none of the service. When Stevens began to speak to the congregation she simply shut down. She could not listen to all the wonderful things she knew were being said about Stewart. She knew how wonderful he was. She knew. And she allowed herself to fall in love with someone else anyway. She was a miserable human being and did not deserve the kindness of anyone here.

"If they knew what I did," she thought, "they would stone me to death. I am such a hypocrite. It should have been me that was murdered for what I did. Stewart could have found someone else, someone who could have given him what I could not. Oh, Stewart, forgive me for giving to Hannah what you so desperately wanted from me. I don't know what's wrong with me."

When the service was over, the group went outside to the little cemetery. Stewart was to be buried next to his parents. As Olivia dropped the first handful of dirt onto his coffin, it took all her strength to keep standing. Somehow, she managed.

She also managed to greet her friends from the wagons. Each hugged her and expressed their love for her. She nodded and tried to smile. It was all so exhausting. All she wanted to do was sleep forever.

As she said goodbye and expressed her thanks to Reverend Stevens, she felt a dizziness overcome her. She told Molly she wasn't feeling well and wanted to get back to town.

Chapter Forty-One

Olivia woke the day after Stewart's funeral feeling the need to be near water. She told Molly she was going to spend time at the river. Molly packed her some bread and cheese and gave her a canteen full of water. She also gave her a blanket on which to lay.

"I know you need time alone, Olivia. Please be careful."

"I will, Molly. Thank you for everything."

As Olivia walked toward the door of the café, Molly hollered out, "If you are not back by mid-afternoon, Sam and I will come looking for you!"

Olivia gave her a weak smile and headed for the river.

The Sacramento River was busiest near K Street at the docks off Front Street. She walked farther north toward Miss Clark's home and found a lovely spot under a grove of trees. She set up her blanket and stared out at the water as it glided southward toward the town. Occasionally, a fish would leap out and splash down. A few ducks waddled toward the edge of the river. Every once in a while, a cloud floated across the sun, and the shadows disappeared.

As she talked to Stewart, she felt the love for him flow out and into the river.

"Oh, Stewart, this is where you planned to build our home. I would have loved to live on the river. You knew that without my even telling you. You knew me so well. You understood my moods and always said or did the perfect thing. How am I to live without you? I doubt there is another man like you in the world.

I wouldn't want one regardless. How did you put up with me? Did you know? Did you see what was happening to me?"

A ferry boat drifted past on the river. One of the ducks waddled over to her, and she gave it a piece of bread. It seemed content with that and went back toward the river.

She dozed and dreamt of Hannah—lying with her and loving her. When she woke, she was more angry at herself than ever. "I didn't understand what happened to me, Stewart. Did you? I so wanted to tell you that I was consumed with desire for her, but I couldn't because of what that meant for us. Did you know? You must have sensed something; you always read me so well."

She was sitting against the tree with her knees bent up in front of her. She hugged them, and the tears began to fall. "I think you did know. Is that why you denied my request to stay with us the night Burt attacked Hannah? Did you know that I was in love with her? Did you gift me that night of goodbye?"

She lay down on the blanket and sobbed. "Why did you have to be so unselfish? How could anyone be? Would it have been easier for me if you had been jealous—if I'd have had to fight for her—if you'd have had to fight for me? Help me, Stewart. Help me make it up to you somehow. Please tell me what to do. I am so lost and sad and . . . and . . . no, honey, I did not ask Hannah to come with us because I knew it would be the end of you and me. I could not bear that on my conscience. You have been my heart. You always will be. For some reason, I just could not find with you what I found with her. It tore me up, Stewart. Please know that it tore me apart. Tell me what to do now. I have lost you forever, and I have walked away from Hannah for us, for you and me. Now I've lost everything I knew and loved and held dear. Mostly, I guess I have lost myself. I no longer recognize myself, or who I have become. Help me, God . . . or have I lost you along with my soul? I have even lost my ability to pray. I am lost. Please, Mother Mary, help me."

Her weeping continued until she felt she had squeezed every last teardrop from her body. She lay, watching the river and the boats move past her toward new beginnings or endings or just into more life.

"Life," she thought to herself, "I feel like I have lost my life." And she fell into a deep sleep.

"Olivia!"

Olivia bolted upright and looked around. She heard her name called. There was not a soul around.

"I must have dreamed that," she thought.

"Go home."

There it was again. Still there was no sign of anyone nearby. She sat perfectly still.

"Go home, Olivia." The voice was inside of her but not in her mind. It was as clear as if someone was speaking to her. It wasn't her grandmother's voice. She knew that voice and had heard it often in the meadow. It wasn't a voice she recognized. But the voice and the words were unmistakably clear.

"Maybe I need to eat something," she thought, and even though she wasn't hungry, she ate the food Molly packed for her. She knew Molly would be upset if she hadn't eaten anything. When she finished the bread and cheese and drank some water, she listened for the voice again. Who or whatever it was, they were apparently done speaking to her. She gathered her things and walked back into town. Two days later she was on the stagecoach to San Francisco. From there, she journeyed back to New York as a passenger on a ship as Rose had done so not long before.

Chapter Forty-Two

It was early evening when there was a knock on the door.

"Are we expecting anyone?" Michael asked.

Maria shook her head. Washing dishes always took her mind millions of miles away. It was a chore she always loved. Perhaps that and cooking. "You can have the housecleaning," she'd told Michael when he first brought her home. The house had been built by his parents. He and Maria lived with them while he finished his education. After his parents both passed away, within months of each other, the house became his. He was an only child. When he started working, they got a housecleaner.

They were still in love, even after almost twenty-three years. When he came home from work each evening from NYU, he always wanted to know how her day was. She loved that he actually wanted to know. He would pour them a drink, and they would share their day. After dinner, he always cleared and cleaned the table, but he knew to let her be with the dishes. He asked her about it once when she shooed him away from helping.

"I don't know," she had answered, "there is something in the ritual of the chore that makes me feel like I did when I would help Mama. I guess it reminds me of Italy, and I drift off into those memories and the love of my family." She was a little teary as she told him. Now, he always finished his part of the after-dinner process and said, "I will leave you to your reverie." Then he kissed her and went off to read.

He went to the door and opened it. Nothing could prepare him for the shock of seeing his niece standing there looking as if she hadn't eaten or slept for weeks.

"Olivia," he shouted.

She fell into his arms, weeping uncontrollably.

"Maria! Maria!" he called urgently as he practically carried Olivia into the living room.

Maria ran to him, her hands still wet, trying to dry them on the dishtowel. She did not at first recognize her niece.

"Madre de Dios, bambina!" she cried as she ran to Olivia and scooped her into her arms.

Michael watched with concern and love. He went out to the porch to bring in Olivia's trunk. The women were now weeping together. Michael went to open a bottle of wine and brought three glasses. He stopped at the dining room entry. He could tell by the look on Olivia's face that something dreadful must have happened. He could hear his wife repeating her childhood nickname for her niece as she held her.

"Oh, Bambina, my Bambina. Whatever it is, I am so happy to see you."

Michael entered when it seemed the weeping was dying down. He set the glasses down and filled them.

"Looks like we have some catching up to do," he said. He

handed each of them a glass and lifted his own. "To family, and the love we share."

They toasted, then Maria asked, "What happened? You look like death."

Olivia took a sip of wine. "I forgot how much I love wine," she said with sad surprise. Then, "You aren't wrong about the death part. Stewart is dead."

"Dios Mio!" Maria cried.

"Tell us what you can now, Olivia, you look like you are exhausted."

"I will tell you that Stewart and I had just left the logging camp. We were in Sacramento getting ready to build a restaurant with Sam and Molly."

"From the wagon train?" Maria asked.

Olivia nodded. "They started a little pastry shop there, and since I had been running the kitchen at the logging camp and experimenting with recipes, we thought it would be the perfect partnership. We hadn't been there for more than a week. Stewart went into town to get nails and supplies for the addition."

Olivia's eyes drifted off as she remembered what happened. Then she told them about Burt and how he came up behind Stewart and stabbed him to death.

Olivia started to cry again, and Maria reached to comfort her. Olivia rested in her aunt's arms and before long was sound asleep. Maria looked at Michael, whose pained look spoke volumes. They sat quietly for some time.

Michael left the living room and returned a bit later. "I have fixed her bed upstairs."

Maria kissed Olivia's head and allowed Michael to lift Olivia from her arms.

"My God, she's as light as a feather," he said with concern.

"I am going to have to take some time off from work," Maria said. "I won't leave her like this."

"I'll stop by your school in the morning and tell them you have a family emergency."

As they took Olivia up the stairs and into her old bedroom, Maria said, "Michael, I can't believe this has happened to her. Of all people, hasn't she already suffered enough?"

"She's certainly shouldered more than her fair share," Michael said sadly. "We will do our best to help her get back on her feet."

"Again," Maria said with a tinge of anger in her voice that her niece had already endured so much.

It was almost noon when Maria knocked on Olivia's door. When there was no answer, Maria cracked the door open and saw Olivia was still sleeping. She went in and put the things she was carrying on the nightstand and pulled back the curtains.

Olivia didn't stir. Maria sat down in the chair in the corner and waited for Olivia to wake up. It was nearly an hour before Olivia began to stir.

Very softly Maria said, "Buena sera, mi amore."

Olivia opened her eyes and saw her aunt watching her. Her eyes filled with tears. "I am so glad I have you to come home to."

"And I am glad you came home. You need time to heal and grieve. Home is the best place for that."

Olivia sat up in bed and saw the plate of anise cookies on the nightstand. She smiled.

"Remember when you brought these to me when I got here?"

Maria smiled and nodded. "You were so angry about what happened. You were still so young."

"Yes, and you knew exactly what I needed."

Maria sighed and got up from the chair and came over to sit on the bed with Olivia. "The espresso was hot when I brought it up. It is probably cold now."

"Cookies are just fine, Auntie." She took one.

"I'm not sure cookies will be much help to you now," Maria said as she reached up to lift a strand of Olivia's dark hair to place it behind her ear. "You have been through so much. All I know to do is to be here for you."

"Auntie, so much has happened. So much. I'm not sure I can even talk about it."

"There is no hurry. When you are ready, you can tell me in your own time and in your own way."

Olivia's smile was so sad that Maria thought her heart would break. "Do you think you might want to get up, maybe have a bath, put on some clean clothes?" Maria asked.

Olivia looked down at herself. She was still in the clothes she arrived in. "Oh! How did I even get up here?"

Maria laughed, "Michael carried you. I have to say, he was

terribly concerned when he lifted you up from the sofa. He put your trunk there," she pointed to a corner of the room. "We will have to make some good Italian dishes to put a little weight back on you, no?"

Olivia attempted a laugh, but it was forced, and she did not recognize her own voice. "I'll bathe and be down in a bit."

Maria found her cleaned and in fresh clothes sound asleep on her bed two hours later.

About a week after coming home to New York, Maria brought a package up to Olivia. It was from Molly. Olivia tore it open hoping to find something, anything from Hannah. There were a few items, but nothing from Hannah. Maria saw the disappointment on her Olivia's face.

"Were you expecting something?"

"Not really," Olivia said, but Maria heard the sadness there.

"I will leave you to your mail, then."

Olivia recognized Molly's hand. She opened that first.

Dearest Olivia,

I hope you found your way home without any problems. I have been worried that I haven't heard from you. Please just drop a line to let us know that you got home safely.

The enclosed items were at the Post Office for you. The postmaster remembered that we were friends and gave me all he had for you.

I miss you, my friend. And I miss Stewart. I guess I am also grieving the loss of our dream together. I do worry that perhaps you had changed your mind about wanting to have a restaurant. You were so distracted and sad when you arrived in Sacramento—even before Stewart died.

Speaking of that, you should know that Burt was hanged. Sam and I didn't go, but it was in the paper. I thought you might like to know that.

Burley comes down from the camp on occasion to pick up supplies and to hire loggers. He is very upset that many of the men he hires quit when they get to the camp and find that the cooks are Chinese. There is concern that the animosity toward the Chinese is growing. It makes Burley pretty mad. He says you were the glue that held that kitchen together, and the loggers knew better than to say anything derogatory about Shu or Mr. Chang.

You were always a force to be reckoned with, Olivia. I don't know what happened before you got here last time, but I know it was something so painful that you couldn't talk about it. I hope being home is helping you to sort things out.

Meanwhile, know that you are missed.

Much love, Molly

PS. Sam sends his love, too.

It made Olivia upset that loggers were discriminating against Shu and Mr. Chang. It's bad enough that they had to leave their home countries to find a way to help their families back home, but to have to deal with racial bias in their new home just wasn't fair. She had no energy to deal with that situation—

and now she was too far away.

She lay on the bed and realized she had given into her melancholy and ignored those who cared about her. She really did not feel that she could tell anyone about her relationship with Hannah. It was her sin to live with, and she was judging herself harshly enough. The agony she felt about the affair with Hannah while she was married to Stewart, and the fact that the affair was with a woman filled her with guilt. My God, who does such a thing? She just did not see that these were things she could, or should, share with anyone.

She sat up again and looked through the other things from the package. She opened Burley's note.

Olivia,

I ain't much for words or writin' but wanted to tell you that we were all real sorry to hear about what happened to Slim. I feel partly to blame. I always knew that Burt was no good. I shoulda tossed him out on his ear some time ago. I am mighty sorry I didn't. Mighty sorry.

Word got up to us at the logging camp after the burial, else I'da been there. Slim was one of the best men I ever knew. And he sure picked one of the best, strongest woman for a wife. You keep your chin up. And know how sorry I am.

Shu wants you to know that she is with child. Still works like an ox, that girl. I wish the men were more appreciative of her and Chang. I fear that with you gone and with the hostility around here, they might leave.

Erik and Hannah took off for Linkville about a week after you left. I know the four of you were close, so I sent a note off to them about Stewart.

You take good care of yourself. Remember you have friends up here in the Sierras.

Yours,

Burley

Olivia put Burley's letter down and went to sit in the chair in her room. "Enough of this, Olivia," she said to herself. "You have got to find a way out of this melancholy." She vowed to write to Molly that very day.

There was one more letter. It was from Rose. She and Rose had kept in touch, but she always read Rose's letters in Sacramento and left them with Molly. She never wanted Burt to find them if he got nosy in the camp. This one was written before Stewart was killed. It probably sat in the post office for a while before Molly was given everything by the postmaster. Then it had to travel all the way back here. She opened it.

January 3, 1857

Dear Olivia,

Happy New Year!

By the time you get this, I hope you and Stewart are retired from the logging business and building a restaurant with your friends in Sacramento. It sounds like a glorious adventure.

Things are going well for me. My parents seem quite happy to have me home, and I have never been happier to be home. We are learning to be a family in a way I never thought we could. That is so gratifying for all of us. Every once in a while, I find myself trying to be my manipulative old self. It is something I may have to work on for some time.

I owe so much to you for your kindness, your generous spirit. You are truly the most amazing person I have ever met. I learned something so valuable from you and your sweet Stewart. If ever you need anything, I hope you won't hesitate to reach out to me. I owe you my life.

Keep me posted on the adventure and know that I think of you often.

With love and affection,

Rose

Olivia dropped the letter in her lap. "Oh, my god, Rose!" she thought. She doesn't know about Stewart or Burt.

Olivia had to let her know. "I can't write this stuff in a letter. That would be cruel."

She looked at the return address on the envelope. She knew Rose lived in Boston, she would look at a map and talk to Maria and Michael about making a trip. Then, for the first time since she had come home, she went downstairs without having to be called or begged to come down.

She found Michael in his office. It was a small room off the dining room. The office was simple with a desk, a leather chair with a reading lamp, and several bookshelves. He finished his

PhD in history when Olivia was still living with them before her journey to California. There was a large globe in one corner of the office.

"Michael?"

"Olivia?" He looked up and smiled, genuinely glad to see her up and about. He always loved to answer her query of his name with his own query of hers.

She smiled back at him. "Do you have a map that might show the streets of Boston?"

He got up and went to a cabinet near one of the bookshelves and opened a large drawer.

"I have maps of many of the eastern states," he stopped and smiled at her, "and one of every place you traveled to get to California. Maria and I followed your journey quite anxiously, you know."

"You did?"

"We did. We even have a detailed map of Sacramento and have marked the place you and Stewart got married." He took that one out and showed her. There, right by the Sacramento River was a small "X" where Miss Clark's home was located.

Olivia tried not to think of the marriage; nonetheless, the information that her aunt and uncle had followed her journey so closely touched her deeply. She turned and hugged him.

"Thank you, Uncle Michael. Thank you for telling me, but more, thank you for doing that. It makes me feel like you and Maria were watching over me."

"We were," Maria said as she walked into the room. "And

we always will."

Maria came over and smiled at Michael as he and Olivia let go of each other.

"I thought I heard voices and came to investigate," Maria said. "Now that I see the map drawer open, I admit to being alarmed. Is someone planning another journey? I don't think I can take it so soon after I have you back!" She looked at Olivia with a tinge of fear in her eyes.

"She has requested a map of Boston," Michael said. He turned to rifle through the drawer. "Here it is," he said as he slid the map out of the drawer. "Now what is it that you are looking for in Boston?"

"I am certain I wrote to you about Rose, didn't I?"

"She is the one who married Burt? The man who killed Stewart?" Maria asked.

Olivia nodded.

"As I recall," Michael added, "he married her, brought her to the camp, and abused her pretty horribly. You and Stewart helped her escape, isn't that right?" Michael added.

"Yes to all of that," Olivia said. "The package from Molly had a letter from Rose. She does not know about what happened in Sacramento. Molly also told me that Burt was hanged not long after I left to come home."

Maria nodded. "You want to go tell her in person."

A heavy silence hung over the room. Finally, Michael broke the quiet. "Olivia, you know this is your home. It will always be your home no matter where you go," he paused, took off his spectacles, and rubbed his eyes. "We are very worried about you. Quite apart from your grief over Stewart, there seems to be more . . . something you choose not to talk about . . . which is fine, we do not need to know all your secrets!" he said quickly. "But going off to Boston when you still do not seem to have recovered—still are not eating and sleeping so much? We are worried." He stopped and put his glasses back on.

Olivia hung her head. Maria saw the tears fall from her face and knew that whatever secret Olivia was withholding might never be revealed. She went to Olivia and wrapped her in her arms. "We love you, mi amore. No matter what it is and whether you feel you can share it or not, we will always love you. We are simply saying it might be too early to think about going anywhere. You are in such a vulnerable state."

Olivia sniffed and said, "I am so lost. I don't know who I am anymore!"

"I know, Bambina, I know."

Over the next days, Olivia pushed herself to stay awake during the day, although dozing in a chair in the living room seemed impossible not to do. She ate at every meal and even helped Maria fix the meals. Maria returned to teaching a week after Olivia arrived, now, on occasion, she returned home to find Olivia actually preparing the entire dinner.

Several days later, Olivia was looking better. She'd begun to put on some of the many pounds she'd lost after leaving the logging camp. She still felt the exhaustion of grief overwhelm her. Mostly, it was the dreams that tortured her. The dreams were not of Stewart or his death. The dreams were all of Hannah. They were dreams that woke her feeling aroused and longing in ways she did not think possible. When that happened, she forced herself to remember Stewart and his sweet, loving nature. He took such good care of her. It was following one of the erotic Hannah dreams that she suffered the most guilt about Stewart.

During dinner one evening about two weeks after she arrived, Olivia asked, "Might I just take a look at the Boston map, Uncle Michael?"

"Let's do that right after dinner and let your aunt do the dishes alone—just as she loves to do."

"Really?" Olivia asked, looking in disbelief at Maria.

"What?" Maria exclaimed. "So, I like to do dishes alone, what of it?"

"Oh, my god," Olivia said, "just like Mama!"

All three of them burst into laughter. It was the first time Olivia had laughed in ages.

Several days later, and following several discussions with her aunt and uncle, Olivia was on the train to Boston.

Chapter Forty-Three

Michael took her to the train station and gave her directions to Rose's home. "You have the address. Boston is large, so there will be carriages outside the train station. Just have a porter flag one down for you and give him the address. And," Michael lifted her chin to look directly in her eyes, "make sure the driver waits to be certain there is someone home. If not, have him take you to this hotel. Understood?"

Olivia nodded. "I promise, Uncle. And I will let you know what happens when I get there."

"Good girl," he said, then hugged her.

The train ride to Boston was short compared to the other long journeys across the country. Nonetheless, once Olivia was in the carriage to Rose's home, she began to wonder if this was a good idea. As she looked at the homes in the area, she understood just how wealthy Rose's family was. These were stately, well-appointed homes. She began to wonder if she shouldn't have sent Rose a message that she was coming to visit.

"Too late now," she said to herself.

The driver stopped, and she asked why.

"We are here, Miss."

Olivia looked at the large home and gasped. "This was definitely a mistake," she thought, but she was there, and the driver waited to help her down. She had a small suitcase, which he handed to her.

"I will wait until you are inside the home or back inside my carriage, Miss."

Olivia nodded and walked up a steep walkway to the front door. She turned once to look back at the driver, hesitating before she turned the ringer on the door. Then she waited nervously.

The door opened. A beautiful woman stood before her.

"Yes? May I help you?"

"I . . . I am looking for Rose Wentworth."

"I am Rose . . . wait, Olivia? Olivia is that you?"

Olivia nodded. Rose was on her in an instant, pulling her into a huge, powerful hug. "I can't believe you are here!" Rose cried. "Oh, my goodness, Olivia!"

Rose saw the carriage waiting and waved the driver off. Then she pulled Olivia into the house and began to pepper her with questions. She stopped suddenly as she helped Olivia out of her coat.

"Olivia," pardon my manners, "but you look like hell."

"So I've been told on more occasions than I can count."

"Come in and sit down. I will make us some tea, and you can tell me everything."

Rose reappeared with a tray holding a pot of tea, two cups and saucers, and a dish of biscuits. "I am the only one here," she said almost apologetically. "My parents went to Europe for a few months, and I only have the help come in a few times a week."

"You live in this house alone for that long?" Olivia asked. "Don't you get lost?"

"Olivia, this is where I grew up. I know the place pretty well." Rose laughed, then asked, "I am more than happy to see you, but why are you here and where is Stewart?"

Olivia told her the whole story except the part about Hannah.

"And," she finished, "I just heard from Molly and Sam that Burt was hanged shortly after I left to come home to New York."

Rose sat in stunned silence. Only the ticking of the large grandfather clock made any noise at all.

Finally, Rose said, "They don't come any more evil than Burt. But neither do they come any sweeter than Stewart. I am so sorry, Olivia. Just so, so sorry." Then, after a moment she said, "Really, sheep?"

"He was an animal. I guess it makes sense," Olivia said, and they both chuckled.

"How long can you stay?" Rose asked. "I have this great, big house and no one to share it with. I hope you will stay for a long time. You know, they say that the ocean has healing powers. I must agree. It took me many months of sitting near it, wading in it, watching it, but somehow it did help me heal when I got home—which I have you to thank for!"

"I don't want to impose, Rose. I really just came to tell you about what happened. It didn't feel right to send it in a letter."

"Thank you. I do appreciate that. I am not sure a letter would have done the story justice. Hearing you talk about what happened was the right decision. Now, the next right decision is for you to stay here with me and allow me to help you. You, Olivia, were my first real and only friend. All other relationships prior to you were somehow connected to status and wealth and looks. You saw me at my very worst and befriended me. I am certain I would have died without you. I want you to stay as long as you want or need to. Okay?"

"Thank you, Rose. I think I would like that."

"Come upstairs," Rose said as she grabbed Olivia's suitcase in one hand and her hand in the other. "We have several guest rooms, but I know which one you might like the best."

The staircase alone was worthy of living in, but Olivia followed Rose to the second floor and down the hall. Rose opened the door and ushered Olivia inside. The room was enormous. It had a large, four-poster bed with a canopy, a dressing table, a writing desk, and a large comfortable-looking chair near a window. Rose walked over to the French doors after setting down the suitcase and drew open the curtains. There, right there, was the ocean. Rose threw open the double doors and stepped out onto a porch. Olivia followed. The cold was bracing, but the view was spectacular.

"Am I in heaven?" Olivia asked, overwhelmed by the breathtaking view, the smell of the ocean breeze, and the sound of the waves rolling in.

Rose put her arm around her friend. "Sounds like you could use a little heaven, Olivia."

Olivia spent the next few days bundled up and walking along the ocean. She sat on the balcony wrapped in blankets, just staring out at the water, resting, and talking with Rose.

Rose was an incredible hostess. She encouraged Olivia to take care of herself. They had long talks about what it was like when Rose returned home, and Olivia shared about her and Stewart's plan to build the restaurant with Molly and Sam.

One snowy, wintry afternoon, they both sat in front of the fire in the parlor on chairs that enveloped them like hugs. Rose brought out some tea, and she opened up about her life after Burt.

"Olivia, you see what I came from. I was so naïve about things. I thought that I'd simply always be in charge of my life and that things would just come to me or that all I had to do was ask for what I wanted. I was ready for an adventure, but what happened with Burt didn't only shatter my view of life—it nearly destroyed me. I was a mess when I got home. But my parents were wonderful. I guess my running away had more of an impact on them than I had intended. It took me a long time to realize that they were as shattered by my leaving as I was by being broken by Burt."

She poured some more tea for both of them, and they stared into the fire.

"You know, living like that—being dependent on others for my safety and well-being—changed me. I was such a romantic. Now I am more realistic, I suppose—and cautious."

"How long, Rose, before you started to feel better? I mean really better? I honestly did not recognize you when you answered the door. All I saw was this beautiful, vibrant woman. It wasn't until I heard your voice that I realized it was you."

"Same here, Olivia. You are a mere shadow of the in-charge woman from the logging camp. It was your voice that I recognized. But, to answer your question, it took months. The nightmares were the worst. I kept waking up screaming, seeing Burt coming for me and trying to run from him. I could never get away from him in the dreams. My mother would come and wake me and then just hold me until I fell back to sleep."

"I am so glad your parents were able to be there for you. My Aunt Maria and her husband, Michael, have been wonderful to come home to, but I needed something else. I still don't know what it is."

"Wait here," Rose said as she got up and left the parlor. Olivia could hear her upstairs. She came back a moment later. "This is what really helped me in the end," she said as she handed a leather-bound journal and a pen and ink bottle to Olivia. "I started writing down all the things that I was feeling. It took me a long time to forgive myself for what I did to my parents and to myself. Something about writing it down, reading it, expressing the anger, the disappointment, the stupidity, the rage I felt helped to, I don't know, wash it from me? Let it go from me? I'm not sure what the right way to put it is; I just know it helped."

Olivia opened the journal. It was empty. She realized that Rose was giving her the journal so that she could write her own feelings in it. A surge of panic welled up inside of her. Rose saw it.

"You don't have to write a thing, Olivia. Just know that if it feels right, you will know, and you will have the tools to do something with it."

Olivia fanned the blank pages. "I feel as empty as these pages right now," she said, "but I will keep the book close and use it. Thank you, Rose."

Chapter Forty-Four

Rose and Olivia enjoyed each other's company when Rose was home. Some days, Rose did volunteer work with a woman named

Lucy Stone.[21] "You would really like her, Olivia. She was the first Massachusetts woman to graduate from Oberlin College. She has been very vocal in her views as an abolitionist, and she thinks women should have the right to vote. I just help stuff envelopes and support her at different rallies, but she is amazing. When you are feeling better, I would love to introduce you to her. She rather reminds me of you in the way she approaches issues that affect those who are downtrodden."

"I'd like to meet her, Rose," Olivia said. "When I have a little more energy, if that is okay." Olivia was having a particularly difficult day. Her dreams of Hannah were becoming stronger instead of fading.

While Rose was gone, Olivia went up to her room, bundled herself in blankets, and opened the doors to her private porch. She sat and watched the waves. The thought came to her that the waves were as relentless as her guilt and as constant as her longing for Hannah. She went inside, closed the doors, and opened the journal on her desk and began to write. Afterward, she fell asleep. She awoke at dusk and got up to see if Rose

---

21 Boston National Historical Park: Lucy Stone was an abolitionist and Suffragist. She lectured tirelessly for the Massachusetts Anti-Slavery Society. She was a principal organizer of the 1850 Worcester First National Woman's Rights Convention and publisher of the *Women's Journal.*

was home yet. It was late afternoon, and she knew Rose would walk in any minute, full of excitement about this Lucy Stone. She had dinner ready just as Rose got home.

Days later, although it was the heart of winter, Olivia sat on her private deck wrapped in several blankets, letting the cold nip her face. She felt her heart turning to ice and felt powerless to do anything about it. She shivered, even within all the blankets. Tears leaked from her eyes. She felt them freeze on her cheeks. That was more a reflection of how she felt than anything. She was certain she would never find herself or even the person she used to be ever again.

"Perhaps I just fooled myself into thinking I was a good person," she thought. "This is my life now. I took a gentle, sweet soul and tossed him away because I found something I wanted more. I hate what I did and can't undo. So, what now? Do I spend the rest of my life wallowing in this pain? Help me, someone, please help me."

Days passed like this with her diving into her own ocean of sorrow. She had to pull herself together to go down and be with Rose. Rose was faithful to her promise to give her time to grieve.

"I know we all grieve in our own way, Olivia," Rose said, "but I am increasingly worried about you. Put these on and let's go walking by the water."

Rose pulled out heavy coats, boots, and scarves. They bundled up and walked to the water. Rose slipped her arm through Olivia's, and they walked. They walked so far that when they turned back, they could not even see the house. Olivia felt both exhilaration and exhaustion. She pushed on. When they returned, Rose opened a bottle of port, and they sat in the parlor near the fire Rose started.

"You are very good at that," Olivia said.

Rose sat down and picked up her glass. "I learned how to start a fire from you, you know?"

"I don't remember teaching you," Olivia said with a puzzled look.

"Olivia, you don't seem to remember a lot of good things you did for a lot of people. I don't know what is eating at you, but if you don't figure it out soon, I fear . . . " Rose couldn't even finish her thought. She could see that Olivia was dying, and she did not know how to help her.

Olivia's eyes drifted off into the fire. She watched the flames quietly for some time and then said, almost as if she were talking to herself, "Sometimes I wonder if we are all just a bundle of contradictions. I always saw myself as innocent. I saw myself as a force for good in the world, but perhaps I was just fooling myself. Now I see that no matter how good I act, or think I am, I have this shadow side that I have kept hidden from even myself. Can a person be both a saint and a sinner? How does a soul reconcile themselves to that? How did I turn from a loving wife to murderer? I destroyed a man so good, so . . . so . . . " Stewart's face filled her gaze. She stopped talking.

Rose watched Olivia disappear inside herself where it seemed she tried and hung herself for what she felt. After a while Rose said, "Olivia, if there is something I have learned, it is that we all have good and bad in us. We all have light and dark. I have personal knowledge of that. I spent the majority of my life acting as if I were the only person on earth who mattered. I was vile. I manipulated and tortured people as if they were nothing but my playthings. I hurt them and thought it was perfectly within my right to do so. I was that monster, and I fed that monster until someone called me out on being exactly what I was. Then I became the victim of a more vile monster. That does not mean I no longer live with my own monster inside of me. But it does mean that I know she is a part of me, and I cannot forget that. My monster is a part of me that I must remember can rear her ugly head. She is not gone, but I am forced to acknowledge that she is a part of me. I must choose, every day, to be better than that part of me that was so ugly and hurtful. Whatever it is you are struggling with, we all have our monsters to grapple with, and unless we do, we only fool ourselves. Stewart is dead, Olivia. Whatever guilt you feel about that will not bring him back. I have watched you. Your grief is more than normal grief. There is an element to it that seems particularly destructive to you. You have seen people grieve, like on your wagon train. Is your grief anything like that?"

"They had no choice but to push on. They were in the middle of nowhere, they had to keep moving or die themselves."

"Do you not have a choice? Are you choosing to stay and die?"

"I am dying Rose!" Olivia yelled. When she heard her voice, it startled her, and she buried her head in her hands. "I'm sorry, Rose, but it does feel like dying. Forgive me, I am tired from our walk," she stopped and drank down the remainder of her port. "I will be better after a short rest. I promise," she lied.

The things that Rose said terrified her. She knew she was letting her feelings eat away at her, but that conversation was a little too close to home for Olivia.

Rose had always been an exceptional observer of people.

That was how she always knew just the right way to get them to do her bidding, to manipulate them into believing her, to get them to turn on themselves. This was different. It was more than grief. Olivia was hiding something, and she decided to figure out what it was.

The sun was nearing the western sky. Rose went up to find Olivia sound asleep on her bed. Even in her sleep, Olivia whimpered and moaned. Rose looked at her friend and prayed for a way to help this woman who once saved her life. The journal was open on the bed. Rose hesitated but picked it up and walked to the window where the light still glowed. She read the first page, and more after that.

JOURNAL of Olivia Russo Anderson

February 25, 1857

broken

I will never

be whole again

consumed with grief

I bury myself beneath

a quilt of despair

sleep is an easy escape

I wake to hopelessness

And rise

because I must

I cannot do this alone

Another reads:

A battle rages within me
a war no one can win
he lies dead on the ground
his heart beats no more
and I hold the knife
that drips with his blood
I turn the blade toward me
my shame a perfect target
but I am a coward.
Relentlessly, the ocean
waves toss me like driftwood
all the day long.
Sleep lulls me to believe
that it holds relief
but I am tortured by dreams
of your body against mine
soft, blissful caresses
and lips hungry for mine.

I surrender to you in dreams

then awaken to war

and enter the battle anew.

Rose's heart was beating faster and faster as she realized what Olivia's struggle encompassed. She looked at Olivia, still sleeping on the bed. Then she smiled, shook her head and continued to the next writing.

H_____

You stir my desire like the wind stirs the clouds

Whipping them into storms that demand release

Lightning

Thunder

And the wash of drenching rain.

I am dry ground

Soaking in every drop of you

opening

quenching

drowning myself in your love

But only in dreams

The pages were full of pain, wanting, and desire. Rose read on:

time and again
I pray for a balm
to soothe the cuts
I have carved upon my heart
I find only salt
and rub it briskly
into the open wounds
help me to stop
beating my heart
against this rock

Rose was moved beyond words and understood, at last, why Olivia was so tormented. She lit the lantern beside the chair and continued to read until Olivia awoke.

"Rose," Olivia sat up in bed, saw what Rose had, and panicked. "What are you doing?"

Rose closed the journal and looked steadily at Olivia. "Your writing is incredible. You never told me you could write."

"How much have you read?" Olivia asked, her heart beating so fast she thought she might faint.

"Enough to understand why you punish yourself so mercilessly."

Olivia waited to hear what she thought she needed to hear.

Someone else berating her for being such a dishonorable woman and wife. There was almost a relief in knowing that someone knew her sin. Perhaps it was like confession when she was little and had to tell the priest what she had done wrong so he could give her penance, and she could move on. Perhaps she wanted Rose to ridicule her, slap her across the face so that she might feel something, anything but what she did feel. Maybe she needed a fight. Maybe she wanted her life snuffed out as Stewart's was. Her mind raced as she realized that Rose might now know her secret. Her shame crushed her, and the physicality of it folded her against the headboard. She shrunk, visibly on the bed and drew her knees up, wrapping her arms around them, curling up like a tiny mouse hiding from a monster.

"Who is 'H'?" Rose asked softly from the corner.

"I don't know what you mean." Olivia's voice was muffled through her limbs.

"Olivia," Rose said a little louder, "who is 'H'?"

"No one!" Olivia practically shouted. "I made her up."

"Bullshit!" Rose yelled. She stood up and walked over to Olivia and dropped the journal on the bed. "I read everything. Maybe that was wrong of me, but I didn't know what else to do to help you, Olivia, and clearly you don't know either."

Rose was quiet for a moment, then sat on the side of Olivia's bed. "I am going to tell you something that still fills me with shame when I think about how I treated people who could have been such good friends to me. When I traveled by ship to California, I was among other women who were seeking husbands, adventure, love, romance—friendship. I was the kind of person who couldn't stand to see anyone else happy, so I drove wedges between every one of those women. I did it by telling lies, starting rumors, trying to make myself a hero by putting a simple dash of cocaine in a sick girl's tea. But the worst thing I did was try to paint a perfectly lovely woman as a lecher for the youngest in the group. These women were friends. Every one of them was scared and eager for friendship, and I singlehandedly destroyed their naivete. They saw through me after I accused the kindest one of them of forcing a kiss on the youngest. The older one exposed me. I had never been humiliated like that before. The captain was sick of the drama and kept me prisoner in my room for the remainder of the voyage. Being alone that long with your thoughts can be frightful, you know?"

Rose waited to see if anything she said had gotten through to Olivia. When Olivia did not respond she continued. "Olivia, whoever 'H' is, you need to forgive yourself. So, you fell in love with someone who was not your husband. You think you are the first person to do so?"

She reached and pulled Olivia's hand to her. "I saw how much you and Stewart had together. You were best friends. I saw your affection and care for each other. That was something I always dreamed of, wanted so badly that I ran away from home to find a dream that became a nightmare. I only thought I knew what humiliation was on that ship. Burt taught me what it really meant. We all have our lessons to learn, but those lessons are not meant to torture us. They are to help us grow. Maybe Stewart was simply the path to whoever this 'H' is. All I know is that the Stewart I saw, who loved you more than anything, would want you to be happy. I know that was his sole aim in life—to make you happy. Right now, you are throwing that gift in his face. You are so in love with 'H'—that . . . "

"Hannah, her name is Hannah," Olivia cried. "Her name is Hannah," she said more softly. "And what you don't understand is that I left her because I could not live with myself if I left Stewart for her. Stewart saved her from Burt and threatened to tell the whole camp about what Burt did if he didn't leave right then and there. He is the one who sent Burt away to protect Hannah. Stewart told me to ask Hannah to come with us to Sacramento, but I couldn't even ask her. I knew I was not strong enough to resist her. You don't understand, Rose. I was beside myself with grief when Stewart and I left the camp. I was so full of sorrow, and he tried so hard to make me happy. All I could do was wallow in my loss of Hannah. And then Burt killed him. I may well have done it myself. I feel like I did. I feel like I killed him. He knew something was wrong. He just didn't know what . . . and he kept loving me."

Rose reflected on everything that Olivia told her. She had put most of that together from Olivia's journal. She still held Olivia's hand. She brought it to her lips and kissed the back of it. "You, my friend, are way too hard on yourself. I know because I recognize myself in you. After all the nastiness and bitterness I created in my life, it took me a long time to find a way to forgive myself. You are right when you write about how it is a war raging within you. But you, unlike me, had a good heart to begin with, and you sowed more beauty in the world than most. Try forgiving yourself a little. Keep writing—you are quite good at it. And realize that you were loved magnificently by two people in this world. Not all of us can say that."

Rose got up and left the room, hoping that something, anything, she said might have made its way through Olivia's guilt. She prayed it did. Time would tell.

Chapter Forty-Five

Maria and Michael were enjoying a pleasant evening meal of wine and homemade pasta when the front doorbell rang.

"I'll get it," Michael said, not too happy about being disturbed.

"Maybe Olivia has come home," Maria offered brightly.

Michael opened the door to find two rather dusty, dirty strangers on his front porch. "May I help you?" he asked.

"Sir," the older of the two boys began haltingly, "we are looking for the home of Olivia Anderson."

"Maria!" Michael called, "I think you need to come here." Michael opened the door wide and invited the boys in.

Maria was startled to find the two unknown boys in her house.

"These boys are looking for Olivia," Michael said.

"Pardon me, sir, ma'am," the taller of the two said, "My name is Erik, this is actually my sister, Hannah." He reached and removed the hat that hid her hair. Her blond locks fell down around her shoulders. We have traveled all the way across the country looking for Olivia. Please tell us she is here."

Maria sighed. "I am sorry, but Olivia is not here. She was, but she left for Boston to visit a friend nearly a month ago and has not yet returned." She looked at the two weary and forlorn souls. "You'd better come in and tell us why you are looking for her."

"We are far too filthy to come into your home, thank you," Erik said. "We have been traveling for weeks to get here. First by horse, then by train, several trains actually. We should have gotten a hotel for the night and cleaned up, but once we knew we were so close, well, we just had to see if Olivia was here. We will leave and come back tomorrow if that is acceptable, or you can just tell us how to find her, and we will be on our way."

Maria looked at Michael, who shrugged and smiled. "No one who has traveled clear across the country looking for Olivia is going anywhere," he said. "Follow me upstairs. You can both have a bath. Maria will leave clean clothes for you. They might not fit, but they will be clean. Then come down and have something to eat."

They both looked at Maria to make certain this was okay with her.

"Go, go," she shooed and smiled. Leave your dirty clothes on the bathroom floors. I will wash them." She went to put more pasta on to boil.

Maria and Michael felt blessed to have not one, but two, bathrooms upstairs. Michael put Erik in the master bath and Hannah in the bath outside of Olivia's room. He called to Hannah through the bathroom door, "We don't have any trousers that will fit you, Hannah, but I put one of Olivia's old dresses on her bed for you."

"Thank you!"

Erik and Hannah came down looking like refreshed human

beings. Michael heard them descending and went to greet them at the bottom of the stairs. "I am Michael, by the way," he said as he shook both of their hands.

When they entered the dining room, Maria looked up and stared at Hannah. "You are lovely," she said.

Michael heard something in Maria's voice but was not at all certain what it meant. He poured them each a glass of wine while Maria dished out the pasta and covered it with her homemade sauce with meatballs."

"Mangia," she said.

"She means eat," Michael said when he saw the puzzled look on their faces.

Except for the clinking of forks and knives on china, it was quiet for a while. The visitors were clearly hungry.

"When was the last time you two ate?" Maria asked.

"I think it was last night," Hannah said. "Once we hopped on the last train to New York, we fell asleep and didn't wake up until it arrived here."

"I see," Maria said. "And you came right to our house to find Olivia?"

"Yes, Ma'am," Erik said, picking up his glass of wine. "This is really good wine, by the way. I've never really had wine before."

"So," Michael said, "how do you know Olivia, and why are you looking for her?"

Hannah hung her head down. She wasn't prepared to

answer that particular question. Her face turned bright red. Maria saw it.

Erik started. "Slim and I were good friends up at the logging camp, even before Olivia got there." He saw the confusion on their faces. "Sorry, Slim was Stewart's nickname at the camp. Sometimes he shared her letters with me. When she arrived, she didn't come right up to the camp. They got married down in Sacramento, but she came up with him and started cooking for the camp. Before her, we had another guy, but he left, and there was only Mr. Chang. Olivia just jumped right in and helped take over the kitchen. She was an amazing cook. The men all loved her cooking. I guess you probably know all of that," he said apologetically.

"That's alright, Erik, please continue."

"Well, after my father passed—you see my mother passed a while ago—and, well, Hannah was in Oregon taking care of both of them. When our father died, I went to get her. She came up to the camp and just like Olivia, she just jumped in and started helping with things that needed to be done. She and Olivia became really good friends."

Erik stopped and took another bite of pasta. When he finished chewing and swallowed, he said, "Stewart and Olivia had friends in Sacramento."

"Sam and Molly?" Michael asked.

"That's them," Eric continued. "They, all four of them, had this idea to start a restaurant in town. Stewart and Olivia had saved enough money to help make that happen. I was also ready to quit the logging camp. I loved being a high rigger, but it is hard work."

"What's a high rigger?" Michael wanted to know.

"Well, there are guys who work at the very tops of the trees. That's me. I kind of rope myself to the tree. I have these boots with spikes, and I work my way up the tree, cutting off the limbs on the way. When I get pretty close to the top, it's my job to cut off the whole top part of the tree. Then the loggers at the bottom can chop the tree down from there. Well, after I get down, of course."

Erik felt like he was rambling, but he was nervous to be eating in such a nice house with wine.

"I'm talking too much," he said, coloring a bit.

"Erik and I left the camp soon after Stewart and Olivia did," Hannah offered. It was weeks after Stewart was killed that we got news of his death. We hadn't made a decision on staying in Oregon, so we went to Sacramento to be with Olivia."

"She was already gone, wasn't she?" Maria asked.

Hannah nodded.

"So, you came to find her?" Maria asked.

Hannah nodded again and looked down at her plate of food. "Will you tell us where she went?" Hannah asked. There was a pleading in her voice. Maria heard it.

"Of course, we will, but you two need a good night's sleep first. She is not far by train. Tomorrow is Saturday, we will take you to the train station and tell you how to find her."

Maria saw Hannah's whole body relax. Erik thanked them profusely. Michael took them upstairs.

"Hannah, you might as well sleep in Olivia's bed. Erik, you can have the floor or the couch downstairs."

"I'm fine on the floor, sir. That'll be the most comfortable bed in weeks."

"Goodnight, then," Michael said, and he went down to talk to Maria.

He picked up a dishtowel and said, "What is going on with you? I saw your face as you watched the two of them. Do you not trust them?"

"They are the missing piece, Michael," she said. She pulled her hands from the dish water and dried them on the towel he held.

"Well, I'm definitely missing something, then, because I have no idea what you are talking about."

"There was something Olivia wasn't telling us. I know my niece. She was hiding something about the whole reason for coming home. I'm not saying she wouldn't have come anyway, but there was definitely more than she told us. I could feel her holding back."

"And now you think you know what that is?" He looked at her with a smile.

"Hannah is the missing piece," she said.

"I don't follow," he said, crinkling up his face. "Her friend, Hannah, is the missing piece?"

"Michael, Olivia and Hannah are in love," she whispered loudly.

Chapter Forty-Six

Olivia went to one of Lucy Stone's meetings and decided she was the real thing. Rose told her that Lucy had met with Frederick Douglass.[22] Olivia remembered Michael talking about Frederick Douglass before she went west to marry Stewart. She knew that Michael was very impressed with Mr. Douglass and was glad she did, at least, know who he was.

The meeting they went to was in downtown Boston. It was an anti-slavery meeting, something dear to Lucy's heart. At the meeting, she was confronted because "this is an anti-slavery meeting, and you have the audacity to dare to speak about the cause of women's rights?" Her answer, which Olivia and Rose both chuckled at was, "I was a woman before I was an abolitionist!"

Olivia found herself enjoying going to the meetings with Rose. Lucy Stone was a marvel of a woman who sparked, or rather, re-sparked, Olivia's sense of justice. The three of them, Rose, Lucy, and Olivia, spent more and more time together either before or after meetings. They had become good friends. Olivia sometimes brought up the topic of the Chinese problems out west. Often, she wondered about Shu and Chang. Were they still at the logging camp? Had they left? Anti-Chinese sentiment wasn't as bad in the east, but so many of the Chinese immigrants

22 Wikipedia: Frederick Douglass was an American social reformer, abolitionist, orator, writer, and statesman. He was the most important leader of the movement for African-American civil rights in the 19th century.

crossed the Pacific and found themselves in California that she was more and more worried about her old cooking friends. She decided to write to Molly to see if she knew anything.

Since Rose had confronted Olivia after having read her journal, Olivia was becoming more engaged with life and living, but she still struggled with her demons. Punishing herself about Stewart was beginning to fade, but she did miss him and wished that she could have shown him more love before he was taken from her. Dreams of Hannah still plagued her nights. It did not make sense to her that those were still so strong. "How am I supposed to forget about her if I cannot stop dreaming about her?" she wondered.

Journaling became a part of her routine. Rose was right, it did help. And she found that she enjoyed writing. It was a creative outlet she did not ever consider or realize she had a gift for. Sometimes, after an anti-slavery or women's movement meeting talk by Lucy, her writing reflected her anger about those injustices.

It had been nearly two months since she arrived on Rose's doorstep. She was still grieving both Stewart and Hannah, but something did change after Rose confronted her. And she felt the grief shape-shifting within her. Some days she went without crying. Mostly those were the busy meeting days with Rose. Other days and nights, she cried herself to sleep. At least now she no longer wished to sleep and never wake up.

Late January came. It was 1857. Three months had passed since Stewart was killed and she said goodbye to all she had known for years. She was having one of her "bad" days. It was gloomy. Clouds were dark over the Atlantic, and the ocean roiled with an anger that mirrored her mood.

"I am not up to a meeting today, Rose. It is miserable out, and I don't want to fight with the weather. Do you mind?"

"You do look a tad pale today. Are you feeling alright?"

"A little tired, I admit, but I promise I will have a wonderful dinner for you when you return."

"I will look forward to that, Olivia. And you know I will hold you to it."

As Rose prepared to leave, there was a tentative knock at the front door. She was right there and opened it to find a man and young woman facing her.

The young man was tall and quite good looking, Rose noticed. "Yes?" she asked expectantly.

"We are looking for Olivia and were told she was here."

"And who told you that?" she demanded, feeling protective of her friend.

The fellow shuffled his feet, clearly uncomfortable. The woman answered, "Her aunt, Maria, told us."

Erik seemed to regain his voice. "My apologies, ma'am. My name is Erik Johannson. This is my sister, Hannah. We are friends of Olivia's from out west. We traveled quite far to find her. Is she here?"

Rose had a vague memory of them but not enough that she recognized them.

"Well," Rose said, "you had better come in out of the cold, or Olivia will never forgive me. Coats there on the hooks and follow me."

Olivia was in the kitchen perusing ingredients for creating dinner. She could make a meal out of anything. Her back was to the kitchen door as she moved things around in the pantry.

"Olivia, you had better make extra, it looks like we are having company for dinner," Rose said matter-of-factly.

"Oh, who, Lucy? She hardly eats at all since she got pregnant."

"Not Lucy, Olivia."

Something in the way Rose said it made her turn around. Erik and Hannah stood next to Rose in the kitchen. Hannah was wearing the dress that Olivia's aunt had given her. She looked beautiful in the dark dress with her long blond hair flowing over her shoulders.

"I'm dreaming," Olivia said and rubbed her eyes.

Hannah walked over to her, reached up, and touched her face gently. The touch stung her, and she jumped back. "No, no!" Olivia cried. "You can't be here. You can't!" Olivia turned and ran out of the kitchen and up to her bedroom slamming the door.

"Well, that was unexpected," Rose said. "I think I will skip my meeting after all." She took her coat off and asked Hannah and Erik to wait in the parlor while she tried to talk to Olivia.

"By the way, Erik, now I remember you from the camp. I'm Rose."

Erik smiled. "I remember you too, Rose. You are looking much happier these days."

"We will talk. I'll be back soon." Rose disappeared up the immense staircase and entered Olivia's room without knocking.

"Care to tell me what is going on with you? The woman

you love just traveled all the way across the country to find you. That was a hell of a greeting."

"You of all people should understand, Rose. She is the reason I killed Stewart! Staying away from her is my punishment."

"Oh, that again?" Rose said rolling her eyes. "I thought you were done flagellating yourself for that. What good does that do anyone—especially you?"

Olivia went to the window and tried to center herself and her nerves. She was raging much like the weather.

"Olivia," Hannah called softly from the doorway. "Please hear me out."

Rose turned to leave. "She is all yours, Hannah. Good luck."

"Do you have any idea how hard I have worked to try to forget you?" Olivia asked, turning from the window.

Hannah shook her head.

"I had to get as far away from you as possible. Stewart was my husband, Hannah. He was my husband, and I gave the love I should have had for him to you!"

Hannah stood quietly and just listened.

"What did you think coming here? Did you think that just because Stewart is dead that we could be together, get married, be happy? You do know that we could be imprisoned or hanged if people found out about us? What did you hope to accomplish by coming here?"

"I hoped that I could help you through your grief over

Stewart. When I found out that Burt killed him, all I thought about was getting to you to comfort you. I needed to know that you were okay."

"I'm fine as you can see."

"I guess our interpretations of fine are quite different." Hannah waited for Olivia to say something that might indicate that she still had any feeling for her at all.

Olivia turned toward the window. She was trembling with rage and burning with fire, and she thought she might explode.

Hannah put her hand on Olivia's shoulder. "I still love you. I will always love you." She waited a moment, and when Olivia didn't move or say anything, she removed her hand, turned, and started toward the door.

"Don't you dare!" Olivia yelled. She had turned and was glaring at Hannah. Her nostrils were flaring. The veins in her neck were popping out.

Hannah stared back at her and felt her own anger flaring up.

"Don't you dare walk out that door without hearing me out!" Olivia practically spit at her.

"What do you think I came here to do, Olivia, play cards? Talk to me!"

Olivia slapped Hannah across the face. "You!" she cried, "This is all your fault!"

Hannah, still stunned and smarting, slapped Olivia across her face and screamed, "This is no one's fault, Olivia. It just happened!"

"Aaaaahhhhhh," Olivia yelled as she tackled Hannah to the floor. "It is your fault! Why did you ever have to come to the camp. Everything was fine until you came!"

Hannah tried to push Olivia off her, but Olivia was holding her arms and screaming into her face. Spittle was flying everywhere. "It's your fault! You made me fall in love with you! I hate you!"

Hannah was stronger and finally pushed Olivia off of her, rolling her onto her back. "Me? Why did you have to be so nice to me and bring me to the meadow?" Hannah screamed as she held Olivia pinned to the floor. Olivia fought with all her might to get out from under Hannah, but Hannah easily held her down while straddling her hips. "Why, Olivia, why? Why did you make me fall in love with you? It's your fault!"

"Don't you dare!" Olivia screamed and kicked, pushing with all her might against Hannah.

It took all of Hannah's strength to hold Olivia in place. Hannah knew she was strong, but Olivia's rage and muscle surprised her. She held her ground. She let Olivia continue to scream and fight. Hannah sat on Olivia's hips and purposely let go of her arms. Olivia flailed them, slapping and punching Hannah with her fists.

"No, no!" Olivia cried even louder. "It's not my fault! I hate you! I hate you!"

After minutes of struggle, Olivia seemed to be winding down.

"It's not. It can't be. I don't know what to do. I am so tired of feeling this guilt. Please tell me it's not my fault." Olivia was sobbing now, and the fight poured out of her along with her tears. "It can't be my fault. I loved Stewart."

Hannah moved off of Olivia, sat beside her, and pulled her up into an embrace. They were still on the floor. They both were crying now.

Hannah sobbed into Olivia's neck, "It's nobody's fault, my love. Not yours, not mine, no one's. We just happened to fall in love. That's what happened. Love happened. Nobody planned it that way. No one did it to cause this horrible string of events to occur. No one wanted to hurt Stewart. We just fell in love."

Olivia was clinging to Hannah, still crying. "I cannot stop loving you. I have tried. It's why I came home. I thought if I left you behind, I might find myself again. I cannot stop loving you, Hannah."

Hannah breathed deeply, and her body finally relaxed. "That, my everything, is why I am here. It seems I cannot stop loving you, either."

They were still sitting on the floor, just holding one another when Rose and Erik silently appeared at the door. "See, Erik. I told you they weren't dead."

Olivia reached over and pushed the door closed on them.

Chapter Forty-Seven

Olivia and Hannah sat silently on the floor in that embrace for some time.

"Home," Hannah finally whispered.

"Hmmm?" Olivia responded.

"This feels like home to me," she said softly. "It's strange, but I feel like I have longed for this all my life and didn't know where to look, or even what it was I was searching for. But now I know. You are home to me."

Olivia pulled away from Hannah's neck and arms just a little. Then she leaned in and kissed Hannah for the first time since their night in the cabin that now seemed so very long ago.

"Grandmother was right when she told me to come," Hannah said.

"What? What grandmother? I thought all your grandparents were gone."

"Let's go find Erik and Rose. I have a story to tell you."

When Olivia and Hannah went downstairs, they were uneasy, sensing the interrogation they would get from Rose and Erik, which began before they even sat down.

"Everything better?" Rose asked.

"Might we have a little of whatever is in that bottle, Rose?" Olivia asked.

"I have a story to tell," Hannah said softly.

Rose poured two more glasses of port wine and slid some cookies over to them. Erik and Rose were sitting in chairs opposite a small Davenport sofa where Olivia and Hannah sat. All were next to the fire in the parlor.

"Is this about the Grandmother?" Erik asked.

Hannah nodded.

Olivia knew that Rose understood that Hannah was more than just a friend, but she had to ask, "Wait, Han. Erik, did you know about me and Hannah?"

Erik smiled and took a sip of port, then he sighed and began. "Hannah was never like other girls growing up. I watched her get hurt over and over because they made fun of her, her way of dressing, the way she always wanted to do the things I did. She pulled inside of herself—dedicated herself to our parents' care. She was a loner. Read a ton. Took care of everything around the house after I left." He set his glass down on the table between them and leaned forward. "I assumed she was happy being alone."

"That's because you're an idiot," Hannah said playfully.

He smiled. "You aren't wrong, little sister." He sat back and continued. "Once I brought you to the camp and I saw how happy you were, saw how you, Olivia, drew her out, didn't judge her for wearing pants, offered her your friendship, well it was like my eyes were opened. I watched my solitary, lonely little sister come alive."

"What," Olivia interrupted, "made you think that it was anything but friendship?"

"You forget, Olivia, that I watched Slim respond the same way every time he got a letter from you. Every day he would remind me how much closer you were. He never stopped talking about you. Han was the same way when we were together. It was always 'Olivia this, Olivia that.' The day Slim left the mountaintop to come down to Sacramento to meet you in person, he was so happy he was almost flying. And when he returned with you, he was changed. The joy just radiated from him. That's what I saw in Hannah."

A silence fell over the room. Hannah sensed Olivia's concern and reached for her hand, but Olivia was uncomfortable with the intimate gesture and pulled her hand away slowly.

"Erik," Olivia said, but she paused for a long time before she asked. "Did Stewart ever . . . did he . . . ?" She could not even say the words. Her fear surged within her.

Erik pursed his lips and ran his fingers through his hair. "One time he said to me that, well, he wondered if I thought that you two were unusually close."

Olivia froze and waited for what might come.

"I said that you two were the only two women in a camp of unruly men. I said I wouldn't worry about it." Erik paused and took a very deep breath, then said, "But he mentioned that he felt you pulling away from him, so I guess," Erik stopped again, then added, "if he suspected anything other than your close friendship, he didn't say anything to me."

"But I wonder if that's why he told me to ask you to come with us," Olivia said, looking at Hannah.

"He did?" Hannah was puzzled. "Why would he do that? Especially if he thought anything more."

"Because," Rose interjected, "that's how much he loved you, Olivia."

Olivia closed her eyes and sank back into the sofa.

"Please don't go there, Olivia," Hannah begged. "Please don't go to that dark place. I have a story to tell."

It took Olivia quite a bit of resolve to bring herself out of the downward spiral that started spinning wildly when Erik told her about Stewart's suspicions. But she took a big breath and nodded.

Olivia, Rose, and Erik all listened as Hannah told them her story.

"When Erik and I got back to Linkville, we rented a couple of small rooms. He set out to find the girl he'd had a crush on.

"I did have one friend growing up named Skybird. He was from one of the three Klamath tribes, a Paiute people. Because I had no friends in town, I would often go into the woods to get to the lake that fed the river. The first time I went, I ran into Skybird. He spoke English, which surprised me. He wanted to know what I was doing on Klamath land. I told him I was looking for the lake. I had my fishing pole and always heard my father and brother talk of the good fishing in the lake. I didn't ask them how to get there, I just went in that direction. I apparently did not go the way that Erik and my father took.

"Skybird went fishing with me. He talked to me like no one else my age ever did. I started going to the lake and through his village often. After a while, everyone knew I was Skybird's friend. Sometimes, I just went to the village to visit.

"When Erik went in search of Martha, I could not bear to stay in that little room, so I went out to walk. Next thing I knew I came out of the woods and onto the Klamath Reservation. I saw some folks I knew who greeted me, but I was being drawn to the lake, right where it fed into the river. I cannot tell you why, but I just knew I needed to be there.

"I went over to the river. I am ashamed to tell you that I

considered jumping in and letting myself be taken over the falls downriver. I was so miserable without you. It was then that I heard her.

"'"Daughter!"' she called to me.

"I turned to see an ancient native woman sitting on a log weaving a basket from the reeds along the marsh. She motioned me over.

"I knew it was proper to refer to all elderly tribeswomen as "grandmother," so I went to where she sat and said, 'Hello, Grandmother.'

"She told me to sit. There was another stump of log next to her, so I sat. She was very old. Her face was lined with so many wrinkles that you couldn't even tell it was skin anymore. Somehow, that just made her more beautiful. It was like she just let the sun weather her into a rare and precious carving.

"'You have black cloud all around you,' she said. 'Spirit of Death follow you.'"

Hannah stopped and took a deep breath. When she started speaking again, she looked Olivia directly in the eyes.

"Grandmother told me I had two choices—to jump in the river or to find what I had lost.

"I wasn't about to tell the old woman that I lost the love of my life—who happened to be married and was a woman. I remember I just bowed my head and said, 'That is not so easy, Grandmother.'

"Then she said the most amazing thing. 'In Spirit world we love who we will. You love her.' I looked up in surprise. She laughed and said, 'Foolish child, give me your hands.'

"I gave her my hands. She closed her eyes and said, 'She carry more than death. Cloud of black guilt consume her. Go to her. She needs you.'

"When the grandmother opened her eyes, they were full of tears. 'Go, go!' she said and shooed me away.

"I ran home to tell Erik that I had to find you, that I knew you were in trouble. That's when he showed me the letter from Burley that said Burt had killed Stewart.

"All I could think about was you and how you must be feeling. I told Eric I had to get to Sacramento to find you. I figured he would try to stop me, but I was not going to be stopped. I was pretty frantic at that point."

"What did Erik say?" Olivia asked.

"He told me he found out that Martha was married and going to have a baby, so he stopped looking for her. He seemed sad, but not heartbroken. Then he said, 'I guess we are heading to Sacramento.'

"I told him I wanted to go back to see the Grandmother first, so he came with me. I was excited for him to meet her. As we walked through the reservation, we ran into Skybird. He was holding a baby. When he saw me, he smiled and waved me over. He introduced me to his baby daughter and his wife. It made me so happy to see him so happy. Then he asked what I was doing there.

"I told him about meeting the weaving Grandmother at the marsh the day before. He looked puzzled.

"'What grandmother?' he asked.

"I told him again and described her to him.

"There is no one like that in our clan, Hannah."

"His wife took the baby from his arms and said, 'It sounds like you met Spirit Mother. I have heard many tales of her.'

"I asked them where could I find her.

"Skybird nodded his head in understanding. 'Ah, my friend, you cannot,' he said. 'Spirit Mother is a Spirit. She comes to those who are in need. You can go look for her near the river, but you will not find her again.' Then he put his hands on my head and said, 'My friend, you have been given a special gift. Whatever she told you, you had best get on with it.'

"Olivia, I will tell you that I ran as fast as I could to the river and to the place where I sat with her. There was no sign of her. All I found was a half-woven basket of reeds. I came as fast as I could."

"I was already gone, though," Olivia said. A memory floated back to her. She remembered how, after Stewart's funeral, Molly had sent her off with a basket of food. She remembered the Sacramento River and the ducks and being awakened by the voice. She smiled and said, "I also had a river message." She closed her eyes again, shook her head slowly, and then told them about how she had fallen asleep along the Sacramento.

"I was awakened by a voice that called my name," she said. "There was no one around. Then I heard it again, but it was like I was hearing the voice in my head, not with my ears. All the voice said, quite clearly, was 'Go home. Go home.'

"I left for San Francisco the next day and boarded a ship for home. How did you two get here? How long did it take you?"

"Molly and Sam told us you'd left for San Francisco several weeks before. I told Erik I had to find you and that I was going to ride across the country whether he was coming or not."

"Like I was going to let you do that," Erik said.

"Molly and Sam suggested that it would be best if I disguised myself as a man and did not think it would be wise to go by wagon train. They gave me Midnight, Stewart's horse, and packed us up with plenty of supplies. Sam knew that the railroad being built across the country wasn't complete yet, but he said that at some point we might be able to find how far the train had been built west from Council Bluffs, Iowa where the train line was started.

"We were very careful. We stayed off the main ruts from the wagon trails but near enough to know we were on track," Hannah said. "It was really rough going through the mountains. I refused to wait until spring. It took us longer than usual, but we still made better time than if we'd tried with a wagon. We actually followed the Pony Express Trail that stopped at all of the forts along the way."

"The horses were much faster, even with the snow in the mountains," Erik said. "Midnight almost seemed as anxious to get us to you as Hannah was!"

"It took a month for us to get to Wyoming, but it got easier once we were more into the plains," Hannah said. "Although a few of the windstorms almost got the better of us."

"Tell them about the Grandmother," Eric said.

"Well, several times when we were camping, I heard the Grandmother's voice. Sometimes she would urge us to keep moving and not camp where we stopped. One time, she woke me up and said, "Go, now!"

"Then, what?" Olivia asked.

"Then we did what she told us to do. We didn't ask questions, but we knew she was watching over us and keeping us safe."

"Once we got to Wyoming we found out that the railroad from Council Bluffs, Iowa had been built faster than the other half coming over the mountains. We heard that it made a stop in Cheyenne, so that's where we headed," Erik said. "Olivia, I am sorry to tell you that we sold both horses in Cheyenne."

"Midnight?" Olivia said, with a tear in her eye.

"Yes, I am afraid so," Erik said. "But if it makes you feel better, we sold both to a farmer. Midnight was intended for his young daughter. She seemed to fall in love with him instantly."

Olivia smiled. "Midnight was such a gentle creature. Stewart loved that horse. I'm glad you found him a good home."

"The train was stop and go to Iowa. We were able to find stagecoaches or just folks with wagons along the way. By the time we got to Illinois, we were able to find small stretches of trains that took us part way. When we finally hit Pennsylvania, it was mostly by train to New York. That's when we went to your aunt's house, Olivia."

"Did they know who you were?"

"We had to tell them, but, yes," Erik said, "they seemed to know who we were."

"They were very gracious," Hannah said. "And they told us how to find you."

"So here we are," Erik said happily.

All four talked most of the afternoon. Rose was surprised that Erik remembered her from the camp at all. She vaguely remembered him, but only because he always seemed to be with Stewart and Olivia.

"I wasn't my normal, charming self while I lived at the camp, but I made it out with Stewart and Olivia's aide."

"So, you and Stewart did sneak Rose out of the camp?" Erik said with surprise. "Stewart never said a word to me."

"We had to be so careful, Erik. We did not want to put you in any jeopardy. Burt was highly unstable."

"I guess that makes sense," he said. "I am glad they got you away from him, Rose."

After a bit, Rose said, "Olivia, you promised me dinner! That means all of us will eat well this evening."

Olivia got up and went to the kitchen. Hannah followed. "Sorry, Liv, but now that I found you, I have no intention of letting you out of my sight for some time."

Olivia pulled Hannah close. "I'll hold you to that promise, Han."

A few minutes later Erik and Rose came into the kitchen.

"Hold up there, Olivia," he said. "I am not about to miss out on the secrets of your cooking." He turned to look at Rose and said, "I don't know how involved you were with this woman's meals, Miss Rose, but I have been craving many of them since she left the camp."

"My memories are foggy from my days there, Mr. Erik," Rose said playfully back, "but I will tell you that when I returned home, and especially since my parents left for Europe, I have attempted to make some of Olivia's finer meals. Sadly, mine never tasted nearly as good as hers."

Olivia shook her head and started plopping ingredients on the large cooking island. "Okay, then, this will be a group effort. Erik, will you please start a good fire going in that oven? Rose and Hannah, start chopping these." She handed them a few cloves of garlic, some onions, a half jar of olives, and a can of tomatoes.

Olivia began mixing some dough. As she kneaded the dough, she began humming. Rose stopped chopping and looked at her. When Olivia looked up, she saw that Rose's eyes were brimming with tears.

"That is a sound I never thought to hear from you again," Rose said.

Olivia smiled. "Me either, Rose. Me either."

When the dough was ready and the oven was plenty hot, Olivia rolled the dough out on the counter. Then she picked it up and expertly twirled it into a perfect circle. When she laid it down, she brushed olive oil over the entire top and sprinkled it with a variety of herbs. She drained the tomatoes and squeezed what juice she could out of them and spread them on the dough. After that, she told the others to spread the onions, garlic, and olives across the dough. Meanwhile, she grated a variety of cheeses left over in the larder. When she was done, she slid a big pan under the dough and placed it in the oven.

"You never made this at camp, Liv," Hannah said. "What is it?"

"It's something my mama used to throw together in Italy. When we had food left over like sausages, peppers, vegetables, anything at all, she would throw it all on a piece of flat dough and stick it in the oven. She just called it," she paused, thinking, "well, the closest thing the Italian comes to is 'mixed-up pie.'"

As they sat down to dinner, Erik held up a glass of wine and toasted the chef. "To Olivia, as always, the best cook around."

They all had wine and a slice of pie. "How could something so simple taste this good?" Rose asked.

"It's the garlic," Olivia answered. "It is a great addition to add flavor to so many things."

"Could you imagine our mother creating something like this?" Erik asked Hannah.

"I am pretty sure that they never heard of garlic in Sweden!" Hannah answered with a laugh.

Conversation flowed as if the four of them had known each other for years and years. There was a warmth and comfort that settled over the dining room table as they shared story after story.

"Olivia," Rose said at one point, "I never heard about your trip by wagon train across the country."

Olivia gave them the highlights and lowlights of their months-long journey, including her happiness at every fort when there was a letter from Stewart. "It's funny. It wasn't until I actually met him and got to the camp that I realized that the scent of his letters smelled just like him. Pine and sawdust. I think I might have told him that once."

Rose talked about her journey home by ship. "It was so different than my trip to California. After Stewart and Olivia saw me to the stage in Sacramento, I was not only alone but broken. That was a feeling I had never known. I stood often on the back of the ship and just stared into the ripples for hours wondering if I would ever be whole again."

Olivia reached out and put her hand on Rose's arm.

"Burt was one of the worst human beings I ever knew," Erik said. "I didn't know that was happening to you Rose. By the time I found out, you were gone. I am sorry you had to endure that."

"On the bright side," Rose added, "I ran into a woman from my passage to California whom I had wronged." She looked pointedly at Olivia. "The youngest woman with whom I traveled to San Francisco apparently fell in love with one of the ship waiters. They married, and she works on the ship now as well. I did get a chance to apologize to her. I was glad of that."

"Until my parents were both gone, my life was so mundane compared to all of yours!" Hannah offered. "Riding on horseback on the Pony Express Trail was the most exciting thing I have ever done. I always envied my brother for being able to go out into the world to explore and meet new people. Not that I would change anything, mind you. I was glad to be able to care for our parents through their illnesses."

"I am so glad you both made it to Boston safely," Rose said. "It must have been dangerous for you both to ride so far on horseback. Did you sleep outdoors?"

"We did," Hannah said. "But I always felt safe with Erik around. Most of the time, anyway. Remember the bear?"

Erik laughed. "That was terrifying enough for a lifetime," he said.

"What happened," Olivia asked, with a look of horror on her face.

"We were coming down the eastern slope of the Sierras and had camped for the night. We both fell asleep by the fire and were awakened by a strange snorting sound," Hannah said. "Erik was up in a flash, grabbed the coffee pot and cook pan, and started yelling and banging things as loud as he could. The bear took off for the woods, but I don't think either of us slept any more that night. Oh, I was screaming as loud as I could, too," Hannah added.

When every drop of wine had been drunk and the pie was nothing but crumbs, Olivia looked around the table and said, "This feels like family. I am so grateful for each of you." In the glow of candlelight, her tears sparkled like diamonds.

Each of them nodded their agreement.

When it was time to retire, Rose showed Erik where he could sleep.

"This is like the fanciest hotel ever!" he exclaimed.

"I assume I don't have to make special arrangements for you, Hannah?"

Hannah blushed. So did Olivia.

"You two are just adorable. Sleep well. Or not," Rose added and turned away laughing.

"You have been to so many places and had so many experiences, Liv. You have touched so many people in your life. Molly told me the story about Esther and Chester and how much help you were to both of them. You are a good woman. I feel so blessed to have you in my life."

"I am so glad you came after me, Han. I was dying, and I knew it. But I didn't know how to fix myself. Thank you for coming to save me."

"I didn't save you, Liv. But I am glad I found you. Oh, I almost forgot." Hannah opened her leather bag and pulled out Olivia's writing box. "Molly said you forgot this."

Olivia opened the box. There, lying on top of her writing things, were the daisy petals from Ben. The bow and arrows from Little Deer were in her trunk at her aunt's, but she had forgotten her writing box when she left Sacramento. She smiled and told Hannah the story behind them.

That night they climbed into bed and just held each other close for a long, long time and didn't fall asleep until after midnight. Around three a.m., Olivia woke up with a start. She was anxious, fidgety. She got out of bed and looked outside. There was a full moon. Its reflection sparkled in the ocean waves. She watched it for a spell, then sat in the chair near the window.

She felt as if someone else was in the room. There was an undeniable presence.

"Who are you?" she asked quietly. "Who is there?"

A single, white orb, like a light, floated through the door

into the bedroom. Olivia thought she should be frightened, but she wasn't. She felt an overwhelming calm and sense of love.

The orb hung directly in front of and just above her head. It stayed there, unmoving for a few seconds.

She could not explain the fact that instead of feeling frightened, she felt so peaceful. Perhaps it was the love she felt filling the room.

She allowed the love to surround and fill her, then the orb shot through the window and was gone. The scent of pine and sawdust filled the air, and Olivia fell asleep in the chair with a soft smile on her face.

EPILOGUE

Shu and Mr. Chang

Shu and Mr. Chang left the logging camp shortly after Eric and Hannah left. The hostility from loggers was increasingly threatening, and it no longer seemed safe to work there.

When the couple left camp, they were worried and extremely cautious about the route to take on the way. Because of the sale of Shu into prostitution, they wanted to avoid Sacramento altogether but instead entered the city from a different route and found their way to Clark's Bakery. It took them a bit longer, but this approach seemed the wiser course of action. Olivia and Stewart had often talked about Shu and Mr. Chang, so Molly and Sam knew who they were as soon as they introduced themselves. They spent one night in Sacramento and left the next morning for San Francisco.

Shu was growing; her pregnancy seemed to be moving along without issue. By the time they reached San Francisco and found a place to live, she was around seven months pregnant.

Shu remembered that San Francisco was full of Chinese. The only reason she remembered was that she had flashback memories of searching for her cousin after he'd sold her. She remembered the sea of Chinese men with queues down their backs and how she could not tell one from another. There were so many Chinese when they reached the outskirts of San Francisco that it was a relief to learn there was an area of San Francisco called Chinatown. They made their way there and found a place to live. It was only a small shanty, but they hoped it to be temporary.

Shu gave birth to a baby boy two months later. By then, Mr. Chang was ready to open their restaurant. They named the restaurant Gum Saan, Gold Mountain. They named the baby Pinyin. Pinyin translates to Stewart. Mr. Chang agreed and just smiled at his wife. She was odd with names. He never could get his wife to call him by his first name, Ling. She learned his name as Mr. Chang and loved calling him that, even after they were married. Many thought it was odd, but Shu didn't care. She fell in love with Mr. Chang, and he would always be Mr. Chang to her.

The restaurant was open for nearly a year and was doing quite well. The Changs were able to hire several employees, though Shu always felt bad for the ones that she couldn't hire. Many of the men were homeless. California had become an unwelcoming place for Chinese. Most of those who'd come to find gold to send money back home were penniless. They could not afford to go back to China, and they could not get work where they were. Many were hired to help build the Transcontinental Railroad. But the work was grueling. They found themselves drilling tunnels through the mountains in up to thirty feet of snow. They thought their work would be appreciated, since ninety percent of the entire labor force working the mountain sections were Chinese. When all was said and done, they were nothing more than a passing mention, just a footnote in history.

No one would hire the Chinese, even though they were the hardest workers. As the Chinese miners and railroad workers returned to town, places that catered to their dietary needs became critical. The Chinese consider meals a social necessity. Gum Saan was very popular. Each evening just before the restaurant closed, Shu always took a big pot of rice and leftover food from the day to the back of the restaurant. There, many men would crowd around for the only meal of their day. Most of them were shabby and lived in the streets, but they all appreciated the generosity of Gum Saan. Shu always made sure that the outside back of the restaurant was swept clean and that no garbage was lying around. She would light a candle on the table where she put the food, and she made sure there were plenty of chopsticks and little bowls to go around.

One evening she was setting up the food table out back when three men came up behind her.

"We hear you feed hungry Chinese," one of them said.

She turned around and looked right into the face of her cousin, Bao. He clearly had fallen on hard times. His clothes were tattered, and he was very thin.

"Shu," he said, obviously surprised and embarrassed by the encounter.

"Bao," she said and bowed to him. She had no wish to shame him in front of his comrades, so she stepped back and gave them privacy to help themselves. She never saw him again.

The protests against the Chinese were rampant in all parts of California. Chinese businesses were being singled out since 1850 for taxes if they were not naturalized. But there was no route to naturalization. Shu and Mr. Chang tried several times.

White workers, including women, formed the Workingmen's Party of California. They did everything they could to drive out the Chinese. Their tactics were low and demoralizing. The WPC, as they called themselves, discredited Chinese by saying that the men were sexual perverts, and campaigns portrayed white working-class women as innocent and chaste victims while depicting Chinese men as menacing perverts.

The Chinese Massacre[23] in Los Angeles highlighted the dangers of being Chinese in America. Nearly two dozen Chinese were attacked with guns or hanged. One was a highly respected doctor. Even though he begged for his life in both English and Spanish, they hanged him. Homes were looted in the search for gold. Shu became physically ill when she heard about the massacre.

Life was difficult for Shu and Mr. Chang, but they never gave up. They managed to weather the hard times and save for when those came. When Yinlin was three years old, a photographer came through Chinatown. He was having a meal at the Gum Saan and noticed little Yinlin helping his mother.

"Would you like to have a photograph of your little boy?" the photographer asked.

"You take family photo?" Shu asked.

"Yes," he said.

"How much?"

The photographer knew that times were hard for everyone. "Free meals?" he asked.

"Okay, three meals," Shu said.

The photo was a tintype of her, Mr. Chang, and Yinlin. She didn't want to send the photo to her family in China. She wanted Olivia to know that she named her son after Stewart. She wrote a letter in her best English and had Mr. Chang check it. She had never discarded Maria's address. Even though she suspected she would never see Olivia again, it made her happy to share her news with the woman who unknowingly saved her and kept her safe.

---

23 Chang, Iris; The Chinese in America, A Narrative History (2003), On October 24, 1871, two dozen Chinese in Los Angeles were murdered by a mob. It is known as The Chinese Massacre

Shu never forgot Olivia's kindness. Or Stewart's. She knew that something special had developed between Olivia and Hannah, but she never said a word to anyone, including Mr. Chang. Shu and Mr. Chang had two more children. Their children grew up as American citizens and so were able to vote when they were older.

Molly and Sam

Molly and Sam missed Olivia and Stewart terribly. Molly, as it happened, was pregnant when Olivia and Stewart first arrived from the logging camp. Olivia's sadness was so painfully obvious that Molly was afraid to mention her own happiness for fear that perhaps Olivia's sadness might be related to a miscarriage. Olivia's melancholy was so opposite of her friend's always cheerful and kind nature that she could think of no other reason. Then, when Stewart was killed, there was no way to share her news.

After Olivia left, she kept in touch by letters through Maria. At some point after she and Sam had their first child, Molly shared the news. They named their daughter Grace after Sam's mother. They had only one more child, a boy, two years later. His name was Benjamin, and they called him Ben. Neither of them ever forgot about little Ben who was killed by the errant wagon on the journey to California.

Their bakery grew as Sacramento grew and as the children also grew. Eventually, Ben and his wife took over the bakery. Grace grew into a fierce, independent type. She was bright and good with numbers. She knew all about Olivia and Stewart. When she was old enough, she took the train eastward and joined her mother's old friend, Olivia, in the causes of the times.

Rose

The Rose who returned safely to her parents was not the Rose who left them. She worked hard to transform herself, though every once in a while, she caught herself being manipulative. When she did, she would stop and say to herself, "How would Olivia manage this situation?" She shared that with Olivia once. Olivia was mortified that anyone would do such a thing.

Rose loved when her home was filled with her friends. She, Olivia, Hannah, and Erik truly enjoyed one another's company. Her parents opted to stay longer in Europe, which alleviated the pressure they were feeling about moving out of Rose's house.

Not surprisingly, Rose and Erik fell in love. Their humor and their protectiveness for Olivia and Hannah were what connected them at first. The more they got to know each other, the closer they became. Rose never thought she wanted to be married again in her life. Erik changed that notion. Erik always thought he would be married but gave up the idea when he decided to follow Hannah in her search for Olivia.

When her parents did return from Europe, they found a completely radiant, happy, and in love Rose. Of course, they were disappointed that he had absolutely no status in any wealthy culture. His education was minimal—and his background was as a logger! Nonetheless, Rose's father found him a situation that paid him and offered opportunities for advancement in banking. Erik had always been good with numbers and was grateful for work that wasn't labor intensive.

Rose and Erik waited until her parents returned to marry. The couple wanted a small, simple civil ceremony, but they gave in to a small church affair to make her parents happy.

Olivia and Hannah were introduced to Rose's parents as good friends. They were aware that Olivia and Stewart had saved their daughter and were saddened by the news that Stewart had been murdered. Because of the role Olivia had played in the life of their daughter, they ignored the obvious signs that the women were intimate. In private, they did raise their eyebrows but over time came to love Olivia and Hannah, overlooking the truth of their relationship. They were, after all, world travelers, and this wasn't their first introduction to such things. They simply weren't used to "those things" being part of their circle.

Rose and Erik had one child whom they named Olivia. The child's godparents were Olivia and Hannah.

Olivia and Hannah

Olivia's orb experience was transformative for her. While she couldn't explain what she saw or the feeling of total love that surrounded her in the presence of the orb, she was absolutely convinced that it was Stewart and that he was letting her know he still loved her.

She and Hannah were so happy to finally be together that they didn't mind all the teasing from Erik and Rose—who never missed an opportunity to poke fun at them. They were able to laugh at themselves and got the chance to return the teasing as they watched Rose and Erik try to deny their feelings for one another at first.

Rose turned out to be a catalyst for many changes. She, Olivia, and Hannah all started volunteering with Lucy Stone. Rose continued only as a volunteer. She had no need to earn a living. However, once Olivia realized how much she enjoyed writing, she found herself penning an article here and there about the issues of slavery and women's rights. Rose encouraged her to show them to Lucy Stone, who hired her on the spot to write for her periodical called ***Woman's Journal***. Hannah took over fundraising for the woman's suffrage movement and found herself to be a valuable asset to the organization.

Maria and Michael often took the train to Boston to visit her niece and Hannah. Olivia and Hannah had taken an apartment downtown. Since they were both earning an income and Rose's parents had returned from Europe, it only made sense for them to be close to work and have their own place.

Some speculated about their relationship, but they were able to conceal the truth because Olivia was an actual widow. As women, it was not that difficult. Male couples had a harder time.

On one of Maria's visits, she brought letters from both Molly and Shu. The letter from Shu was heavy. Olivia was so excited to hear from her that she opened that one first. She read it aloud to Maria and Hannah.

Olivia,

Mr.Chang and me leave camp. It hard because men get so mean about China people after you leave. We visit Molly but not let people see us. She have nice baby. We live in San Francisco. Open a food house for China people. We okay. Want you to know we have son. Call him Yinlin. It mean Stewart in China. He good boy. This picture of family. Things hard in California for Chinese. Get murdered. No good for us here, but we okay. We still send money to family in China. We lucky. Cousin Bao not so lucky. He kill self. I see him one time. You friend, Shu.

Olivia had written to Shu in the camp but never heard back. She was teary on reading the letter and soon started to do some research on the struggles of the Chinese in California. She found that Chinese prejudice was not confined to California and began writing articles about Chinese women's issues in the *Woman's Journal*. In fact, any kind of injustice riled her up these days, and she was only too glad to have a platform in which to create awareness for the issues.

Now that she had Shu's address, she would be able to write to her and keep in touch. She always admired Shu's resourcefulness and hard work and always thought of her as a friend.

Olivia kept in touch with Molly and Shu for the rest of her life, especially after Sam and Molly's daughter, Grace, arrived via the Transcontinental Railroad. Olivia and Hannah helped Grace get settled in a women's boarding house near them. They watched over Grace like parents.

Though she and Hannah got the opportunity to travel for their work, most of the travel was limited to the eastern seaboard. Sadly, neither of them lived long enough to see women earn the right to vote in 1920. In New York, on a combined family and work visit, Olivia and Hannah were taking the Brighton Beach Line subway to a speaking engagement in Prospect Park. The elevated line, whose cars were made of wood, entered a tunnel.

The transit company employees were on strike. The company decided to use a crew dispatcher who had no experience operating the line, but the company was trying to keep the service running with non-striking personnel. The dispatcher (suddenly line operator) attempted to negotiate a six-mile-an-hour curve at speeds between thirty and forty miles an hour. The resulting crash involved six hundred and fifty passengers. Ninety-three of them were killed.[24] Olivia and Hannah were two of the deceased.

Olivia and Hannah died together. They would have had it no other way.

---

24 The crash is known as the Malbone Street Wreck. It happened on November 1, 1918.

Acknowledgments

Heartfelt thanks to my wife, Peggy, for traveling the Oregon Trail with me without complaint, so that I was able to stop at old logging and historical sights, drive through the Sierras, and imagine and learn about the hardships of the pioneers.

Grace Youngblood Hollen, you are a treasure. Not only are you a fabulous editor, but your encouragement encourages me. I am not certain this book would exist without your support.

Pamela Warren Williams, publisher extraordinaire at Mercury HeartLink, a million thanks. The character of Stewart (named for my sweet friend and your late husband) kept me writing. I wanted to honor him. He knew that I had planned to name the character after him and seemed pleased. Your support of my work means everything. I am sorry I made you cry.

My daughter, Emma, keeps me grounded, honest, and laughing. She has taught me not to take myself too seriously. I am so grateful to have you in my life.

My aunt and uncle, Lloyd and June Anderson, long deceased—you are honored here as Stewart's parents. Our missing years were filled with love when we were able to reunite.

Patti Brenneman, you are—and have always been—my touchstone. We have been friends for almost seventy years. Not sure I would still be here without you.

Joanie Kavooras, you, Patti and I met so long ago in grade school that it seems impossible that we could still be this close. I am honored by your love, support, and friendship.

reputation

About the Author

Maggi Petton is a poet and author of historical fiction. Her novels tell of the struggles of disenfranchised women throughout history . . . women of strength, courage and determination. Whether she is illuminating women's struggles during the Inquisition in Italy, or the American Civil War, her stories weave a tapestry of truth that resonates still. Today, more than ever, we need the depth, faith, and insight of women pushed to the breaking point, who discover their strength and purpose. Maggi's characters give us that and more—they give us honesty and insight as they grow and learn about themselves and the times in which they live.

Five of Maggi's books have been finalists of the Arizona/New Mexico Book Awards. Born in Chicago, Illinois, Maggi has made her home in New Mexico since 1985. She lives with her wife of forty-two years. They have one daughter.

www.ingramcontent.com/pod-product-compliance
Lightning Source LLC
LaVergne TN
LVHW041109080826
845145LV00007B/1744